A Sleuth in the Summer of Love

a Gwen Harris Mystery

by Carol Sheldon

A Sleuth in the Summer of Love

Published by Houghton, 501 Via Casitas, Greenbrae CA 94904

All characters are fictitious.

ISBN-9781730878549

Other Books by Carol Sheldon:

Mother Lode
Driven to Rage
A Sleuth in Sausalito
A Sleuth in The Haven
Exposed: The Poetry of Carol Sheldon

Children's Books
Penny's Christmas Tree
Craig's Crazy Cruise

Website/blog: www.carolsheldon.com

If you enjoy this book, why not get the others in the Gwen Harris Mystery Series? These are available at Amazon.com.

It's Sausalito in the sixties. Poets, painters and philosophers dot this artsy town, After ten years of not knowing what happened to her mother when she disappeared, Gwen Harris is notified that recently discovered remains might be those of her mother. Gwen begins a long and arduous journey of discovering what happened, and who is responsible. Eager, but young and vulnerable, her trust in several people is shattered by secrecy, betrayal and deception.

A SLEUTH IN THE HAVEN is the second in the Gwen Harris Mystery Series. Bizarre and fatal events threaten the residents of *The Haven*, a retirement home where her Aunt Megan lives. Agreeing to help with the investigation, Gwen gets caught deeper and deeper in the attacker's agenda as the tightrope she's walking gets higher and higher

CHAPTER 1

Gwen Harris was just getting ready to step into a cool shower when her boss from the San Francisco Chronicle called. "There's been a murder in the Haight. Can you get over there and get the story, Gwen?"

"Oh, my God. I just got back from there, Martin."

"A *murder*, Gwen."

"OK, OK, I'm on my way."

Skipping the shower, she got into the clothes she'd just discarded, tied her auburn hair back in a ponytail and gave her partner a quick kiss.

"Sorry, Mark. I have to go back. Vandermeer wants me to cover a murder in the Haight!"

"Murder? Not another one."

She knew he was thinking of the murder at *The Haven*, where he was the director. And where she, too had been involved.

"The Haight—that's where all those hippies are," he said.

"Right. I have to go."

Her handsome dark-haired partner caught her arm.

"Be home for supper?"

"Sure hope so."

"I'll fix something for later."

"That would be wonderful." She kissed him on the forehead.

"Be careful."

Gwen ran down the steps of the old house, almost tripping on the loose floorboard. When was the landlord going to fix it? The house they were renting was old and in need of repair, but close to San Francisco via the Golden Gate Bridge.

Although still warm in August, signs of fall were beginning to be seen. A few leaves swept across her path and nights were getting cooler and days shorter.

Firing up her Hudson, she adjusted the seat, as Mark, who was almost a foot taller than she at six feet two, had driven it last. She sped back across the Golden Gate Bridge to San Francisco and into the district known as The Haight.

Murder!

It hadn't started out this way. Gwen remembered her first venture into the Haight two months ago, in June.

~~~

That day she left her usual work garb in the closet and donned a full print cotton skirt and white blouse. Not wanting to stand out, looking like a reporter in the land of the free she was about to inhabit, she undid her ponytail and let her long hair flow freely down her back, tied a ribbon across her forehead and around her head. She'd pass, she figured. That's how these kids dressed these days, and she wanted to fit in, at least not stand out. The tailored blouse didn't quite work, but it would have to do for now.

She wore the sandals she usually reserved for the beach and put on some long beads she hadn't worn since high school. Beads, flowers, scarves served as the membership card for this loosely formed community of people who'd come from all walks of life and all over the country to sing in the new social order of the century. Peace and love were their mantras.

She wouldn't carry a notebook; that would be too obvious. Anyway, she was going there to get a general feeling of the lifestyle of these people, the mood, the ambiance. She didn't need to take notes for that.

Gwen left sunny Marin that day in her Hudson, crossed the Golden Gate Bridge, and even as she did so, could feel the drop in the temperature. San Francisco, with its usual oyster-grey sky was cool. As someone had said, "The coldest winter he'd ever spent was a summer in San Francisco."

She threaded her way through the city, and over to Haight Street. This was the hub of the populous that had created this social revolution. She wanted to get the feel of this place, try to find an angle on what exactly was happening, and what had brought thousands of kids to this city.

It seemed unreal, that so many people could gather together, and live peacefully. So far there hadn't been any serious crimes—at least none that she'd heard of. Everyone was peaceful, young adults came with their toddlers, and all got along.

She wanted to tread carefully, avoid stepping out on a loose limb. Everything seemed so idyllic. But was it? There must be some dark corners too, and she would seek them out.

She found a parking spot a few blocks down on Delma and strolled back to the heart of the Haight, which was the corner of Haight and Ashbury. Still fairly early in the morning, the streets were almost empty. Vestiges of the previous night littered the streets—paper cups, used needles, even sleeping bodies. Quiet, but for a lone blind man sitting on the corner playing a harmonica.

So many buildings painted in bright colors—a purple store, neighbored by an orange one, adorned by big, bold psychedelic lettering announcing their wares. She passed a second-hand clothing store, a fortune teller's den and a tea shop, then ambled further on Haight Street, and continued inhaling the essence of this village within the city.

She watched an industrious soul in the window of his shop pounding leather on a large work table. The sign above his shop said, "Lyon's Leather". The sign in the window said, "Custom-made leather goods for you."

A man in his early twenties with long dish-water blond hair approached her with a friendly grin and said 'hello'. Her first instinct was to move on quickly, not to talk to strangers as her mid-west upbringing had taught her, but on second thought she decided that if she was going to get a handle on this nascent society, she was going to have to talk to the inhabitants.

"Hi," she said. "You new here?"

"Yes. Is it always this quiet in the mornings?"

"Pretty much. This town doesn't wake up 'til noon. Concerts run late, other activities. Late to bed and late to rise."

"What kind of activities?"

"Parties, drugs, sex."

"How long have you been here?" she asked.

"Three months. Came from Maine."

"All that way?"

"Yeah. It's dead there. Back east, they're social Luddites. You know what I mean?"

Gwen nodded. "I think so."

"I love it here."

"What do you love about it?"

"Everything. Hey, you can be yourself. Nobody judges you. Anything goes, as long as you're kind and peaceful, and everybody is. It's a paradise, man."

"What do people do about lodging?"

"Lots of the houses up the street have opened their doors to strangers, for a night, maybe forever."

"And nobody pays rent?"

"Nobody I know."

They passed a shop with Indian clothing for women. Beautiful, they came in bright colors, the dressier ones enhanced with bangles or sequins. On closer look, she could see they were actually the kind of dresses Indian women wore. They were made of exotic materials like satin with full-length skirts and short sleeves. The midriff was bare.

As Gwen had never seen this type of work, she was fascinated, stopped to study them. "I think they're called saris."

"Beautiful, aren't they?" Hank said.

"They certainly are. Do you suppose they dress like this every day?"

"That's the only kind of dress I've seen them wear."

A couple of small tables were on the sidewalk outside. "Would you like a cup of tea?" he asked.

"Thank you, yes."

She decided she was lucky to encounter this friendly person and would learn as much as she could from him.

They sat outside. The tea came, and to Gwen it had an unusual sweet taste.

"You'll get used to it. It's hot."

Two girls, arm in arm strolled down the street in their direction. Both had long, blonde hair, with ribbons and beads. The only difference between the way they were dressed and herself was that they were barefoot. For the most part, Gwen was reassured that she fit in.

"How did you know I was new to the neighborhood?" she asked her new friend.

"You had that look. Gazing at buildings—a giveaway. And you didn't walk like you had any purpose."

She smiled. "Oh, I have a purpose."

"No doubt you do. I'm sorry."

"It's OK."

"Where you from?"

"I live in Marin—across the bridge."

"What are you doing here? Checking us out?"

"Sort of. Doesn't everyone?"

"Yeah. In fact, they have tourist buses that come here every day." Showing in quote marks with his hands he said, 'No passport needed for this foreign country.' They even hand out leaflets to the passengers defining the vocabulary used around here."

"Like what?"

"Joint, meaning a marijuana cigarette, a toke is a hit on a marijuana cigarette and stoned is an altered state. Those are a few."

"Yes, I've seen a couple of these buses. I never saw anyone get off them, though."

"Not often. Occasionally, a couple will get off the bus and walk around the streets to fine-tune their impression of Hippyville. But for the most part, they remain safely in their seats, perhaps afraid that if they venture into this foreign land they'll be swallowed up in some vortex and never return to Kansas, or wherever they're from."

Gwen said, "I've seen anxious parents peering into the face of some long-haired bearded youth and wondering, 'Are you my Tommy?' It almost makes me cry. They've come all the way from whatever state they live in, spending days walking the Haight, holding pictures up to strangers. 'Have you seen her?'"

"What about all the drugs, even LSD?"

"It wasn't even illegal until recently. Some spokesman said psychedelics are a gift to mankind. And lots of folks think drugs are a sacrament."

They were quiet for a while, sipping their tea and people-watching. Never a dull thing to do in this part of San Francisco.

He surprised her with what he said next. "What do you do?"

Not yet ready to reveal her real purpose she hedged. "Right now I'm trying to learn something about this phenomenon known as the summer of love. And you've been a big help." She turned the question back on him. "Let me ask you. What do you do?"

"Partly what I'm doing now— introducing myself to new arrivals, and telling them about the Survival School, where I work part-time. It's all about how to stay alive on Haight Street. We cover topics like sex, drugs, street smarts, how to avoid getting arrested, and what to do if you are. It's an organization to steer kids out of trouble. I needed to know some of this stuff myself when I got here. I figured no better way to learn than to work with those in the know."

"Sounds like a good-neighbor kind of thing to do."

"You know, the feeling this community evokes inspires the best in all of us. Makes you want to help others."

"Does everybody feel that way?"

"No, not everyone. There are givers and takers, like everywhere. But I'd say more givers here than in most places."

Gwen wished she could take some notes. But she would just have to keep it in her head. It would not be cool to pull out a notebook.

"What did you do before you came here?"

"I was a bookkeeper for some big shot outfit. Couldn't be more boring. There's just no comparison. Here it's so alive, so much happening. Like tonight, there's a concert in the park. You oughta go if you can."

"Who's playing?

"The Grateful Dead."

"Really?"

"The park will be jammed."

"Thanks. I'll try to make it."

Hank looked at his watch. "Now I gotta get down the street for my shift with the Survival School. It's been great meeting you. Come by sometime, and I'll show you our pamphlets."

"I'd like that."

"It's at 901 Cole Street."

"Well, thank you for spending half your morning educating me on the multi-faceted aspects of this amazing community."

When he left, Gwen wandered down the street and into a shop selling used musical instruments and was amazed at how inexpensive they were. Three dollars for an old violin that needed new strings. Two young men in the back were strumming away on what she first thought were guitars. On further investigation, she saw that one of the instruments was a mandolin. It reminded her of the one that had hung on her Aunt's wall in Michigan.

The store next door was selling smoking gear, water pipes and such. Perhaps they sold the pot to go with it, but she didn't ask.

On the street, pedestrian traffic was picking up. It was getting near noon, and singles, groups of two or three were beginning to fill the streets.

She kept ambling and came to the Golden Gate Park. No wonder this area of the city had been chosen to live in; it was right next to the park, where famous musicians were giving free concerts. The Haight was their home; the park was their playground. The enormous Golden Gate Park with its spacious meadows, ball fields, gardens—even a patch with real buffalos.

Around noon she left the Haight and went back to the office. She had a feel for the neighborhood now, at least during the morning, but would need a lot more visits to get the pulse of the people who occupied it.

Why had they come?

What were they looking for?

Could this peaceful society exist for long?

These and other questions filled her head. She meant to find the answers. She would grapple with them until she could grasp the essence of what was happening this summer in San Francisco.

~~~

Sophie Bennington endured the last humiliation her father inflicted on her, went to her room and slammed the door. Standing outside chatting with her friends, he'd come out and said in front of them, "You have to come in now, Sophie." He pointed to his watch.

She went to her room and slammed the door. She was tired of her family, the Presbyterian Church, and her all-white community in Illinois.

An attractive girl, tall with curly brown hair, she'd been a star on her basketball team. In her next and senior year, she would be captain. All that paled, as she and her friends kept hearing about the great revolution in San Francisco. It was like a dream. Its tendrils were spreading all over the country. Young people were pouring into that city from everywhere, getting free food, places to live, going to concerts and all in a very peaceful manner. It was called the Summer of Love. She had dreamed about it long enough. Now she would go. She'd been saving her baby-sitting money all last year to buy a new bike, but now, since she'd heard about the excitement in San Francisco, going there was much more important. She had almost one hundred dollars. If she hitch-hiked, she figured she could make it. The love-in community would take care of her after that.

She was sure her father would kill her if he found out what she planned to do. Grounded today because he discovered she'd gone to an outdoor concert last night and the newspaper had reported that one could get high just breathing in the marijuana smoke of those around you, she was furious. Furthermore, he was always ranting about how any slip in her behavior would reflect on him at the college, where he was the dean. And her mother acted like she would turn into a pumpkin if she got in after ten thirty.

She was sixteen and a half, and they still treated her like a little girl. She pulled her suitcase out from the back of her closet and began choosing clothes from her dresser and the things on hangers. It didn't take long. When she finished, she shoved the suitcase under her bed and then slipped under the covers. When sleep didn't come, she got up and flipped through her last issue of *Seventeen*. Just a month ago she'd loved this magazine. Now it seemed totally stupid. Full of hair styles, plaid skirts and insipid stories, she threw it down in disgust.

She would make her exodus after her father left for work in the morning, and her mother drove her little brother off to school. Then she would sneak out the back door, hurry down the street and take the bus to the highway.

Should she leave a note? She thought about the pros and cons of this and decided against it. Where would she say she was going? She certainly didn't want to leave bread crumbs for them to follow.

~~~

From the Chronicle office Gwen called Mark in Marin. She knew she could reach him at work where he was the manager of a retirement home called *The Haven*.

"Sweetie, how would you like to go to a concert tonight in the Golden Gate Park? The Grateful Dead are playing."

"It's going be awfully crowded."

"But it will be fun, and also I want to write it up for the paper."

"OK, I'll pick you up around five. Shall I bring Alfi?"

"Why not?"

Until six weeks ago Alfi had been a resident of the Humane Society due to the death of his owner. Now happy to be with his new owners, Alfi proved to be a delight to both Gwen and Mark.

Although Gwen had first known Mark through a computer class they were both taking, they had renewed their acquaintance several months ago at *The Haven* when she was helping her aunt to move in and he was the director. An immediate attraction had evolved into a serious relationship. When Gwen's roommate got married, Mark moved in and took her place.

When he arrived at the Chronicle to pick her up, he'd brought Alfi their lab with him. Confined to the back seat, he sat forward and licked Gwen's neck as way of welcoming her.

They drove through town, dodging the busiest streets, and turned into the Golden Gate Park. Driving through the tree-lined streets they were immersed in cars trying to park and pedestrians overflowing the sidewalks. Gwen noticed the pedestrians were dressed in everything from T shirts and shorts to flowing skirts with headbands and flowers in their hair. Even many of the boys and men had eschewed conventional dress for the freedom this time and place allowed them.

As they inched their way along, Gwen said, "You were right, it's very crowded. But just think—Jerry Garcia and The Grateful Dead. They're here tonight, and I can't wait to hear them."

He smiled and took her hand.

Parking took longer than they'd expected. They had to hike close to a mile to join the excitement, but if nothing else, the smell of marijuana led them to that part of the great expanse where everyone in this new tribe gathered regularly for wild celebrations of love, peace and live music.

As the rock 'n roll got louder, and the smells stronger, they passed by a lighted stage and adorned with microphones. Happy hippies were chanting and carrying signs of 'Peace' and 'Love'. Gwen saw more eye-catching attire, as some wore diaphanous robes, and a large group were adorned in historical costumes.

They passed a food stand where Mark purchased hotdogs with some strange sauce, and some spicy Indian dish they'd never tasted before.

"This is the Summer of Love," Gwen declared. "And now I'm having the real experience."

Mark grinned, squeezed her hand. When they found a place to sit, he arranged the blanket he'd brought, and they sat down to enjoy an evening of Jerry Garcia and his band.

Maybe it was inhaling other people's smoke, or maybe just the atmosphere, but Gwen and Mark were in as much a state of bliss as those all about them. So many people, all in harmony. Alfi too, seemed to pick up on the surrounding vibes and fell into the same state. Nearby children came over to pet him. Life was good.

Most folks remained sitting when the band took a break, but here and there Gwen could see groups making their own entertainment. Nearby, a circle of kids danced as they sang one of Janis Joplin's songs, *Peace of my Heart.*

When the band resumed most of the crowd stood, entranced by the sound, swaying, singing, in rapture. Balloons rose in the air, along with the smoke from hundreds of pot smokers.

After listening to the music for a while, Gwen's attention was drawn more to watching the people around her. The meadow was expansive. As far as she could see the ground was covered with a sea of people. Her only experience with such large crowds had been at football games. The University of Michigan, where she'd attended college, possessed the largest college stadium in the country, seating one hundred thousand people. The atmosphere here was entirely different. No shouting and stamping, no pushing to get ahead. It was unbelievable how content, generous and happy everyone seemed.

A huge bag of popcorn was passed around her immediate neighbors. A laughing toddler, wearing only diapers stumbled by in front of her, as his long-haired father followed in close pursuit—a game of tag. Sweeping the child up in his arms, the squeal of laughter filled the air.

In the distance she could see some giant puppets moving by mysterious hands to the delight of children, and not too far away happy kids were climbing through a large paper tunnel. All the work of the Diggers, she'd heard.

The moon came up, and although the sounds of *The Dead* went on for hours, the evening seemed to end all too soon.

They walked back to the car holding hands, swinging them between them.

As they left the park Mark said, "I'm really glad we went."

"I am too, and the best part is now I can write about it for the paper."

Ever since Gwen had written feature articles on the murder and resolution at *The Haven*, her boss had been very interested in her ideas.

When they arrived at their apartment, Mark said, "I've had my music fix for tonight. Now I want my fix of you!"

He carried her into the bedroom. They laughed and rolled around, "Can you tell that I'm crazy about you?" he said running his fingers through her coppery hair.

"Well, you've given a few hints," she laughed.

As their love-making turned serious, their hands explored each other with passion and urgency, culminating their love in a riot of color and heat.

CHAPTER 2

Sophie's trip to California was anything but dull. After a couple of brief rides with locals who got her out of the city, she was picked up by a boy in a psychedelic painted VW van. On the side was written, "Going to San Francisco?"

Sophie climbed in eagerly. Smelling of French fries, she noted that she was not the only passenger in the van. Two other girls and another boy were in the back, playing cards. Laughing and talking, they stopped to introduce themselves to her. She found a seat, crushing some potato chips as she did.

"Hi, I'm Tru, short for Trudy," the pretty black girl said. "What's your name?"

"Sophie."

"Hi. Me Justin, her Mavis."

"Where you from?" Tru asked.

"Illinois."

"I'm from Michigan,"

The other two looked up long enough to say, "We're from Pennsylvania—Eerie."

The driver spoke up then, saying, "And I'm Marcus, most recently from New Jersey. Before that, Florida, New Zealand—Oh, you don't want to know."

Marcus slowed down as the highway took them right through the center of a town.

They pulled into a Standard Oil station, and as the attendant filled the tank Mavis and Justin handed Marcus a bill to help pay for it. Sophie knew that she'd have to contribute in some way too.

At noon, they pulled off the highway and looked for a grocery store. "I'll go," Tru piped up. She jumped out of the van and ran into the grocery store.

"Should I go too?" Sophie asked.

"Your turn will come," Marcus smiled.

When Tru returned, they put the lunch meat between slices of white spread, smeared the bread with mustard and chowed down. Previous stops had provided them with condiments. A sandwich never tasted so good to Sophie. A box of half-eaten cookies completed their simple meal.

In the afternoon, they began talking about San Francisco, what they expected, and what they hoped to find.

"From what I've heard, everything is free. Even drugs. Even LSD. Can you imagine? I can't wait to trip out on that," Mavis said.

"Totally," Justin agreed.

"Go easy; you can get hurt on that stuff. Wake up and not know who you are. Or not wake up," Marcus said.

"Hey, everybody's doing it."

Mavis turned to Sophie. "Why are you going?"

Sophie shrugged. "Anything's better than living at home. Besides, it sounds super cool."

"That's what I figure," Mavis added. "You can't imagine what it was like in my house. So many kids, my dad couldn't remember our names. But that didn't stop him from taking the belt to us whenever he felt like it. And once he said to one of the boys, 'You go on home now. I got enough kids to feed without taking in the neighbors.' He was talking to my brother!"

"Incredible."

"I'm just looking for some peacefulness," Justin said. "Being surrounded by peace-loving people. Hey, that's groovin'."

They were quiet then, and Mavis and Justin drifted off to sleep.

~~~

Martin Vandermeer hoisted his considerable bulk out of his chair to shake Gwen's hand. It was an unusually warm day. Martin mopped his bald pate as the anemic fan turned lethargically above.

"I like it, Gwen. You've done a fine job on the article about the concert in the park."

"Thank you."

"How would you like to do a series on this Summer of Love?" Vandermeer inquired.

"You mean it?"

"Yes, of course."

"I would love that!" It was exactly what Gwen was hoping for.

She had started working a reporter assigned to the insipid tasks of writing up the construction of new buildings, social events in the city and other events of mild interest to the readership of the Chronicle. She had gotten her break a few months ago when she had covered the events at her aunt's retirement home in Marin, when a murderer had gotten into the building. She'd actually been caught up in the events that followed. Martin Vandermeer had quickly recognized her talent, given her a by-line and a fairly free hand in what she covered.

She decided to spend that afternoon around Haight and Ashbury. She'd been there in the morning, but the community wasn't quite awake then. Maybe she'd catch more action in the afternoon.

She was right. The Haight had awakened. The streets were overflowing with hundreds of young people, some sauntering down the street, others hanging out in small groups.

Since she'd left from the Chronicle, she wasn't dressed in a way that would make her even vaguely fit in. She stood out like an outsider in her suit and heels. It wasn't going to be so easy starting a conversation with someone dressed as she was.

Just as she was wondering if she looked like a reporter, an overweight and somewhat older woman standing in a doorway in a large Hawaiian muumuu asked her if she was a tourist.

"Not really. Just checking out the scene. And you?"

The woman nodded to a sign in the window that said, 'Free counseling.'

"That's me," she smiled. "The shop sells used and vintage clothing, but the owner lets me put up my shingle. It brings in business for her too."

"You do this au gratis?"

"Yes."

"That's very impressive"

"Not uncommon around here." Her round, freckled face glowed in the sunlight.

"Utopia?"

"In a way. Think you'll want to be part of it?" she asked Gwen.

"Not sure yet. Just getting a feel for it. I don't exactly blend in, dressed as I am."

"If you want to—blend in that is, come with me. By the way, I'm Sheila."

"And I'm Gwen. Where are we going?"

"I'll show you where you can get some free clothes."

"Really?"

She followed Sheila for a block and a half, where they entered the Free Store. No glamourous window displays were needed. People were looking through a few racks of clothes, but mostly through the boxes, as there weren't enough racks to hang them all up.

"They get new stuff every day," Sheila explained. "And it's all free."

"How can it be?"

"It's donated. Folks come in and give their clothes away. Not just ones who live around the Haight. Business people, teachers—everybody. Lots of folks support the movement even if they can't be part of it."

Sheila began digging through the boxes, pulled out a long, cotton skirt she thought would fit Gwen and held it up.

"What do you think?"

"Nice."

" Thanks."

"None of this stuff ever fits me. I'm too fat."

Gwen did some of her own digging and found a couple of T-shirts and some beads she thought would do.

"Here, you can go behind this screen to try this stuff on."

Gwen did. The skirt was red in flared panels and Gwen decided it fit well enough.

Glancing at Gwen's 'professional' style heels, Sheila said, "If you want something for your feet, the shoes are over there. Or you can go barefoot."

"I think I'll look at the shoes."

She found a pair of tennis shoes that were a bit large, but when tied up they felt OK.

Gwen had never experience such instantaneous friendship. She wanted to ask Sheila, "Why are you doing this for me?" but decided it would be off-putting. Instead, she said, "You've been very kind. Can I buy you a cup of tea?"

"Sure, if you want. You don't have to."

"I'd like to."

"Then come with me."

"What shall I do with this stuff?" she said, referring to her office clothes.

"Maybe they'll have a bag. Or you can donate them if you like."

This was such a foreign concept to Gwen; after all, she'd paid quite a bit for this summer outfit.

"Will anyone want them?"

"Sure. Regular folks come here too."

Still, if she were going to get in the swing of things, why not? It would be a rite of passage, something she knew meant more than leaving some clothes on top of a box. She left her clothes.

As they were leaving the shop, Gwen spied a box of watches. "What's with all these? Are they broken?"

"No, it's another aspect of the counterculture. A lot of folks don't want their lives run by man-made timepieces," she explained. "The sun and the moon are good enough for them."

"I guess that works if you don't have a job, or any commitments."

"Want to get our tea at the Indian spice place?"

"Sure."

When they were seated, Sheila said, "Do you want to pick your own flavor, or can I recommend something?"

"Happy for your advice."

Sheila pulled some cookies out of the voluminous folds of her muumuu. She unwrapped the wax paper and put them on the table. "Help yourself."

As she sipped the tea Gwen recognized the flavor of ginger, but something unfamiliar was added to it. "Have you been here long?" she asked.

Lighting a cigarette Sheila said, "About a month. I flew here from Maryland."

"I bet there's a story behind that."

"I didn't run away from home like so many of these kids, my folks know where I am. I'm not as young as some of these kids, I'm twenty-nine. But after finishing two years of college, I still didn't know what I wanted to major in—was generally bored. I guess I was looking for some kind of adventure."

"And you've found it."

Sheila nodded. "I'm fed up with the war. Lots of us are protesting it. What the hell are we doing in Viet Nam? My little brother's over there." She grew inward, sad. "Wonder if I'll ever see him again."

Then she looked up and smiled. "How about you? Do you live around here?"

"Across the bridge in Marin County. Sausalito."

"I'd like to go over there someday."

"Maybe you'll come visit me."

"You grew up there?"

"For a while. Then I went to live with my aunt in Michigan. I came back a couple of years ago. I love the Bay Area."

"Me too."

They chatted some more, and then Sheila said, "How'd you like to come to a party tonight?"

"Really?"

"Sure. A friend of mine has get-togethers on Fridays at his pad. Come by about nine o'clock."

Sheila scribbled down an address on a napkin and handed it to Gwen.

"I'd love to. I'll try to make it. Really."

"It's not far from here. About two blocks."

~~~

The long stretch across the United States went by quickly, as the occupants of the VW van played cards, told jokes, and slept in the van. They sang songs. In fact, Sophie got them all singing—Beatles songs, folk songs of Joan Baez and Joni Mitchell.

"I can't wait to hear the bands in San Francisco," Sophie said.

"Like Jefferson Airplane and Big Brother and the Holding Company."

They knew the names of most of the popular bands and musicians making a name for themselves in San Francisco.

As they neared their destination the seductive signs declaring, San Francisco fifty miles, then twenty caused growing excitement. Then, in the distance the marker of any large city, tall buildings, began to appear eliciting squeals from the occupants.

When they arrived in the golden city, none of them, except Marcus, had a clue as to where they should go. Marcus was joining a friend who had invited him to come out.

Tearfully, the girls hugged him and said their goodbyes, as Marcus dropped them off in the Haight.

"Stay in touch," they called after him. But who knew if they'd ever meet again?

It was the middle of the afternoon. Hauling their duffel bags along, they set out to look for lodgings. Sophie was embarrassed that she was lugging her suitcase. How out of place can I be? she deplored. Besides, the suitcase itself was heavy, never mind its contents.

They were so delighted and amazed at the colorful scene— both of people dressed in all manner of costumes, and the buildings painted in every color of the rainbow, that they forgot they were looking for somewhere to stay.

Suddenly, in a store-front window, Mavis spotted a poster that said, "Can we help?" They went inside. A pleasant looking woman with braided gray hair was almost lost among the colorful clothes that adorned her shop.

"Can I help you?" she said.

"Yes. We've just arrived. We're looking for a place to stay," Justin said.

The woman sighed. "A few weeks ago, I could have directed you to a few places. Now, with such an influx of people, it's getting harder and harder to find spots for the newcomers. Let me think."

Mavis was fingering some of the clothing. "Isn't this cool?" she called out. "Bell-bottoms with studs."

"Let's focus on where we're going to sleep tonight," Justin told her. "Oh, right." She joined the others, popping her bubble gum.

"I can probably take two of you, but not all four. I think a couple of my residents are leaving this week."

The foursome looked at each other. Justin spoke. "Tru, why don't you and Sophie go? Mavis and I will keep looking."

"If that's OK with you," Tru said.

"Sure," Mavis said.

The shopkeeper spoke up. "My name's Marjorie. What's yours?"

The girls gave their names and Marjorie gave them her address. "It's an old Victorian on Ashbury, basically tan but with lots of colorful trim." She laughed. "Some of the boys offered to paint all the gingerbread trim on the house with different colors. You can't miss it. Now we're a real hippy house."

"Do we need a key?" Tru asked.

"Heavens no. Make yourselves at home, but first floor only."

Hugs, as Tru and Sophie bid Mavis and Justin goodbye. They promised to meet the next day on the corner of Ashbury and Haight at noon.

"At least that goodbye doesn't feel so final," Sophie said.

Sophie and Tru proceeded down the street until they found the colorful house Marjorie had described.

"Wow, did you ever see anything like that?"

"Not in Illinois," Sophie answered.

They could see the front door partially open as they walked up the steps. Even before they entered, they could hear the sounds of the inhabitants talking, laughing.

Stepping in, a pretty girl looked up and came over to meet them. "Hi. I'm Rebecca. Are you going to be staying here?"

"Yes."

"Most of the kids are out, so it's kind of quiet now."

Sophie and Tru surveyed the room. But for a small portion where a few sat talking, most of the floor was covered with sleeping bags and blankets, duffel bags and backpacks. The adjoining room held more of the same.

"You gals bring a bag?"

Still overwhelmed by the sight, Tru said, "A what?"

"If you don't, it's OK. There are a couple over there in the corner, left by previous residents. Used, of course, but if you don't have anything else—"

"That will be fine. Really appreciate it, "Sophie said.

That night, trying not to notice the snoring coming from across the room, and trying to get comfortable on the floor,

Sophie thought, *So, this is my new home. Well, freedom comes with a price. But it's worth it, worth every sacrifice.*

CHAPTER 3

Gwen would like to have brought Mark to the party, but Sheila had only invited her, and she didn't want to risk offending her new friend by asking if she could bring a guest.

She figured this kind of party was not a dress-up affair. She didn't know what to expect, but she thought it would be casual. She donned some old jeans, and the top and tennis shoes from the Free Store.

She arrived at the right address at nine fifteen, an old Victorian house painted purple. By now she was used to seeing these old ladies in this part of town adorned in primary colors. Sheila had told her to use the outside entrance and go up to the third floor, to Tyson's apartment. Climbing the stairs, she could hear guitar music coming from the top floor. A friendly young man with a ponytail and a cowboy hat let her in. Without questioning her credentials, he said, "Sit anywhere. Can I get you something?"

She wanted to say, *like what*? But shook her head instead. She looked around, saw in this crowded room that all the chairs were taken, but she found a cushion on the floor and plopped on it. She didn't see Sheila anywhere. Through the cloud of pot smoke, she could make out the guitar player strumming some Joni Mitchell song, and Gwen found herself humming along. It wasn't long before Sheila popped out of the kitchen, spotted Gwen and came over to her.

"I'm so glad you came. Here, have a funny Brownie."

Gwen knew that meant it was laced with marijuana. She hesitated, but decided that couldn't be too bad, and anyway she wanted not only to see, but feel what it was like to live this lifestyle.

Sheila sat on the floor beside Gwen. "That's Tyson playing the guitar. It's his pad."

Gwen took a closer look at him. His clear blue eyes made a stunning and unusual contrast to his long, dark hair.

"Does he throw these parties often?"

"So far, every Friday night. Fun, huh?"

"Yes, great."

Even more folks arrived and crowded into this homey, but small room. Gwen moved over on the floor to make room for two young boys.

Just then a pretty girl with streaming black hair intertwined with ribbons stood up beside Tyson and began to sing *I've Looked at Both Sides Now.* Such a clear and radiant voice Gwen couldn't remember ever hearing.

"That's Rebecca," Sheila whispered. "Isn't she divine?"

"She is."

"She wants to get some experience here, and then she's going to audition for one of the major bands. Someday we might hear her play in the park."

"She sure has the voice for it."

The music that night was soft and lyrical.

"I know what you're thinking," Sheila said. "Where's the rock? That's what you hear at the park concerts, but Tyson's landlord wants to keep the roar down, and we like the soft stuff too."

"My favorite," Gwen said.

"There's more food in the kitchen. Just help yourself. Someone will probably offer you some LSD, but don't take it unless you're comfortable with it."

"I think I'll pass. Do you use it?"

"I've tried it a couple of time. You have to be careful. If you're in a good space, you can have a great trip. But if you're not, you can have a very depressing, even scary trip."

"It's not legal, is it?"

"Not anymore. It was until last year when Governor Reagan made it illegal. But that doesn't stop people from making and distributing it. People think it's going to change the world. Make everybody look at everything totally differently. Like maybe we won't even need governments. We'll grow up and govern ourselves in responsible ways."

"Is that what you think?"

Sheila rolled her eyes. "We'll see."

Gwen nodded. From what she'd seen so far, there was no kind of governance—from above or self-imposed. Still, she wanted to withhold judgment as much as she could.

Suddenly, everyone stopped talking. Rebecca was singing *Amazing Grace* in her crystal-clear voice. Even to the assembled, many of whom had discarded religion in favor of drugs and new epiphanies, this was something sacred. Whether it was the song or the singer, it needed listening to.

When she'd finished, applause and loud 'bravas' from the two girls sitting next to her.

A small wisp of a girl who'd been waiting in the kitchen doorway came around passing out donuts. "They're day-old," she said, "But still good."

"Smoking gives you the munchies." Everybody with a joint in hand took one.

"Have you ever even smoked pot?" Sheila asked. "Once," Gwen admitted. "It didn't do anything for me."

"You probably didn't have very good stuff. You can get some top-drawer weed tonight if Kenny comes."

"Doesn't anyone charge for anything?"

"Sure, some do, or they'll take donations. But we're trying to become a free society, where we take what we need, and give what we can. Tyson gives guitar lessons to the landlord, so he lets him stay here free of rent. And he helps out at the Free Clinic. Doc Smith treats over two hundred kids a day. Can you imagine? And he doesn't charge a cent. They go there with VD, bad acid trips—you name it."

"What does he live on?"

"I don't know. But I've heard some agency or charitable foundation contribute funds to his clinic."

"Sounds like a very dedicated guy."

"And he rounds up a bunch of interns who bring him penicillin, tranquilizers and supplies from whatever hospital they're working at."

"Sometimes Tyson goes over, takes down initial information, washes feet infected from going barefoot, anything to help."

"Cool. What about this place? Tyson doesn't have it to himself, does he?"

"No. There are a couple of regulars who stay here, and any number of others who crash. He might wake up next to a dozen strangers."

"Really?" Gwen asked in surprise.

Rebecca was making her way through the crowded room, stopping to chat with various friends. As she came near, Sheila called her over.

"I want you to meet a new friend. Rebecca, this is Gwen."

Rebecca took Gwen's hand in both of hers. So soft and warm, so gentle. Her long eyelashes framed her large dark eyes, and her smile was radiant.

"I loved your singing. You have a remarkable voice. Have you studied music?" Gwen asked.

"My musical education was in a church choir. And a few lessons."

They chatted a bit, and then Rebecca said, "Have you met my friends?"

She introduced them to her roommates Sophie and Tru. "These are my number one fans," she added.

Sheila said, "We are so lucky to have her here. She'll be famous someday."

Gwen turned her attention back to Sheila.

"Do the kids pay you anything for your counseling?"

"If they can, they give me food, cigarettes, feathers—whatever."

"A barter system."

Sheila nodded. "I try to help them find their path, whether that's back to Mom and Dad, or staying here. And if they need medical help, where to find the free clinic. They come with all sorts of problems— pregnancy, VD, overdose, infections from walking barefoot. You name it."

"That's great that you help them."

"I'm a counselor. Not a social worker or psychologist. I have no real training for it, except a couple of psychology classes, but it sort of comes naturally."

They leaned against the couch, and Gwen felt a sort of high. Whether it was from the brownie, or the general loving atmosphere she wasn't sure. Soon sitting on the couch behind her someone was massaging her shoulders. She didn't care who was doing it; it just felt so good.

She was introduced to a lot of people. She said, "I'll never remember all these names."

A short girl laughed and wiggled her hips. "You won't need to. You'll know if you know us by just looking at us. And if you don't, that's OK too."

When he took a break, Sheila introduced Tyson to her. She could tell he was seriously stoned, wondering if that enhanced his musical expression.

He said, "I saw you the other morning. You were strollin' along with Hank."

"Yes, yes I was."

Sheila said, "If you have any favorite songs, Tyson will play them for you."

"Oh, requests. Let me think. No, I'm not really up on the new ones. I'll enjoy whatever you play."

The esteemed Kenny arrived, and Sheila rose to greet him. "Come meet my new friend," she said, guiding him over to Gwen. "Gwen, this is Kenny I told you about. He has the real stuff." She turned to the young man. "Let her try some, Kenny."

"No, no, not tonight," Gwen said. "I have to navigate back to Marin. I need to stay alert."

"Want to take it with you?" Kenny offered.

"It's tempting. Maybe another time." But Gwen couldn't imagine that she'd ever try it.

"Anytime," Kenny smiled.

It was eleven o'clock, time to go home, Gwen decided. She'd learned a lot, made new friends and had a good experience. She couldn't wait to tell Mark.

"Weren't you taking some risks?" he asked Gwen when she got home.

"How so?"

"Walking around alone after dark, meeting with strangers. Anything could have happened to you."

"It feels so safe, Mark. People take care of each other. And as far as I know, there isn't any crime."

Mark just shook his head.

"I thought you were happy for me that Vandermeer's letting me write articles on the Summer of Love."

"But going out at night alone is risky."

"I'll see if they'll let me bring you. I don't see why not."

Mark grunted. "Did you imbibe?"

"On what?"

"Pot, LSD, whatever they had."

"I ate one funny brownie."

"It could impair your judgment."

"Well, it didn't."

He took her in his arms. "I just don't want anything to happen to you, Sweetheart. You understand, don't you?"

"I think you're being overly cautious. Thousands of kids are roaming the street. Nobody's been attacked, murdered. The whole point of the movement is peace and love."

"Just be careful."

"I am."

~~~

Sophie met Rebecca the day she arrived at Marjorie's. The two didn't take long to become close friends and share their stories.

On this sunny day they were sitting in Marjorie's backyard drying their recently shampooed hair in the sun.

"Why did you come to California, Rebecca?"

"To get away from my dad. On Fridays, after he got his pay, he'd get drunk and come home loaded. Then all hell broke loose." She paused.

"Are you serious?"

With her perfect skin and radiant smile Sophie would never have imagined that Rebecca had such a background.

"Sometimes he'd just and collapse on the couch and fall asleep. But other times he'd pick up whatever was handy—a broom, a vase, his belt and start beating Mom, shouting stuff we couldn't understand. One night I just couldn't stand it. I couldn't let him hurt her anymore. I came up behind him with a chair and tried to hit him from behind to give her a chance to get out of his way. He turned on me, grabbed the chair, and knocked me over with it."

"Oh, my God!"

Rebecca said, "Then after slapping me around, he raped me. The next day I left town."

Sophie marveled at how Rebecca seemed to be taking this in her stride.

"It seems like a long time ago. Anyway, I'm doing everything I can to forget it."

"Oh, Rebecca, I'm so sorry. I ran away too. But my story is so pale compared to yours."

"Everyone's story is important for them."

"Well, my folks were strict, that's really all. I had to keep stupid hours, wasn't even supposed to date boys. But hearing your story, I feel kind of ashamed."

"Do they know where you are?"

"No. At least I didn't tell them."

"Maybe you should."

"Yeah. But I'm so glad I came. Just think—do we want to live like *Leave it to Beaver* or like Janis Joplin?"

They giggled, and then Rebecca said, "Let's go to the concert tonight."

"Sure. Maybe Tru will come too."

Rebecca was particularly interested in the Swans, an all-girl band, and they were on tonight. She was hoping she had honed her singing skills enough to sing with a band, and the Swans would be a perfect match. Their type of music, less intense and more lyrical than some of the other groups matched her own style. She meant to approach them after the concert.

That evening in the part she sat with the others, listening carefully to the nuances the lead singer was employing. Rebecca did not hope to replace her, but perhaps if she could become a backup singer . . . Oh, just thinking about it gave her goosebumps.

When the concert was over, she told Sophie and Tru she was going to talk to someone in the band.

"Do you want us to wait?"

"No, you go on back. I won't be long."

"OK."

Rebecca approached the stage. One of the members came over. "I'd like to talk to you about --- trying out, to" she stumbled for words, "to possibly work with your band."

"In what capacity?"

Rebecca was a little intimidated. "As a musician."

"What's your instrument?"

Rebecca felt her face go red. "Oh, sorry, I sing."

The woman sat down on the edge of the stage, dangling her feet. She stretched out her hand. "I'm Janet. I'm on bass."

"I'm so glad to meet you. I've been following your group and really admire your style."

"What's your name, Honey?"

"Oh, sorry. Rebecca, it's Rebecca."

"And you sing. Do you have any experience—on stage?"

"Well, church, but I don't suppose that counts. And at a small group that meets in someone's home."

She dropped her eyes in embarrassment. How lame it sounded. She knew if she were to get anywhere, she had to come across stronger, more competent.

She looked Janet straight in the eyes and said, "I'd love it if you'd listen to me sing. I don't mean on stage. Just somewhere where you could hear my voice."

After a few more questions, Janet said, "Well, sure, if you'd like to come to my apartment, we'll give you a listen. I'll get the others to come, too."

She smiled brightly and turned to the drummer and the saxophone player behind her packing up their equipment. "Hey, can you gals come over on Friday, say two o'clock to hear this gal sing for us?"

They agreed. Janet wrote down an address for her on Gough Street, and said, "It's a fair ways from here. But you can take the bus. Bring sheet music if you can. One of us will accompany you on the piano."

Rebecca ran all the way back to her friends. They could tell by her expressions that her talk with the band had gone well. Together they jumped up and down and squealed in jubilation.

Then they skipped and ran all the way back to Marjorie's.

~~~

Rebecca worked at the ice-cream store on Ashbury. Her shift was from two in the afternoon until ten. It had been a hot and busy day, and she was glad that it was getting near closing time.

Looking up at the next customer she paled. "Thought you'd seen the last of me, Beck?"

"What are you doing here?" she hissed.

"Same as you, I suppose. Came to see the sights."

Rebecca glanced at her fellow worker who was watching. Turning back to the intruder she said, "I can't talk now."

"I can wait. Meanwhile, fix me a double dip chocolate."

Skittishly she carved out a scoop of ice-cream, then put another on top.

As she presented it over the counter he said, "That top scoop looks like it might fall off. In fact, I didn't see you pack the first scoop down tight. I think you'd better start over."

Seething inside, but not wanting to invite a scene, she dumped the ice-cream back in its bin and began again. She was careful this time to push the first scoop down and press the second firmly on the first.

But when she tried to give it to him, he said, "Those scoops look awful small. Fix them bigger. I'm hungry."

She felt her face turning beet red, as again she dumped the ice-cream and started over.

Finally, he seemed satisfied, and put some coins on the counter. "There's a tip there for you." He winked. "See you outside."

She could feel her uniform sticking to her skin.

"Who's he?" her co-worker asked.

"Somebody I went to high school with."

"Good looking."

"Yeah, but a real jerk."

She dreaded going outside when her shift was over. She could see him sitting on the bench out there, chatting up anyone who would talk to him. Cheerful and cool, it turned Rebecca's stomach.

When it was time to leave, she took off her ruffled apron, hung it on a hook, picked up her purse and left the store. She would walk right past him.

He stood up, feet spread, blocking her path.

"Don't be in such a hurry. Aren't you glad to see me? Have some good 'ole times?"

"I don't want to see you ever again." She tried to brush past him.

He blocked her path. "Oh, Beck, don't be like that. We used to really rumble." He grinned and shook his hips.

She was frightened. He could be charming, and that's why she'd dated him in high school, but there was another side to him, too. Their friendship had not lasted long.

"Look, I don't know what you're doing here, but I don't want to see you anymore."

She tried to step around him, but he stepped in front of her.

"Let me pass."

"I'll walk you home, Beck."

"I don't need your escort."

"Oh, but I think you do. It's dark, dangerous for a pretty girl like you to be out on the streets by herself."

As she moved away from him, he stepped beside her, keeping pace with her. She considered going somewhere other than home, but she didn't know where. Proceeding on toward Marjorie's she knew that when she opened the front door there would be others in the front room, some talking, some trying to sleep. He wouldn't dare force his way in.

It worked, at least for tonight. But what about the future? He knew where she worked, and he knew where she lived. He'd probably show up again, and then what?

~~~

The night before she was to sing for the Swans Rebecca found it hard to sleep. In the morning she got up early, went in the backyard and practiced singing her audition piece. It was her own song. She hoped she wasn't making a mistake not singing something familiar. Then she went in the house, drank some tea and honey, and finished writing out the sheet music.

She left in plenty of time to catch the bus and reach her destination. Rebecca rang the bell indicated for the first-floor apartment, Janet let her in and took her to a room with a piano that overlooked the street.

Due to the heat, the windows were open which was somewhat disconcerting as the traffic outside was noisy. Janet introduced her to the others.

Rebecca gave the music to Patty who said, "Just let me play this a couple of times, to get familiar with it."

Rebecca tried to relax. She focused on her breathing, as she listened to the music. When Patty felt she knew the music well enough to accompany the singer she said to her, "Are you ready, Honey?"

"Yes."

As she began Rebecca felt a little nervous, but as she registered encouraging smiles she gathered courage. Her voice was clear, and Rebecca knew she was singing well. When she'd finished, they applauded.

"That was lovely" Patty said. "Who wrote it?"

"I did."

"You did!" Janet gasped. "You wrote this beautiful song?"

"Yes."

"And it's about this awful war. You couldn't have chosen a timelier subject."

"How long have you been singing?" asked Patty.

"For quite awhile, in my church choir back home."

"And where is that?"

"Nebraska."

Peggy brought out a tray of cookies from the kitchen, along with a pitcher of iced tea.

"Sit down, Rebecca, help yourself."

They all did, and more questions were asked. Rebecca couldn't remember eating anything, if she had.

"Have you had professional training?"

"Only one year, just before I came out here."

When it was time to leave, Janet said, "You have a gifted voice, Rebecca. I'll be in touch. Do you have a number where we can reach you?"

She gave them Marjorie's number. For something so special she didn't think Marjorie would mind.

As Janet walked her to the door she whispered, "I think you're in luck. Our lead singer is pregnant, and she'll be leaving the band soon."

Rebecca was so happy she skipped down the stairs and along the sidewalk. Suddenly she heard steps catching up with her. She turned to see her nemesis.

"Are you following me?"

"Is that a crime?"

"Look, I don't want anything to do with you."

"Don't be so hasty. You sang beautifully and I was enchanted. Did you tell them that you wrote that piece?"

She didn't answer.

"You did. Now what would those ladies think if I told them otherwise? That you actually stole that song from one of our classmates."

"You know that's not true!"

"— stole her work. Said it was yours. How do you think they'd feel about taking you on then, Beck?"

"That's a lie!" Every fiber in her being was on fire.

"They wouldn't know who to believe, would they? There'd be enough doubt to drop you like a hot potato."

She attempted to get rid of him by hastening to the bus stop, but he was following her.

"That would be awful, wouldn't it?" he said. "Just when you might really make it big time. But you can avoid all that unpleasant disappointment. You just have to keep me company for a while."

No!

"You want to sing with the big girls, don't you? So, you'll think about it. See you tonight—eight o'clock, in front of your place." He smiled, turned abruptly and left.

Bitter tears filled her eyes as she waited for the bus. She'd focused her whole life on becoming a singer, studied, worked as a waitress to pay for lessons, given up all other interests to pursue her ambition to sing.

And just when her dream was about to come true, he was about to smash it.

~~~

Gwen was planning to go to the concert that night to hear Grace Slick. Absolutely a stunning beauty, some folks came just to watch her sing. But her voice was bewitching too. She sang with Jefferson Airplane's Band, and people loved her.

"Mark, do you want to go with me?"

He agreed and picked her up at the Chronicle. By now, Gwen kept some hippie clothes at work, so when Mark picked her up she was in jeans, beads and sandals. They were more than a costume, they were another persona that she was gradually adopting.

As a reporter she didn't want to just stand aside as an observer and fake a costume; she wanted to immerse herself in the whole picture, be a part of it. She was beginning to feel the zeitgeist of this place.

"Are you trying to look like a hippie, or are you a hippie?" he asked with a touch of sarcasm.

When she went to her first park concert, Gwen enjoyed it thoroughly, but she was an observer of a happening new to her. She'd been to a couple of others since with her new friend, Sheila. Now she was immersed in this Paradise. Objective enough to separate herself from the euphoria of it to write about it during the day, she was totally entranced in the evening concerts. She was no longer just an observer of this heady time. She was a participant.

Going tonight with Mark was very different from the first time. Then they were both spectators. Now she felt constrained. She wanted to get up and dance with a circle of folks nearby but knew Mark would disapprove. This was hard. They'd gotten along so well in the previous year, seemed to be on the same page about everything. No struggles, no arguments.

He'd brought a picnic, and the wine was good. Wanting the evening to go smoothly, she smiled, squeezed his hand, and said, "Thank you."

Timothy Leary, expelled from the faculty at Harvard for inducting his students with the visions of a new society available through LSD, was on the stage telling the assembled to "Turn on, tune in, and drop out."

Gwen winced when she heard those words. She knew the effect they'd have on Mark. Straight as an arrow and conservative in politics, right on cue, he was ready to leave.

"This is anarchy," he said.

"Let's just listen to the music."

He remained in stoic silence for the duration of the concert. When they got home, he said, "You're loving this, aren't you? You're not just reporting—you're in it, up to your eyebrows."

"I'm enjoying it, yes. I think it's cool that people are learning to re-think their values and not just adopt the status quo."

"That's hippie talk."

"Mark, I wish you'd open your mind to new ideas. Everything is changing—politics, spirituality, ideas about materialism—"

"Yeah, I've heard. 'Down with capitalism.' That will lead to communism. Did you see the posters pushing anarchy? Wouldn't that be wonderful?"

She found it harder and harder to talk to him. In the morning she was still upset with his stubborn refusal to discuss anything calmly. After walking Alfi, she did some karate kicks in the backyard. First taken at the university to satisfy a phys ed requirement, she'd kept it up, both for exercise and self-defense. Now it was serving as a healthy release of her frustration.

CHAPTER 4

Rebecca was an emotional wreck, trying to think of what to do. If she just stayed in the house, would he dare come in? Why had she been so foolish the night before as to lead him right to her door? And then he'd followed her to her audition. Now he was here again. Was it worth giving up her career to get rid of him? If she refused to see him, he could go to Janet, and that would be the end of everything she'd dreamed. Of course, she didn't know for sure if she'd get the job with the band, but from what Janet said, it looked quite likely. With difficulty she decided to see him, try to placate him, and see if she could put him off. When eight o'clock came, she stepped out on the porch. Sure enough, he was waiting for her. In her mind she had it all planned what to say.

"Let's go for a walk," she said. "I want to talk to you."

"Fine. We'll talk and walk."

He took her by the arm. When she balked, he said, "You don't want to cause a scene, do you, in front of your friends?"

"I don't want to go anywhere with you!"

"You want to be a singer, don't you? A famous one. Nothing to stop you now, with that great audition. I just need a little cooperation from you, a little payback."

"What are you talking about?"

He held her tightly by the elbow, marching her along, turning down a quiet side street.

"Where are you taking me?"

"Just a stroll in the park where we can make a deal."

"I don't want any deal with you and I don't want to go to the park!"

Indeed, they were very close to the Golden Gate Park. She tried to pull away, but he held her tightly. She looked desperately for someone who might help her. She wanted to scream for help, but there was no one around.

"No concerts tonight. Hardly anyone here. We'll have to make our own music."

She started to break out in a sweat. If only she could run, but she knew he'd catch up.

"Let me go. Please let me go. It's all over with us."

"You got that wrong, Beck. It's just beginning."

What would he do if she screamed? Did she dare? She did. But no one heard her; they were all too far away, why hadn't she screamed earlier? He laughed.

Now they were alone in the park. He kept marching her further in, away from the lights of the Haight, away from the joy-makers and parents with strollers. Far in the distance, she could hear a small group singing "We Shall Overcome."

How shall I overcome?

He guided her forcefully toward some bushes.

How could this be happening? What of her plan to make it clear that she wouldn't see him under any circumstance.

"This is a good spot," he grinned.

She pulled against his iron grip. "Let me go!"

"You're going to cooperate, aren't you?"

"What do you mean?"

"Oh, Sweetie, don't be so naive. You remember the good times." Rebecca cringed. "We didn't have any 'good times'!"

He grabbed her, forcing her into a dance step. "Remember the prom, Beck? How much fun we had," he snarled.

He stopped abruptly before the bushes. "Behold. The way has been prepared for us."

He pushed her through the thicket to a spot well-worn prepared by a host of previous lovers. "See, we're shielded on every side. The perfect spot for out trysts."

Rebecca was crying.

"Stop that now."

He was carrying a backpack. "I came prepared," he said, deftly slipping his backpack off his shoulder, while not releasing his hold. "Now you unzip it."

She screamed and pulled against his grip. He was hurting her arm. "Now do it."

She stared at him, then blindly unzipped the backpack. Inside was a blanket.

"Think I'd make you lie down on the cold wet grass? No, that's no way to treat a lady. Now spread it out."

Shaking, she did so.

"Lie down on it like a good girl."

Her adrenalin kicked in. She pulled away from him and started to run. He laughed, letting her get a few feet ahead of him. Then he caught her, forced her back to the blanket and pushed her down on it.

He knelt down beside her. "I'm glad you're wearing a skirt. I want you to always wear a skirt. Now pull it up, Beck. Let's see your lovely white legs."

She lay frozen.

"I'm going to count to five."

Still, she didn't move.

"I can see you're going to learn your lessons the hard way."

He slapped her hard in the face. She whimpered and turned away.

He pulled her back gently.

"I don't want to hurt you, that's not my thing, but we can't have any fun if you don't play by the rules. Now, once again, lift up your skirt."

Whimpering, she did so.

"Now slide down those pretty panties. I'm gonna watch you do it."

"No. Please."

"See, I'm not going to rape you, Beck. That wouldn't be nice. And besides it's against the law. You're going to get ready for me, all willing, and then not resist me at all. In fact, you're going to participate."

"You're crazy!" She rose to a sitting position.

Another slap, this time harder.

"You have to show some respect, Beck. Respect is very important."

Her hands went to her face, and she sat sobbing. How had her intention to have a civil talk with him, ended in this nightmare?

He pushed her down again. "How many slaps do you want, Beck? Now, do you remember what you're to do?"

Slowly, she slid her panties down to her knees.

"And the rest of the way. Take them all the way off, I want to watch you do it." He smiled as he sat back on his haunches.

A waning moon shown down on them. "You're so pretty when you're scared, Beck."

She slid them off. He looked at her a long time, casting his eyes up and down her body, relishing her humiliation and fear.

"Is this hard for you, Beck? It was hard for me too, the night of the prom, when you walked out on me. When you shouted, 'Stop it!' and left me standing there, everybody laughed at me, Beck. You didn't know that, did you? They laughed. And later, when they saw me in the halls at school, they laughed again. Even after graduation they laughed. Nobody respected me. So, you have to pay, Beck. You're going to show me some respect now. Yesserie, you're going to show me respect."

She stared at him in disbelief. "Now spread your legs."

When she remained still, he raised his hand to strike her. Before he could do so, she quickly did as she was told.

"Now you're learning," he said as he leaned over and gently spread them further apart. Then running his finger from her navel to her pelvis, with both hands he separated her lips, pulling them painfully apart.

"Pretty, pretty pussy."

He took her then, while she watched the stars above, trying to block out the pain, remembering another time back home, trying to believe it wasn't happening.

When he finished she still lay imprisoned beneath him.

He said, "Now that wasn't so hard, was it? Next time, though, I'm gonna expect a little more action from you. Know what I mean? You gotta get into it, Beck, show you're enjoying it. Move that sexy ass of yours around. You're gonna learn to do it real good. Before we're finished, you'll be a pro. And always, always, Beck, you're going to show me respect."

"Let me up!"

But he held her down. His hands found her neck, squeezing, releasing in a pulsating rhythm. "And when you stop co-operating, Beck, there won't be any Beck. You understand what I'm saying?"

He held her down for several more minutes. When he rose, he said, "Now get up and fold the blanket."

She did so and put it in the backpack. When she started to run off, he grabbed her by the arm and said, "Not so fast, Beck. I'm going to walk you home. It's dangerous to be out at night. Something bad could happen to you."

All the way back he held her hand, like they were going together. He gripped it mercilessly, as he talked about other things, how he'd hitchhiked to California, how he was doing some volunteer work here—*it makes you feel good, you know*— and how he enjoyed the services at some church, not because he believed in anything they said, but because he liked the music.

When they reached Marjorie's, he said, "Now give me a good-night kiss, Beck."

This time she managed to summon her remaining fragment of will, pull away and run up the steps. Behind her she could hear his high-pitched laughter. Going directly to her sleeping bag and burying her head in her pillow, she concealed her sobs as best she could until finally, she fell into a sleep so wrought with nightmares, that for the rest of the night she lay awake.

~~~

The next morning, Sophie found Rebecca in the bathroom applying cold cloths to her face. She could see that she had a big bruise. "My God, Rebecca, what happened to you?"

"You don't want to know. It's nothing."

"It doesn't look like nothing. Did your boyfriend do that to you?" Rebecca handed her some pancake make-up. "Help me cover it up, will you?"

Sophie dabbed the make-up on Rebecca's face as Rebecca winced in pain.

"That's the best I can do. It just looks like makeup trying to cover up a bruise, I'm afraid," Sophie said.

"Better than before."

"Do you want to talk about this?"

Rebecca shook her head.

Later when Tru was alone with Sophie in the kitchen, she asked, "What happened to her?"

"I don't know. Just be nice to her." Sophie sipped her water and wondered what in the world Rebecca had gotten herself into. She wanted to help, but how?

~~~

In the next week Gwen made several more sojourns into this happy land. It reminded her of King Arthur's Camelot, a place spun up like cotton candy, and from an outsider's point of view, never meant to last. She saw quite a bit of Sheila, and they found themselves sharing much of themselves with each other.

One day when Gwen stopped in to see Sheila at the vintage clothing shop, Sheila said, "I'm ready to call it a day. Why don't you come home with me? I'll fix you my special tea."

Walking the two blocks to place, Sheila told her about her latest client.

"Poor kid. He's only thirteen, hitchhiked all the way here from Iowa. He's so scared. Scared to stay, scared to go home. By the way, I'm not telling tails out of school—no names— confidentiality."

"I understand."

On Sheila's back balcony over the India ice-tea Sheila had prepared, she said, "My parents were great. Not perfect, no one is, but really nice, supportive and cheerful. I didn't inherit any of their talents. My dad was a violinist in the symphony orchestra, and my mom did large murals for banks and places like that. I couldn't do any of those artistic things."

Cool summer breezes fanned their faces. "Did you have anything in common?"

"We're all overweight."

They laughed. Sheila said, "I write to them every week. What are your folks like?"

"I was raised in Marin until I was ten, then when I lost my mom I was taken to Michigan and my aunt took care of me."

Sheila wanted more. "What happened to her?"

Gwen swallowed. So few people knew. Was she ready to tell her new friend?

"She disappeared. No one knew what happened to her. And I didn't know who my father was."

"How awful. Did they ever find your mother?"

"Years later they found human bones, and they matched my mom's X-rays."

Sheila put her hand over Gwen's. "I am so sorry."

"Please don't tell anyone."

"Oh, never!"

~~~

They sat in Marjorie's backyard manicuring their nails. Sophie was applying a bright red to her short stubby ones.

"What's that color, Rebecca? It looks heavenly."

"Satin Rose."

The day was warm, but Rebecca was wearing a turtleneck. When she turned her head, Sophie could see the bruise on her neck. Small, but dark and angry.

Sophie caught her breath. "He did it again," she burst out.

Rebecca pulled her collar up. "Does it show?"

"When you turn. What did he hit you with?"

"His fist. Not very hard—the mark is from the ring he wears."

"Big ring."

"Yeah."

"How did it happen?"

Rebecca swallowed hard. "You wouldn't understand, Sophie. I have to do what he says. If I don't . . ." she shrugged.

"Is he holding something over you?"

"He'll spoil everything for me."

"Like what?"

"You know my dream to sing with the Swans—"

"Yes."

"He's going to tell them I didn't write that song, that I stole someone else's song." She burst into tears. He would, too. And then they'd have nothing more to do with me."

"Don't be so sure of that. They like you."

"That's not enough! They'd throw me out like last week's garbage."

"Rebecca, please stop seeing him," Sophie pleaded.

"I can't."

"Just because of that threat?"

"No." In a whisper, "He said he'd kill me."

For the first time, Sophie realized how genuinely frightened her friend was. Sophie put her arms around her. After a moment, she said, "You can't let him treat you like this. Can't you see? He's just like your father."

The tears cascaded down Rebecca's face.

Sophie said, "I left home because of my dad, too. He never beat us, but it was suffocating in that house. Oh, damn, I've smeared the polish all over my fingers. I'm no good at this. I could never do it right."

"Here, let me."

Rebecca removed the messy job with nail polish remover. When she finished cleaning her up, she said, "Want to try some of mine?"

"Oh, thank you."

Rebecca began painting Sophie's fingernails, slowly, perfectly. When she had finished Sophie said, "You're good at everything, you know that? Singing, fingernail polish—"

They burst out laughing. Then Sophie said, "I wish I could do one thing as well as you do so many."

"Don't compare yourself to anyone, Sophie. You're a dear friend, and you have a lot to offer. Take a big bite out of life. If it's sour, spit it out. If it tastes good, have more of it."

~~~

That evening Rebecca said, "Sophie, want to go with me to get some sodas?"

"Sure. Where we going?"

"This Mom and Pop store over on Cole."

The streets were alive with the jangle of kids laughing, even dancing. Several wannabe musicians were practicing their craft on the sidewalks.

"This is so great," Rebecca said. "Aren't we lucky just to be here, be part of this scene? It's going to go down in history."

"You think so?"

"I do. Everything we were brought up to believe in is turned upside down. The movement is reaching not only all over our country, but even to Europe. It's washed over the planet like a tsunami."

"I didn't realize that," Sophie said. She wasn't sure it was such an earth-moving happening, but maybe Rebecca was right.

"And just think, we can tell our grandchildren we were part of it." They turned the corner and strode arm and arm down Cole Street.

The store was so narrow that it would be easy to miss it, but Rebecca knew where it was, and they stepped inside, as a bell jangled from the door to announce their presence. A sleepy looking man in his fifties emerged from a back room. Small, but wiry and spry he hastened to the counter.

"Oh, Pop, are we keeping you up?" Rebecca asked with a grin.

"I guess I nodded off. Had a late night last night. Mother's been sick."

"I'm sorry to hear that. Is there anything I can do? Bring her some soup or something?" Rebecca asked.

"No, we got plenty of that. Thanks, though."

They headed for the refrigerator where an assortment of wine, beer and sodas were cooling.

Just then the bell on the door jangled again, and a young couple stepped in. The man, in a leather jacket, strode purposely toward Pop. The young girl followed.

The man approached Pop and demanded that he turn over all his cash.

"Look, kid, I ain't got any. And if I did, I wouldn't give it to you." The man pulled out a gun and pointed it at the grocer.

"I'm warning you, Pop. Trigger here, don't like to be kept waiting. he's gonna go off real soon if you don't cough up."

A few seconds later the sound of the shot reverberated through the whole store. Sophie and Rebecca ducked behind the free-standing snack shelf and held their breath.

The bell jangled again as the girl screamed and ran out of the store. Sophie and Rebecca remained frozen, waiting for the man to leave.

They could hear him fiddling with the cash register, attempting to open it, release its contents. Finally, they heard him leave. Then Rebecca rose and went to the grocer. Blood covered his chest and spilled all over the floor. She felt for signs of life but found none.

"He's dead!" she cried.

Looking fearfully at the door Sophie cried, "Let's get out of here."

"We can't just leave him."

"But if he's dead— let's go back and call the police."

"His mother, someone has to tell his mother."

"The police can do that." Sophie pulled on Rebecca's arm.

The girls raced all the way back to their lodgings, ran upstairs and pounded on Marjorie's door.

"We need to use your phone," they said panting.

She shook her head. "I told you—no phone calls. I've been burned with long-distance bills when the kid said it was local."

"A man's been murdered! We have to call the police."

"What!"

They were admitted to the rarified atmosphere of the second floor. Warm and cozy, it smelled of fresh flowers.

Marjorie picked up the phone herself and turned to the girls. "Now who did you say got murdered, and where did this happen?"

Marjorie managed to give the message to the police, including her address if they wanted to ask questions. But she was as shaken as Sophie and Rebecca.

After the call she said, "Stop pacing, Sophie, sit down. You girls want some cocoa? I could use some."

Marjorie was heating some milk in a pan. "Now tell me everything. Why were you there? What did you see?"

Seated around the round kitchen table they told her the story.

"Just like that? He shot the guy? I can't believe it. I mean we don't have crime in the Haight. Not like murder. Everybody treats everybody else respectful and pleasant, right? What was he thinking?" she said, twisting her braids.

She was in her own reverie, and the milk began to boil and threaten to rise above its confines.

Sophie dashed to the stove and turned the gas off just as the bubbly stuff cascaded down the side.

"I'm sorry dear, I got distracted." Marjorie spooned three large scoops of cocoa into the milk and stirred it.

When she got her cup, Sophie knew the taste would be tainted from the boiled milk, but she was shivering from shock, and hot liquid was a welcome warmth.

"Comfort food," Marjorie said, putting a plate of cookies on the table. "Now tell me again. Who was in that store first—you gals or the killer?"

CHAPTER 5

G wen was about to get in the shower when she got the call. Someone had called in a heinous murder in the Haight, and Vandermeer had contacted her. She went back to the city.

She'd never been at the scene of a murder before. Nervous, uncertain as to how to proceed, she headed for the Haight. Would she be allowed into the crime scene? Would there also be a photographer there to take pictures? She checked her purse. Yes, her trusty notebook was there. She'd take notes of the scene, of ambient atmosphere of the neighborhood, talk to people, if she could.

Blinking red lights guided her to the exact address. She had to park almost three blocks away, then rush back on foot to get to the scene. She tread gingerly through the gathering crowd on Cole Street. Yellow tape forbade the entrance of anyone beyond it. Inside, someone was being lifted onto a gurney, and carried to the entrance. A policeman released the yellow tape, and like a wave, the crowd parted allowing the paramedics through. As the ambulance rolled away screaming sirens and bright lights faded in the distance. The yellow tape was reapplied.

The police remained inside for some time, and Gwen, displaying her press badge was, at first, not allowed admittance. She waited, while the crowd dispersed. Finally, a police officer motioned for her to enter. She saw the very narrow, but homey little Mom and Pop store, the shelves lined with the necessities of living, the cooler with beverages. And then, as she dared approach the counter, she saw on the wall a pattern of red that had created a ghoulish abstract painting. And on the floor, more blood.

Querying the police, she asked if the killer had been apprehended, if they knew the motive for the crime, if there'd been any witnesses.

"Apparently a couple of girls saw what happened."

"Do you know who they were?"

The officer shook his head, dismissing her.

Walking through the Haight she felt a changed atmosphere descend on the neighborhood. The usual exuberance and noise of the streets was missing. The unthinkable had silenced the sounds of joy. Even the air felt heavier.

Gwen queried folks about the man who'd been killed.

In whispers she heard things like, "Everybody loved Pop. If you didn't have the money for something, heck, he'd give it to you."

The Haight was stunned. It couldn't happen here. Not in Utopia. Not where the very mantra was Peace. A cloak of mourning had engulfed the Haight.

~~~

About an hour after Marjorie had made the phone call, they heard her door buzzer from below.

"Probably the police," she told the girls.

"Do we have to talk to them?" Sophie asked. She rose so abruptly from the table that she spilled her cup of cocoa.

"It will be OK. Just sit tight." Marjorie said, splaying her hands. Then she left them and descended the stairs.

She came back with a policeman. Although young, he appeared tired; apparently he'd just come from the murder scene. Marjorie offered him a seat.

"These are the two girls who witnessed this awful crime," she told the cop, twisting her braids. She was the last to sit down.

"What time was this?" the officer asked.

"Just before I called the station," Marjorie said.

"Could you give me a description of the killer, miss?"

Rebecca spoke. "I didn't get a very good look at him, mostly from the back. We didn't pay attention to him when they first came in the store."

"They?"

"He was with a girl. As soon as we saw the gun we hid behind some shelves."

"Please describe them as best you can. Were they white?"

"Yes, both of them." Rebecca looked at Sophie. "He had dark hair, I think."

Sophie nodded in agreement.

"How tall would you say he was?"

"I'm not sure. About your height, I guess."

Writing notes, the officer said, "Five feet, seven."

"And the girl?"

"She was wearing a scarf over her head. I don't know what color her hair was. Did you notice, Sophie?"

Sophie shook her head. "She had on a coat, though. It's warm out, but she was wearing a coat."

"She seemed pretty shocked when the gun went off. She yelled his name, screamed and ran out of there," Rebecca said.

"Did you catch his name?"

"I couldn't make it out."

"Was it one syllable or two? One like Mike, or two like Michael?"

Sophie and Rebecca looked at each other. One, I think," Sophie said.

"Did they leave right away?"

"She did. She ran out of there," Sophie said.

Rebecca added, "But he went behind the counter and opened the cash register. We couldn't see him, but I heard the sound it makes when it opens. Then in a couple of minutes he left."

"Do you remember anything else?" Sophie shook her head.

"Thank you, miss. Would you mind coming down to the station and looking at some mug shots tomorrow?"

The girls looked at Marjorie. Marjorie nodded. "I'll go with you."

"I guess so," they said in unison.

When the policemen was gone, Marjorie said, "Listen, girls. You've been through a lot. I'm going to let you have the boys' room. They're somewhere over there in Vietnam, so you girls take it for now. I want you to have it. There's two twin beds in there. You'll have to take the sheets to the laundromat every week or so, and you can take mine, too. But otherwise, it's free to you."

Rebecca and Sophie thanked her, and after lying in separate beds for a while rehashing the horror they'd witnessed, Sophie said, "Rebecca, can I come to your bed? I know it's not cold, but I'm shivering to death."

And so, the two curled up together, offering what comfort they could to each other simply by their close presence.

~~~

The next day Gwen went to the Park Police Station. Signs of *Wet Paint* were posted along the wall. But Gwen didn't need any signs to tell her that. Sensitive to smells the noxious odor of fresh oil-based paint assaulted her nostrils as she waited in the outer office to speak to an officer. Seated across from her was a young woman sobbing in the arms of a young man. The efforts of the young man to comfort her did little to assuage her despair. Gwen wondered what calamity had occasioned such a torrent of emotion from the woman. So many stories, so much unhappiness.

Finally, Gwen was led into an office, where she met a small officer with a mustache extending so far to either side it was comical.

Offering her no seat he said, "I'm due at a meeting."

Flashing her press badge, she said "I've come regarding the murder of the grocer—"

"I know why you've come."

A bit taken aback by his abrupt attitude Gwen decided to waste no words. "Do you have any leads on the killer of the grocer?"

"Not yet, no." He stood, and she knew she was being dismissed.

But leaving the building, on the wall she noticed about a hundred notes and photos of missing kids, sent by desperate parents from all over the country. Some showed the shining faces of daughters in their cap and gown, others of sons standing proud in their football uniform. Gwen could feel the fear and heartache of the parents.

One read, "Suzie, please come home. Everything will be different now. We love you." Another said, "Derek, your father said you can go to whatever college you want. Please let us know you're OK."

Gwen read several more, and then she spotted a picture of Rebecca. She read the note accompanying it. "Rebecca, if you don't come home, your father's going out there to fetch you. We know where you are. Your friend Alice told us."

She relayed this information to Sheila. "Do you want to tell Rebecca about the note? You know her, I don't."

Sheila's lip twitched as she debated.

Gwen continued. "She should know, don't you think?"

"You're right. I'll tell her when we see her Friday night at Tyson's."

Writing an article for the Chronicle she spun this dark story against the background of peace, poetry and liberation. How could this atrocious crime have happened in the *city of love*?

She wrote another article for *The Oracle*, a paper printed in the Haight, and read by its inhabitants. Using a pen name for fear the Chronicle would not approve of her writing for another paper, she wrote a more personal piece, including the testimonies of several people who lived there and knew the grocer.

~~~

The next morning, Sophie and Rebecca were led into room at the police station, where a very large book of mug shots was laid on the table before them.

"Take your time. Look at them carefully."

After an hour, when they saw no one that they could say definitely was the killer, the policeman thanked them and let them go.

"If you think of anything else—a tattoo you saw, a scar, anything, please contact us."

"Of course," Rebecca said.

"Wait a minute," Sophie said. "I remember this sickly-sweet after-shave, or whatever. That smell wasn't there when we first went in."

"That's right. I don't think he was one of us, I mean I don't think he was a hippie, or anyone who's a regular around here." Rebecca turned to Sophie. "Did you ever smell after-shave on anyone at the park?"

Sophie shook her head.

Rebecca looked at the policeman. "Was that at all helpful?"

"Could be. Details are important. Sometimes they solve the case."

~~~

Friday night came, and Gwen was about to leave for Tyson's. An angry Mark questioned her. "Drugs, sex. Why do you need to immerse yourself in that Dionysian culture?"

"Mark, please, it's not like that."

"Do they have Bacchanalian orgies?"

Determined not to echo his roiling emotions she tried to calm him down. "It's music, and it almost feels . . . spiritual. Why not come with me? I'm sure it will be alright," she said.

He shook his head, "I'm not interested in that hippie stuff, and I wish you'd confine your interest to daylight hours."

"I'm sorry you feel that way. I really am." She walked over to where he was sitting and put her arm on his shoulder.

Even before she was at Tyson's door, she could hear the angelic sounds of Rebecca's singing. This time lyrical strains of *White Rabbit* was coming through. As she entered the room, she heard the words clearly: *One pill makes you larger, another makes you small.* After that she sang, *You Need Somebody to Love.* The usual smell of pot permeated the crowded room.

There was hardly a place on the floor to sit. Each Friday more and more people were coming to hear Rebecca.

When she finished singing Rebecca headed over to chat with Sophie and Tru.

"You tell her," Sheila nudged. "You're the one who saw the note."

When the opportunity arose, Gwen said, "Rebecca, I was at the police station a few days ago, and I saw a bulletin board full of notes from parents, pleading for their children to come home. There was one there from your mother. She wants you to come back."

"I know she does," Rebecca said sadly. "I can't do that." She turned and walked away.

Gwen and Sheila exchanged looks of surprise.

CHAPTER 6

Mark had softened for a bit, and on the previous Wednesday night asked her if she'd go with him to a party.

"What kind of party?"

"Company thing. Administrators and department heads of our three facilities."

"Where's it going to be?"

"At the Saint Francis Yacht Club on Saturday night. A black-tie event."

That meant she'd have to get something really dressy to wear. She felt like she was in a play, or maybe two or three plays, always changing costumes, even personas.

Surprisingly, she found the perfect gown where she least expected. Looking for more hippie clothes in a box at the Free Store, something glittery caught her eye. She pulled out a long silver gown covered with sequins. If only it would fit. Going behind the single screen, she slid out of her street clothes and tried it on. Except for it being too long, it was a perfect fit. My gosh, she thought, *I could have paid a hundred dollars for this.*

As she sat shortening the gown that evening, Mark was impressed, but not entirely supportive of her new shopping methods.

"Hey, I'm saving money. And I'm going to clean out my closet and donate all the stuff I never wear anymore. Do you have anything to contribute?"

He smirked, but the next morning, there were two pair of shoes and some trousers on the table.

"Are these for the Free Store?"

Without looking up from the newspaper he said, "Whatever you want to do with them."

"Thank you."

On Saturday, as she dressed and began applying mascara, she felt like she was preparing for another role. She would have to be the perfect, supportive partner for Mark tonight. She felt confident she could handle this part too.

They took the Hudson through the Rainbow Tunnel and across the bridge. Already the sequins were causing her skin to itch. Well, beauty has its price.

The Yacht Club was exquisitely decorated for the occasion, the dining room was in shades of mauve and pale green. The windows looked out of the Bay, where many sailboats were enjoying the last rays of sunlight. She looked around at the well-heeled assembled and wondered if they even knew about the cultural revolution in this very city.

Gwen was surprised at how easily she was adapting to the role of partner of an important businessman. It made her smile. She was introduced to the managers and their wives of the other two retirement homes in their group. When the women discovered she wrote for the Chronicle they were duly impressed and wanted to know what she was working on.

When she told them, she heard remarks of the same tone:

"I've heard those hippies are causing an awful disruption to that neighborhood—just invaded it and took it over from the poor people who live there."

"Yes, and they're not taking any responsibility for anything. Just going for the drugs and sex."

"I hope you're writing about that. I'll be watching."

"Absolutely. So much to write about," she nodded.

It would have been fun to spread the philosophy of the Summer of Love, but this was not the time and place. She had no intention of embarrassing Mark.

The seating arrangement placed Mark of her right, and one of the managers, Mr. Riley, on her left. Mark had consumed about three drinks before they started eating and kept going during dinner. This, in turn affected his choice of conversation.

Mrs. Anderson was sitting on his other side. After saying more than he should have about her attractive gown, he announced, "Gwen here, found her getup in a pile of rubbish on Haight Street. It's smart, though, don't you think?"

Gwen blushed all the way down to her toes.

"To explain, my dear Gwen has taken to becoming a hippie. She's exchanging her lovely wardrobe for love beads and feathers, sandals and ribbons. Aren't you, Sweetie?" He squeezed her thigh, hard.

She wanted to get up and run. She said nothing the rest of the evening. When they reached home, she closed the bedroom door in Mark's face and yelled at him. "Sleep on the couch!"

In the morning, he staggered into the kitchen with a hangover. "Do you have any aspirin?"

She didn't answer him.

"Look, I'm sorry about last night. Don't know what got into me. The booze, I guess."

"Why were you drinking so much? I thought you wanted to be on your best behavior in front of your boss."

"I need some aspirin."

"And even when people have too much to drink, they don't become something they're not. Some real part of you leaked out through the booze. Why did you need to humiliate me?"

"I'm going to the store to get some aspirin."

When he left Gwen burst out crying. What was happening to their relationship? Why was he so angry?

Maybe she *had* become one of the new order. She no longer thought that her values, behavior should be dictated by society; she felt it was her right to determine for herself what they should be, according to her beliefs and needs.

But what was the cost? Was she losing the man she loved?

~~~

The hunt for the killer of the grocer continued. Police officers, seldom seen on the streets of the Haight made their presence known now. They questioned shop owners, posted signs asking anyone who knew anything to please come forward. They took a dog to the shop to pick of the scent of the after-shave and walked him around the Haight Ashbury district.

Although most of the people who lived here had a suspicion of police, backed up by a general belief that government and any representation of it should be abolished, they were of mixed minds when it came to doing something about an outrageous killing. And so, the police were tolerated.

However, this was not the only crime in the city of San Francisco, and after a week it was decided by the powers that be that their presence was needed elsewhere. The mystery of who killed the grocer remained unsolved, as life went on.

Sophie, Tru and Rebecca hadn't forgotten, though. They were careful to stay together when they went out and to avoid dark and lonely places.

Gwen, knowing nothing at all of the witnesses to the shooting continued her own efforts at finding the assassin. She wrote pieces for the Chronicle to keep the story alive, and personal, human stories for *The Oracle*. She talked to folks who knew the owner of that little store and got their stories of him. She put them together and created a persona of this man. Using this, she wrote a piece about Herman Schmidt that made him come to life. How he was from Germany, came to this country when he was twelve, began working right away at a butcher's in San Francisco. How he'd saved money until at age forty-five he was able to buy his own little shop. And how his mother was so thrilled, she cried. He'd never married because he didn't think he'd ever get his shop if he was raising a family. And being an owner of a proper grocery store was what he wanted more than anything. That was the American dream, wasn't it?

If this little village had been united before, it was even more so now. Readers of her articles in *The Oracle* approached her on the streets, asking for more information. They posted signs in their windows urging anyone who knew of the killer to come forward.

As a friend and as a sleuth she met with Sheila.

"Have you heard anything? From the folks who come for counseling?"

"No. If I do, I'll let you know."

~~~

Sophie didn't want to be in the spotlight. She saw the notices, heard people talking and read the paper. But she didn't want the publicity. Besides, she'd told the police everything she knew. Rebecca felt the same. They had talked to the police, looked at mug shots. She didn't want to be in the spotlight either.

Anyway, if they were open about what they'd seen, the killer might come after them.

One night Sophie, Rebecca and Tru decided to go hear Jimi Hendrix in the park. Dynamic, charismatic, the girls couldn't wait to be among the lucky ones to hear this beautiful black man work his magic with his guitar.

They sat next to a young family sitting on the blanket next to them.

A toddler wandered over to Sophie and gave her a popsicle stick. "Thank you," said Sophie. To the mother, she said, "What's her name?"

"Fawn."

"That's a pretty name."

The woman went on, but Rebecca was watching someone walking through the crowd carrying a sign, "Who killed Pop?"

"See, my name's Doris. But everybody calls me Doe. So, when she was born—you know . ." The woman smiled and shrugged.

Rebecca nudged Sophie and indicated the man with the sign. "Yeah. I'm expecting again. My husband says if it's a boy we should call him Bambi."

"I was kidding," the husband said.

The girls looked at each other and shook their heads. No, they couldn't get any more involved. Anyway, they couldn't answer the man's question. They'd done what they could.

"You girls care for some weed?" the father asked them.

"You mean marijuana?" Sophie asked.

"Yeah."

"No," they answered simultaneously. "No thanks."

~~~

Sophie looked for her friend upstairs, downstairs. Nowhere in the house. She went to the backyard. There she was, sitting forlorn under the pear tree.

"Are you supposed to see him tonight?"

"Yes."

"Don't go, Rebecca."

"I have to."

"No, listen. This is what we can do." Sophie told Rebecca her plan.

"That will never work."

"Of course, it will. What can he do? He can't stop you."

"It's too risky, Sophie. Besides, I haven't told Tru any of this."

"We'll just tell her we're playing a joke on your boyfriend."

Just before eight Sophie and Tru came bursting into the room. Each took one of Rebecca's arms, and laughing they pulled her down the stairs. Somewhat frightened, but going along with it, Rebecca put up little resistance.

When they got to the bottom, Sophie said, "You ready? Open the door and see if he's there."

She opened the door, nodded. The trio came down the steps arm-in-arm, her escorts laughing and singing. They ran right past him and continued around the block.

When they returned to the house he was gone.

Back in their room Sophie was still laughing. "That ought to cool his heals--hopefully, you've shaken him for good." She looked at Rebecca.

"What's wrong?"

"It was insane."

~~~

"You didn't think you could get away with your little game, did you?"

He had tailed her from the ice-cream store. Rebecca froze, startled and afraid.

"I thought you were smarter than that, Beck. But we can make up for your indiscretions. We have ways." He held her arm firmly in his grip.

Rebecca stood in shock. "What do you mean?" she whispered.

"You'll see. Come along like a good girl, and it will all be over quickly."

She tried to pull away.

"You know what happens when you try to resist me. It never works."

"Please," she whimpered.

"Don't try my patience, Beck. You might incur my wrath."

In fear, she allowed him to lead her.

What could be worse than what she'd already endured?

As they walked toward the park he said, "What do you imagine an appropriate discipline would be for breaking the rule?"

"I don't know," she mumbled.

"I could whip you. But not tonight. Tonight we're going to do something that will remind you who your master is."

They were in the park now. Any illusion of escape vanished.

He guided her toward their special place. When they arrived, he said "Look at me, Beck."

She remained with eyes cast downward. Seeing him raise his arm toward her, she quickly looked up.

"That's right. Now listen carefully to what I'm going to say. "You broke the cardinal rule, Beck. You remember what it is, don't you?"

She nodded.

"Say it, Beck."

Her lips quivered, but she said nothing.

He slapped her. "You can't have so quickly forgotten. What's the rule, Beck? Say it."

"Respect," she muttered.

"And to whom must you show respect?"

"You," she whispered, dropping her gaze.

He pulled her chin up sharply and held it. "Now put it altogether. Say, 'I must at all times respect and obey you.'"

Somehow, she managed to choke out the words.

"But you forgot that rule, didn't you, Beck? You flagrantly laughed in my face. And that's sad, 'cuz now I'll have to do something to help you remember it."

He handed her the backpack. Shaking, she performed the ritual of removing the blanket and spreading it on the ground.

"Get the corners straight. Make the whole blanket nice and smooth. We don't want any wrinkles in our love nest, do we Beck?"

When he was satisfied, he said, "Now lie down and close your eyes."

She did so, waiting for his next command. Fully dressed he straddled her. Then she felt him tying something tight around her arm.

Trying to sit up she cried, "What are you doing?"

He pushed her down. "Just relax, Beck. We'll do this often to help you remember the rule."

She watched in horror as he took a syringe from the pocket in his backpack. He pulled her arm toward him.

"Please don't do this to me! I'm sorry, it was a joke!"

"A joke? I don't like jokes, Beck. And it's too late for 'sorry', Beck. Now you have to pay for your transgression. That's kind of the way the world works, you know?"

"Then whip me!"

He laughed. "Oh, but then you might run away from me again. No, I'm not going to hurt you, Beck. But I have to make sure that that doesn't happen again." He was removing the cap from the syringe. "Because if it does, there won't be any Beck."

"Please!" She pulled her arm away.

"This will help you remember in the future."

He forced her arm back across his lap. "You're going to love it, Beck. It'll make you feel euphoric."

"What is it? "

"Heroin."

"Please, no!" She tried to jerk away.

"Hold real still now. After a few times you won't have any more trouble remembering the rule. Pretty soon you'll be begging for it. You'll do anything for me, Beck, just to get it."

CHAPTER 7

Sheila called Gwen. "I've got to see you."

"OK. Where?"

They met at the same shop where Sheila did her counseling. As she spotted her friend, Sheila said apologetically, "Do you mind if I smoke? I gave it up, but sometimes I just have to."

She pulled a cigarette from its pack. "Listen, Gwen, you'll never guess who came to see me."

"Who?"

"The grocer killer's girlfriend," Sheila said, lighting the cigarette.

"You're kidding."

"I shouldn't be telling you any of this—confidentiality of a client, you know. But this is too big for me. I'm not sure what to do." She inhaled deeply.

"Go on."

Sheila didn't wait to finish her cigarette before opening and chewing a Snickers bar. A puff, a bite.

"She saw my 'Free Counseling' sign in the window. I saw her mince by several times, like she was debating whether to come in or not. She didn't look more than fourteen. Of course, I didn't know who she was. Finally, on the third day she did come in. It took her a long time to get to the point, to let on what was troubling her, although it was obvious that something was. I kept smiling and saying, 'Take your time.' She kept twisting this dirty handkerchief in her hands and looking at the door. I was afraid she was going to run for it."

Sheila started coughing and wheezing. She put out the cigarette and whipped an inhaler out of her purse. In a few moments she was breathing normally.

"Sorry," she said, referring to her asthma. "Acts up when I'm excited."

"Take your time," Gwen said. She wanted to say, "Hurry up, tell me!"

"The girl said, 'Did you hear about the grocer who was killed?' I said, 'Yes, I did.' Then she whispered, 'I was in the store too, and saw him do it.' I was stunned, as you can imagine. Trying to keep calm I said, 'Could you identify him?' She looked up terrified, and said, 'He's my boyfriend.' Gwen, my heart was beating a mile a minute."

"She told you this? Incredible!"

"Then she said, 'I can't decide whether I should go to the police or not.'"

"Oh, no."

"I know. I asked her what her hesitation was, and she told me she still loves the guy. She's real torn up about whether to turn him in or not."

"She still loves him even though he killed someone?" Gwen asked incredulously.

"Love can be an awful affliction."

"Did she make a decision?"

"No, and I don't know if she's coming back. Gwen, I'm in the same dilemma. I don't know whether to go to the police."

"To report her, you mean."

"Yeah, to get her to help them catch the guy."

"Is she an accessory?"

"I don't think so. From what she said, she was blown away when he pulled out a gun. She didn't even know he had one. And when he pulled the trigger, she was out of there."

"Then she shouldn't be afraid of the police."

"She's afraid of the boyfriend."

"Did you give her any advice?"

"I was so in shock, I said something like she should listen to her conscience and do what felt right. I understand her fear. Between the time that she reports him, and they catch him, he could kill her."

~~~

Gwen continued to talk to people, trying not to sound like a reporter. She was, like they, also in deep distress over this unlikely murder. Treading the murky waters of investigating it she followed every lead she could, however slim. She heard people's compassion, their shock, but no one was coming forth with any significant information. She spent a great deal of time in the Haight observing, gathering information, talking to people, then returning to the office to write up articles.

She was not just on the trail of a murder; she was still searching for the heart and soul of this counter-culture. It soon became obvious that the inhabitants of this village were there for different reasons. She sought out Sheila, who'd been here longer than she, to help her get a handle on the disparate elements of this community.

"You're right, Gwen, lots of different motives draw people here. Some are here for the music, some for the drugs, or drugs and free sex."

"Is there a lot of that—free sex?"

"Oh, yeah. It's considered an act of generosity."

Shaking her head, Gwen had to share Sheila's laugh.

"Then there are those with the highest of purposes: to create a revolutionary change in the way we think, behave and govern ourselves. Started by the Diggers, a dedicated group of visionaries, they want to invent a new culture from scratch."

"Yeah, I kind of picked up on that."

"And as a way of putting their actions where their mouths are they serve up heaps of free food every day to feed the masses."

"What about all these stoned-out kids, sleeping on the sidewalk and in doorways?"

"That's not a pretty sight, is it? But it's just as common to see others working in a free store or harvesting food supplies from grocers inclined to give away day-old baked goods and wilting produce."

"Whatever their purpose, the inhabitants of the Haight seem to get along well together," Gwen mused.

"Yeah, some who only came for the adventure have found themselves drafted into doing useful things, like cleaning up the park after a concert."

"That reminds me, Janis Joplin is singing tonight with Big Brother and the Holding Company." Gwen remembered. "Wanna go?"

"Sure. I've heard stories about this young woman. Did you know she was voted 'most ugly man' by a fraternity?"

"Ugliest *man*? Oh, that's sad."

"Yeah, and her self-esteem is terrible. But wait 'til you hear her. She's got a golden voice, and everyone loves her—audience and fellow musicians—everyone but herself."

Before she went to the concert Gwen wrote an article for the Chronicle. "The Haight district in San Francisco has been invaded by great numbers of kids from all over the country. Statistics run anywhere from seventy-five thousand to a hundred thousand. Where do they all sleep? A few owners in the area have opened their homes to the new people. But the others? In doorways, in the park.

"And how are they fed? It is the founders' belief that everything in society should be free—food, clothing, all of the necessities and many of the pleasures, like the wonderful concerts. But how do you feed a hundred all these people? The founders are given left-over food from grocers, which their girlfriends make into stew every day, but that can't possibly be enough to feed all the hippies in town. One is reminded of Jesus and the twelve loaves.

"On the surface, The Summer of Love in the Haight Ashbury district is a real love-in, as it is intended to be. But there is a very dark underbelly to this modern Garden of Eden. The streets are spotted with young people zoned out on drugs, some so stoned they are lying in doorways. A murder has been reported, and so far, there has been no arrest."

That evening as she and Sheila joined hundreds of Joplin fans trapesing through the streets on the way to the park, Gwen felt a joyous lift in her spirits after the sobering article she'd written. Listening to the concert that had attracted thousands, Gwen could understand why this woman was so loved. As she sang her whole being opened up, and she spread the holy fruit of her talent to all who were listening.

~~~

Jennie Lopez was so conflicted she didn't know what to do. She couldn't believe she'd gotten involved with a killer. When she first started seeing Bud, she knew he was on the tough side, a member of Hells Angels, and wasn't going to brook any trouble from his girlfriend. She'd seen him get in a couple of fights with the flower people, but he'd never hurt her, and she thought he subscribed to a certain code of honor that the Angels had. She wasn't sure what that was, but he'd mentioned it, and she knew he believed in it.

Plain, with thick dark hair, she had a decent figure and a strong appetite for sex and obedience. She was attracted to the sheer brawn and masculinity of this man. Bud wasn't a talker, he was all about action. Not tentative about anything, he went after what he wanted and got it, like he'd gotten her. She liked that, liked his dominance.

She'd met him, hanging out in a gas station on Nineteenth Street. She went there to have somebody to talk to. The owners were Mexican, and she felt at home with them. They were among a fading breed who still pumped gas for people. Sometimes Jennie would wash the customers' windshields, and once in a while earn a tip for doing so.

One day Bud came vrooming in on his Harley. Jennie ran out to look at this beautiful beast. Although basically shy, she was so impressed with his black and glossy bike that the words burst forth.

"Do you mind if I look at your bike?"

"Go ahead."

"Is it yours?"

"Yup."

She watched the bike while the owner filled his gas tank and he went inside to buy some Camels. When he left, she waved as he drove off. That was about all there was that day, but the next time he came in, she went out to him again.

"Can I wash your windshield for you?"

"If you want to."

"Sure."

She did it very carefully, and cleaned the rear-view mirrors, too. When she finished, she said,

"Thanks." He laughed at her for saying that.

"You're so lucky to have this bike." She was practically salivating.

"Ever ride on one?"

"No."

"Want to?"

"Really?" she squealed. "Sure, I do."

"Hop on."

And that's how it started. She'd noticed the bike before the man. He was on the short size, dark-haired and slender. He was OK to look at, but it was the bike she'd fallen in love with.

They drove down Geary to the beach and rode for a few miles along the ocean drive. Jennie thought it was the best time she'd ever had in her whole life.

He said, "You have to be home any certain time?"

"No, I'm on my own."

"Where do you live?"

"In the Haight."

"You a hippie?"

She shook her head.

They rode to the Haight. When they reached the house where she was staying, he said, "You ever had sex?"

Jennie was uncomfortable. "No!"

"You a virgin?"

Nodding, she was embarrassed to be having this conversation.

"Want to—have sex?" He held her chin up.

"With you?"

"You see anybody else?"

She knew she wanted to see more of this man, so she said, "I guess so."

He followed her into the house, which like so many others, was an old Victorian-- this one sprouting yellow blisters of paint. This old lady was badly in need of a facelift. The owner was housing a dozen or more kids. Jennie shared a room upstairs with three other girls. Being four o'clock in the afternoon, the other girls were out.

"We have the room to ourselves, but I can't guarantee how long that will last."

"Sex doesn't have to take long."

And it didn't. It was over all too soon to suit Jennie. She wished he'd stayed longer, but soon after he'd finished, he said, "I'm off."

She walked out to his bike with him. "Will I see you again?"

He smiled. "I'll be by."

That wasn't very specific, but Bud did come by, every day for a while. She stopped going to the gas station, for fear of missing his visit. He didn't even need to come to the door. She'd hear him vrooming up the street and she was down the stairs and outside to meet him. Sometimes they'd go for a ride on his bike, and sometimes they'd go straight to her room.

Jennie had not traveled across the country to wear flowers in her hair and join the new social order. She grew up in the canal district of Marin County, a community of mostly Mexicans, sometimes four families in one apartment. Her father had raised roosters for cockfights, and one night after a cockfight that ended in a dispute, he died in a knife fight. She lived with a mother who was always sad and often crying. Jennie was only three at the time, so she'd never had a masculine influence in her life. Not until Bud.

When she was fourteen, she left home and went to San Francisco because she'd heard they give away food in a neighborhood near the big park, and free places to sleep, too. After she met Bud, she went everywhere with him whenever he let her and stayed away when he told her to.

One afternoon when it was over, she said to him, "I like the way you make love."

He said, "Call it that if you want. I call it sex."

Well, OK, he wasn't the romantic type, but she liked it anyway. It made her feel loved. At least she could pretend.

She knew he didn't share everything with her, but what he did share was so much more than she'd ever had before, that she accepted it.

"He could be real nice," she told Sheila. "He bought me stuff, you know, like ice-cream cones and banana splits. I love banana splits. And he bought me a teddy bear because I told him I'd never had one. Wasn't that sweet?" Her eyes filled with tears as she remembered.

Now something had happened that she couldn't blindly accept. She knew she should report Bud to the police. But she loved him. She didn't want him in prison, she wanted him with her. How alone she'd be again without him.

And maybe if she turned him over to the police, she'd be arrested as an accessory. After all, she was with him when the shot was fired. Maybe he'd blame her for what happened. Or worse, maybe he'd kill her if he found out she'd told the police. He'd already threatened her. It was after they'd made love one afternoon, Bud was restless, tossing and turning in her bed for a long time.

"You're thinking about it, aren't you?" she ventured.

"Thinking about what?"

"You know—the grocer."

"Why do you say that?"

"I don't know. You seem kind of nervous."

"Naw. Who's gonna tell—you?"

He turned toward her. "Don't even think about telling anyone. One word and you're toast—you got that?" He held her jaw tightly in his hand.

"I'm not telling anyone. I don't want to lose you …but   "

"But what?"

She tried to turn away. "Come on, say it."

"We weren't the only ones in the store."

"What are you talking about?"

"There were two girls—"

"What!"

"Hiding. But I saw them when I came in."

"Jesus! Why didn't you tell me?"

"There, there wasn't time—" she stuttered.

"What did they look like?"

"I didn't really notice, and then they hid when you asked Pop for the money."

He held her jaw even tighter. "Don't you remember *anything*?"

"One of them had black hair. That's all I know."

"Would you recognize her?"

"You're hurting me."

"Well, would you?"

"Maybe," she managed to squeak.

"You find her, and you show her to me. You got that?"

She nodded as best she could within his vice-like grip. *My God, she thought. Why did I tell him? Now what am I going to do?*

~~~

Rebecca did her best to wipe chocolate ice-cream off her apron. She was feeling so clumsy today. A hot day, the fan from above did little to cool the shop. She was sweating. Her wrist hurt from scooping the hard ice-cream from the bins from the last four hours, and besides she was having cramps; today was the first day of her period. Suddenly she looked up and saw two people who looked vaguely familiar.

"I'll have a banana split," the girl said. She turned to the young man. "What do you want, Honey?"

"A double chocolate."

Something very familiar about this couple! Rebecca stood absolutely frozen, staring at the pair.

And then she remembered.

The man said, "Are you deaf or what?"

Hands shaking, Rebecca picked up the scoop and twisted it in her hands. Willing herself to act, she began to attack the vanilla and the chocolate. Before she could get to the strawberry, she dropped the scoop on the floor. Hastening to retrieve it and wash it under the sink, she turned back to find the couple had disappeared.

~~~

The question of what Rebecca was to wear for her grand debut with the Swans had been settled the week before when she, Sophie and Tru had visited the free stores, searching through racks and boxes for the perfect outfit for Rebecca. When she discovered the blue bell-bottom trousers with matching top she was in heaven.

"It couldn't be better!" she squealed.

On the day of her debut with the Swans Rebecca couldn't stand still, she was so excited. Both anxious and happy she paced the floor. She sang the scales up and down, then sang her audition song. She was so wired she couldn't eat any lunch.

"You have to eat something, Dear," Marjorie said.

Rebecca looked at the salami sandwich. "Not now, I'm sorry."

Sophie said, "Let's go get you some new make-up. And there's this hair spray now that has sparkles in it. It will make you look fabulous."

With giggles and butterflies, somehow the afternoon went by.

~~

In a hotel room on busy Lombard Street Doug Barton threw his jacket on the bed, and said to himself, "Dirty San Francisco, the asshole of the country. Queers galore, and now this—a whole village of low lives with free sex, drugs, V.D. The Sodom and Gomorrah of the 20th century."

The phone rang. "Yeah, I got here alright. I've been walking around that freak neighborhood. Already found out she's gonna sing somewhere tonight. Can you believe that? There's posters around, advertising a girl band concert on some stage in the park. In small print it says 'Introducing a new singer, Rebecca Barton' . . . Calm down, Marla, I won't interfere with her singing tonight, but it's the last time she's gonna do that in this god-forsaken place. She can sing when she gets back home—at that church. . .I'm not gonna hurt her. I'll find out where she's staying . . . Tomorrow or the next day I'll get her and bring her home . . .if she doesn't *want* to? It doesn't matter if she *wants* to! She's a minor and I can make her. . . Did I say anything about hurting her? If she co-operates, I won't have to … Shut up, Marla! You're making me mad."

~~~

"You have to sit still long enough for me to do your makeup, Rebecca," Sophie implored.

Rebecca complied. Sophie examined Rebecca's face and neck carefully.

"Hey, thankfully, I don't see any bruises needed covering up."

"No."

"In fact, you had any in a long time, right?"

"Right."

"He must be treating you better." Rebecca pulled at her sleeve.

As this was such a special night for Rebecca, Sophie took her time applying foundation, rouge, lipstick and eye-shadow.

"Hurry up, Sophie, we'll be late!" Rebecca implored.

"Just a minute. Hold still while I do your mascara."

When the time came to leave, Sophie, Tru and Rebecca skipped to the park together, with Marjorie bringing up the rear.

"This is the beginning of my life," Rebecca said to herself. "I am so blessed."

"I know a star, she's famous," Sophie said as they skipped along.

"I'm not a star, I'm just beginning." But then under her breath, "Maybe someday."

An unusually warm evening, even in her sweater she was shivering. That's just nerves," Tru said.

They arrived early, as was expected of performers.

Janet called out as soon as Rebecca was in sight. "Glad you're here. Don't want to worry if you'd show." She gave Rebecca a big hug.

"There's no way I wouldn't be here," Rebecca beamed.

"Love your outfit. You're going to take your sweater off when you sing, right?"

"Right."

"You can watch in the wings, and when it's time, I'll introduce you."

"OK. Can I help you set up?"

Janet was surprised. "Well, sure. You can help Peggy drag those drums up here."

Rebecca was glad to have something to pass the time. She helped position the mics too. The stage seemed a little shaky. Or was it her?

The crowd was beginning to gather. "Are you nervous?" Janet asked.

"Yes, can you tell?"

"That's natural. It's your first time. You'll get used to it. You know, we have big plans for you. When Lottie leaves, you might become the lead singer. Then you'll be singing lots of songs every time we give a concert."

"Oh, my gosh!" Rebecca covered her mouth in exhilaration.

"Rebecca," someone called to her.

She turned to see Tyson, Sheila, Gwen with her little band of fans from the Friday night gatherings.

They smiled, all thumbs up. "We're here for you, girl. Can you come down here a minute?"

"Oh, my gosh," she said again, slipping off the stage. She accepted their hugs as tears of joy and gratitude trickled down her face.

"Be careful there," Sophie said. "You don't want to ruin your makeup."

Gwen handed her a tissue to wipe her face.

"I'm so nervous." She was jumping up and down in small steps.

"You'll be fabulous," Gwen said. And Tyson threw her kisses.

Rebecca talked with them a few minutes and then, as the park was filling up, went back onto the stage and into the wings.

The concert started with Lottie singing the first song. Rebecca listened carefully. She liked her style, the way the woman could spin a note into two or three. She could learn a lot from Lottie, she decided. But tonight, she'd stick to her own style—no experimenting on her debut.

Each time a number ended, Rebecca sat on the edge of her chair, wondering if she'd be called up next.

Finally, she heard Janet say, "It is my pleasure to introduce a new singer to you, making her debut tonight on our stage. I'm proud to say we discovered her and mean to keep her." She gestured to the wings. "I bring you the talented and beautiful young Rebecca."

Rebecca walked on stage, aware that folks were clapping. She listened for the band's intro, opened her mouth and sang her heart out. All remnants of the jitters had vanished. This was her moment and she was owning it with every fiber in her body.

Near the end of her piece as she made eye contact with those in the first few rows, her eyes locked on someone she hadn't seen before. Rebecca faltered briefly, and then continued to the end of the song.

When she left the stage, Janet had to push her back on for a bow. Although her little band of fans was yelling 'Encore', that was not to be tonight.

"What's wrong?" Janet asked when the show was over. "Nothing."

Janet didn't want to bring attention to the fact that Rebecca had missed a note, but she did wonder why.

When the show was over, and Rebecca had received congratulations from the adults and hugs from her friends, Marjorie announced, "Surprise, Rebecca! Our little tribe is having a party for you!"

They traipsed back to the house, laughing, whistling and singing. Marjorie presented a cake with "Congratulations Rebecca" written on it. Everyone cheered, gorged on the cake and ice-cream. Sophie even had provided noise-makers, which everyone, even Marjorie, blew.

Rebecca felt a kind of high like no other. Was she seeing things through a rose-colored glass, or was her life going to be like this—beautiful, exciting and gloriously happy?

After the party, and back in their room, Rebecca and Sophie talked late into the night.

"You were so wonderful, Rebecca. Someday I'll be able to say, 'I knew her when.'"

"That day will be a long way off. Sophie, did you notice when I missed a note just before the end of my song?"

"Yeah, I did. You looked like you'd just seen a ghost."

"I wish he *was* a ghost."

"Who?"

"My father."

"You're kidding."

"No. I don't know how he found out, but he was there."

"All the way from Nebraska. Has he tried to contact you?"

"Not yet. He'll probably want to drag me home."

"Will you go?"

"Absolutely not."

They turned the lights out and climbed under the covers. From her bed, Sophie called, "Sweet Dreams."

Rebecca had completely forgotten that she was to meet her nemesis after the concert.

~~~

Rebecca worked a double shift that day, covering for a girl who couldn't come in. She hung up her apron and left the shop at ten o'clock. Exhausted after being on her feet for so many hours she took the shortcut through the alley. It was a lovely evening to be out, balmy and warm with just a slight breeze. Such a nice feeling after being cooped up in the ice- cream shop for so long. A happy couple passed her, laughing. They threw her a kiss and she threw one back. It's good to be alive, she thought.

So focused on the new song she was writing she didn't hear the footsteps behind her. Suddenly someone was grabbing her neck, squeezing it. She couldn't see who, and she couldn't make a sound.

CHAPTER 8

As she climbed the stairs to Tyson's the next night Gwen could feel something had changed even before she got to the top. An entirely different atmosphere permeated the space. Everyone was quiet. No music, no laughing. Some were sniffling. One girl was sobbing. Gwen stood riveted in the doorway. It was obvious that something odious had happened. But what? Finally, Sheila saw her, and quietly wound her way over to her, pushing her back into the hall, where they could talk.

"What happened?"

"It's terrible, Gwen."

"Tell me."

"Rebecca is dead."

Gwen's hand went to her mouth. "No!"

"Yes."

"Oh, my God. How did it happen?"

"We don't know. She was discovered in an alley not far from here this morning. We just found out. Everyone is stunned."

"I hadn't heard. Why wasn't the Chron informed?"

"I think the police are keeping it from the press pending notification of nearest kin."

Sheila led the way back into the crowded room. A heavy silence hung over the group like a dark cloud.

Sheila sat down on the floor leaning against the couch. As Gwen squeezed in beside her a feeling of terrible shock and sorrow engulfed her. She was no longer the objective reporter, she'd become emotionally involved.

People were beginning to whisper.

Soon Tyson spoke up. His deep blue eyes penetrated those in the room.

"Look, we need to talk about this, so let's share what we know, questions too. If anyone knows anything, even the last time you saw her, please speak up and tell us all."

For a moment it was quiet. Then someone in the back said, "I saw her yesterday where she works at that ice-cream store. She waited on me."

It was quiet again, and Tyson asked, "Anyone else?"

"Did she O.D?" someone murmured.

"She wasn't a user. She never touched the stuff."

"No." He swallowed hard and then went on. "Rebecca was strangled."

A loud gasp filled the room. "Murder!"

"How do you know?"

"Somebody who lives here heard she'd died, so I called Doc to see if he knew anything." Tyson said.

"Did he say how long she'd been dead?"

"I didn't ask."

"Who found her?"

"Some guy discovered her about seven o'clock this morning."

"Did he take her to Doc's?"

"Yes. He said he couldn't just leave her there."

"Does anyone know where she was living?"

Sheila spoke up. "Yes, she stayed at my friend Marjorie's house." She wondered if Marjorie knew.

"Do we even know her last name?"

A shuffling, and murmuring, but no one seemed to know. In the new paradigm last names were seldom used. It was like baggage from the past. Who needed it?

"How did Doc know who she was?"

"She'd been there a couple of times with a foot infection. He knew her." Tyson said.

"How about her folks, where do they live?"

"Somewhere in the Midwest, I think she said."

The questions and partial answers continued. Shock reverberated through the room. Who'd want to hurt Rebecca?

Tyson drew the evening to a close by announcing that there would be a memorial service for Rebecca on the next Friday night.

When she came home that night and told him, Mark said, "No crime, huh? Just a city of brotherly love? If I could, I'd forbid you to go there at night."

"Well, luckily you can't. Anyway, she was found dead during the day." Gwen said, although she knew the murder had probably happened during the previous night.

"Then I'd forbid you to go at all."

Exhausted, she plopped down on the sofa. "Look, I'm glad you care, but life goes on, and so does my reporting. This isn't nearly as dangerous as what I was involved in at *The Haven*. The criminal was right there inside the retirement home, and I was at risk, if you recall."

Mark came to sit beside her. "Of course, I do. I was hoping we were in a safe zone now. You're a reporter, Gwen, not a detective."

"Sometimes the lines get blurred."

He stared at the far wall. Was he losing the woman he loved to the career she loved?

~~~

In the morning Gwen wrote an article for the Chronicle about the death of this young singer. She felt her information was woefully skimpy, so after submitting the meager article, she sought out Sheila to see if she could tell her more about this young woman. She went by the vintage clothing shop in the hope that she'd be there by her counseling table. Not in today. She experienced first-hand the frustration of not knowing someone's last name, not knowing if she could be reached by phone.

The only other person she might contact was Tyson. But it didn't feel right to just show up on his doorstep. Then she remembered that Sheila had said that he's used to people coming and going. So maybe it would be OK to go there. She walked down Haight and over to Ashbury where he lived. Life seemed to be going on as usual, as though no life-altering event had taken place at all. I suppose it's like that when we die, it has to be that way, she mused.

She reached Tyson's house, and climbed the steps to the third floor. It was ten-thirty in the morning, but when she rang the bell, a girl in pajamas let her in "Is Tyson here?"

"In the kitchen. Come on in."

She stepped gingerly between the late sleepers on the floor and into the kitchen, where Tyson was brewing something that might be coffee. He was wearing khakis, but nothing else.

"Hi, Tyson, do you remember me?"

"Yeah, sure. You're Sheila's friend. And you've been here on a couple of Friday nights."

"Do you mind my coming over, uninvited?"

"Not at all. Nobody stands on ceremony here."

"I was wondering if you know any more about why Rebecca was murdered."

He was silent, and Gwen wasn't sure he'd heard her. Or maybe he didn't want to answer the question.

"Look, if I'm out of line—"

"No. The same question's on everybody's mind."

He poured two cups of his brew, set them on the oilcloth-covered table, and motioned for Gwen to sit down.

"Who could have done such a thing?" Gwen asked.

"That's what everyone's asking," Tyson said.

"Do you know anyone that she had a problem with, or who didn't like her?"

"No. I've talked to some of the folks who come here. No one knows anything."

"Has anyone claimed her body?"

"I called the coroner. He said her father's coming out to claim her body and take it home. And by the way, I got her last name from Doc. It's Barton."

"Well, that's something."

He stirred his cup of brew endlessly, seemingly unaware of Gwen's presence.

Finally, he said, "We're all keeping our ears and eyes open, trying to find out whatever we can that led to her death." He looked up. "We could use your ears and eyes, too."

Gwen perked up. "You have them."

Tyson continued. "Sheila says you've done some sleuthing. We'd appreciate it if you do what you can to help us get to the bottom of this."

"I'm happy to do what I can. But you know these people, Tyson. I don't. I don't know where to begin."

He had fished some weed out of a small canister and was putting it a cigarette paper and rolling a joint. Finally, he said, "Hang out with us. Get to know folks."

"But you don't think it's one of your friends."

"No, but somebody might know someone. We get a lot of strangers in here too. I don't know everyone. And the more people you can get to talk outside our group—well, that would help, too."

"Can you tell me anything about her background? How well did you know her, Tyson?"

"Sadly, not well enough."

"Where she was from?"

He shook his head. "We take people for who they are. Not who they were, or the baggage from their past."

He lit the cigarette and offered Gwen a toke. Shaking her head she said, "Did Sheila tell you I write for the Chronicle?"

"No."

"I have to be up front with you. I write the dark side of this Camelot, too."

"I understand. As long as you're honest, and I'm sure you are, I don't have a problem with that. In fact, it should be in the papers. Are you familiar with the *San Francisco Oracle*?"

"Yes, I wrote an article for them about the grocer who was killed, and then a couple of follow-up pieces."

"Could you write up something about Rebecca —ask that anyone who knows anything or saw anything come forward?"

"I've already started it."

Tyson said, "Be sure Allen gets it. He's head honcho over there."

"OK. Do you have a picture of her?"

"No. I could kick myself. All the opportunities we had to take one."

"Never mind. I know where I can get one."

This was all new territory for Gwen. No last names. No addresses. She guessed it all worked fine until something happened. Something terrible, like murder.

When she left Tyson's, she went to the police station. Among the hundreds of others, she found the notice and picture of Rebecca that her mother had sent and took it with her.

Returning to the tea shop she and Sheila had been to, she sat down and wrote something to take to *The Oracle*. It was more than a plea for information. It was a feature article, describing Rebecca's radiance, her beautiful voice, her debut at the park. If you could hear the violin strings, well that was OK. She wanted to move people to action.

She took both the picture and the article to *The Oracle*. Speaking with Allen, she elaborated on what he already knew, and told him that it was urgent that the word get out, and the culprit found.

"Thank you. I'll make sure this gets printed in tomorrow's run."

She left feeling drained of all energy. Still, she felt the need to go back to the Chronicle and write a follow-up article for that paper. With a much larger readership than *The Oracle* she hoped to reach a different audience. A feature article, but not nearly as personal as the one for *The Oracle*.

When she got home Mark had already eaten, was sitting at the kitchen table with a cup of coffee. The remains of scrambled eggs were visible in the sink. Popping a couple slices of whole-grain bread in the toaster, she fixed the same for herself.

"Where were you?" he said.

"At the office. I had to write up an article for the Chron."

"About the murder?"

"Yes."

"Is that all you're doing—reporting?"

She left the stove to face him "What's that supposed to mean?"

He jiggled the coffee in his cup, "Surely you're not going to get involved in this murder."

"You didn't object when I was helping you deal with the one at *The Haven*."

"Actually, I did, if you recall. Anyway, your Aunt Megan lives there, and you said you were doing it to help her stay safe."

"I need to do this, Mark. Give me some space."

"And give me some piece of mind—knowing you're safe."

Gwen's attention was drawn back to the stove by the smell of burned eggs. She turned the burner off and escaped to the backyard before the argument could escalate. Here she did some vigorous karate kicks, a way of dispelling her roiling emotions.

When she returned a stormy silence ensued. She loved Mark. He was a great friend and lover, but she couldn't have him trying to control her life. Maybe it was a mistake letting him move in with her when Denise got married and moved out. They'd only been living together a month, and already there were dark clouds hanging over them.

~~~

Gwen visited Tyson again.

"Any news?" she asked as he let her in.

He shook his head. "Nada."

He led her into the kitchen where the aroma of something good was brewing on the stove.

"Want some soup? It's a hodgepodge of leftover veggies."

"I'd love it."

She sat at the table and he spooned the collage into two mugs.

"Have you talked to anyone who knew her, well, better than you did?"

Tyson blew on his hot soup. Then he turned to her.

"No. Not a soul. I'm beginning to rethink this belief that we didn't need to know anything about each other. Hell, we need to take care of one another; that's part of our motto, isn't it? Loving each other. That means taking responsibility."

He finished his speech and seemed to be out of breath. He closed his eyes and took some deep breaths.

Gwen couldn't help wondering if the grocer and Rebecca had been murdered by the same killer. Probably not. She couldn't think what that connection could be. But she wanted to run it by Tyson.

He said, "It could be the same killer. It doesn't seem likely, but maybe the man's on a killing rampage."

"But usually, there's an M.O. The grocer was shot. Rebecca was strangled."

"But a gun makes a lot of noise outdoors."

Gwen said, "There's probably no connection. I think the probability of these two being connected is very slim. There are killings in the Bay Area almost every day."

"But not around here."

They spooned up the soup, each with their own thoughts.

Then Tyson said, "I thought she didn't have an enemy in the world. But then, I didn't know her friends outside of our little group," He looked up. "Allen at *The Oracle* hasn't received any leads?"

"He said there were a couple of crank calls—vague and unbelievable."

"Well, we'll keep digging," he said. "Until we know."

~~~

Sophie couldn't believe what had happened to her friend. My God, what had become of this village of peace and love? First, a murder in a little Mom and Pop grocery store, and now her new friend was dead. Was there a connection? She and Rebecca had witnessed that grocery store mayhem. Had the killer noticed them—behind the snack shelf? Wasn't he too busy to get out of the place to see them? Maybe he saw them when he first came in, before they were hiding.

If this was true, then he must have seen her, too. And her life was in danger. She went to Marjorie. Marjorie, who had empathized so strongly with what the two girls had been through, had afterwards invited them into the rarified air of the second floor and offered them sleeping arrangements there.

"I don't know what to do. I'm scared."

"Listen, Honey. We don't know it was that grocery store killer who got Rebecca. Rebecca had a nasty boyfriend. It could have been him."

Sophie remembered the bruises. This offered some consolation, but not a lot. She thought about going home. But she couldn't face her parents.

She looked down at her nails. The polish was chipping, and her nails didn't look good. But she didn't want to remove the polish. It was a gift form Rebecca had left her mark on her. She wished she could keep the polish on forever.

When she was at her lowest and totally depressed about losing her friend, she remembered what Rebecca had said that afternoon. *Take a big bite out of life. If it's sour, spit it out. If it tastes good, take more.*

Rebecca wouldn't have given up. Rebecca was always taking big bites. If only she, Sophie, could follow her advice.

She didn't go anywhere alone, and nowhere after dark. She and Tru stayed close together, and Marjorie let Tru come up and take Rebecca's place in the spare bedroom.

One day they were waiting for the sheets to dry at the laundromat—theirs and Marjorie's.

"I feel like I've got to do something," Tru said. "We can make some signs asking if anybody knows anything, they should contact us."

Sophie looked at Tru. "The way I see it there are three different people who could have killed her."

"Three?"

"The guy who killed the grocer, her boyfriend, and her father." She looked around to make sure no one was within earshot.

"Her father?"

They heard the buzzer on the dryer, collected the sheets and went to the folding table.

"Tell me." Tru shook out a sheet and together they folded it.

They shook out another sheet and Sophie whispered, "Yeah, he was a bastard, from what she told me."

"What? I can't hear you."

"We have to be careful; someone might hear us."

Tru looked around. "There's no one close. And anyway, the machines are making an awful lot of noise. Now, what did you say?" Sophie repeated what a bastard Rebecca's father was.

Tru frowned. "She never told me anything so personal. What else did she tell you?"

"How awful he was. He even raped her."

Tru buried her head in the sheet she was folding. "Oh, my God. So, you think he's a suspect."

"So that's how I count three. And her father was there that night—at the concert. But I can't help thinking about the guy who killed the grocer. We were in the store, you know, Rebecca and me. If he saw us, then he knows we were witnesses and so maybe he did it."

"Oh, my God!"

"And if he did, I'm next."

"Sophie, no! You don't mean it."

"Yes, I do!"

"What are the police doing?"

"Probably waiting for someone to come in and confess," she said bitterly.

Tru put her arm around her and tried to comfort her, feeling that their world of happiness and peace had crumbled around them.

CHAPTER 9

Gwen tried to talk to Mark that evening about what being free really meant. She shared the conversation she'd had with Tyson.

"I think they're nuts," he said. "Total chaos, anarchy—bedlam would result. New social order, my eye. There wouldn't be any order at all. Do what you want? 'I want your new car. Or maybe I want your baby.' The whole thing's insane. Mark my words. This Nirvana won't last out the summer."

Maybe Mark was right. But she wished they could have a rational dialogue, instead of a statement of judgment that precluded any discussion.

Because of his growing belief of what he thought young people were all about—anarchy, sex and drugs, Mark refused to go to any more concerts in the park with Gwen.

But Gwen was not going to let that stop her. She enjoyed the music, the energy and she enjoyed the feeling of community. She knew that not everyone had the lofty vision that the Diggers did. Many were there for a good time and would return home when the summer was over.

The next day, after sitting at the tea shop writing up another article, Gwen called *The Haven*, where Mark worked and left a message for him that she was going to a concert and would be late coming home. She knew he wouldn't like it, but it was part of her job. Besides, she admitted to herself, she was becoming part of this lively, energetic community.

That night, while listening to the soulful voice of Janis Joplin, Gwen mingled through the crowd carrying a large cardboard sign upon which was written "Does anybody know anything about Rebecca's death?"

A few people spoke to her, expressed sympathy, and asked what Gwen knew.

Looking around, she saw a whole contingency of Hells Angels mingling through the crowd and guarding the stage. What strange bedfellows—the flower children and the Angels. What was the common denominator? Although it struck her as odd, she'd been told that the Angels were hired as bodyguards by the musicians for some of the concerts.

She looked up at the stage to watch Joplin for a few minutes and saw a drunk or stoned woman trying to crawl up on the stage. One of the Angels pulled her off twice. When she tried a third time, he pulled her off and gave her a fist in the face which decked her. How can they be so cruel? She shuddered.

A nice-looking boy of about nineteen tapped her on the shoulder. Referring to the sign she was carrying he said, "That's Rebecca Barton, right?"

"Yes."

"We were friends, through church."

At last, someone who knew Rebecca. "Can we talk?"

"Sure. I'm with my friend over there. But I'd be happy to meet you tomorrow."

"OK. Where?"

"How about Mac's on Page Street? One o'clock?"

"That will be fine. Thank you so much for coming forward."

The boy extended his hand to shake Gwen's, then waved and was gone.

Gwen was so excited she wanted to yell to the heavens. She reminded herself that a friend didn't mean he knew anything about how Rebecca had met her demise, but this did little to diminish her excitement.

Returning to her spot on the grass the two young men sitting next to her started up a conversation.

"That's awful, about that girl's murder," one said. "Did you know her?"

"Yes, I did."

They nodded sympathetically, then whether they were flirting, or just so into the love-everybody scene, she wasn't sure. They were smoking pot and offered her a toke.

Gwen had reached the point that she knew she wanted to experience the effects of marijuana. She wanted to fully engage in the culture of this summer, and that was definitely part of the experience. But she wanted to do it with someone she knew, and not have to find her way home alone in the dark. She politely declined, saying that she had to drive back to Marin.

On the way across the bridge that evening she thought about who that person would be who she'd be most comfortable with. Tyson, it would be Tyson.

~~~

Tru posted signs about Rebecca up and down Haight, Ashbury and a few other streets in the neighborhood. Store owners were happy to put them in their windows, especially when Tru told them, almost crying, how Rebecca had been her housemate and what a beautiful singer she was.

"Somebody must have seen something," she told Sophie.

Sophie began not going out at all. She stayed in the house almost all the time, refusing even to accompany Tru to buy necessities.

Tru spoke to Marjorie. "Please talk to her. She's wasting away, just living in fear."

Marjorie said, "I have, Tru. But I can't make her change. Her fear isn't entirely unfounded."

"But she used to be such a happy person. If anyone could make you laugh, she could."

"She witnessed something terrible, Tru. And then her best friend was murdered. When things like that happen, it changes you. Life will never be quite the same for Sophie. You can't expect her to just put it behind her, forget it ever happened. Especially as long as the killer or killers are still out there."

~~~

On the next day Gwen could hardly wait for one o'clock to come. She got directions to Page Street, which wasn't far, and at twelve forty-five, she entered the little deli. Choosing a table by the window, she waited impatiently for the young man. She realized she didn't even know his name. Finally, it was one o'clock, but still the boy did not come. She waited ten more minutes and concluded that he wasn't coming. Maybe he'd forgotten. Maybe he'd decided it was a bad idea. Then at one fifteen he appeared.

"I'm so sorry. Excuses are odious. But here's mine: I was helping in one of the free stores. If you can't find something and ask for the manager, they say 'You're it.' If you don't like the way things are, you're the one who has to fix it. He was out of breath from running and took a deep breath. Let's sit down," he said, motioning to a recently vacated table inside.

As they sat down, he continued, "On a larger scale, that's what the whole paradigm of social change is all about, isn't it? No bosses, everyone equal. Anyway, I was sorting out clothes, trying to make some sense of the mess. I forgot about the time, sorry."

"You're forgiven. Just glad you came."

He took a deep breath and pushed his thick shock of blonde hair away from his forehead. "I'm Kevin, by the way. Kevin Jones. I don't think we introduced ourselves."

"And I'm Gwen. Tell me what you know about Rebecca."

"I couldn't believe it, when I read about her death in the paper." The boy rubbed his chin and looked genuinely distressed.

"How well did you know her?"

"As I said, we went to the same church here. We'd get together once in a while. She wasn't interested in anything romantic—she had a boyfriend. But we were pals."

"Did you ever meet the boyfriend?"

"I did. He didn't impress me as anyone who'd be good for her, or good to her."

"In what way?"

"His face was hard. He was wound up tighter than a drum. I don't know. And he gave off vibes that let me know he didn't want any other guys in Rebecca's life."

Kevin noticed an employee staring at them.

"Let me buy you a coke or something. We're taking up a table."

"A coke would be fine."

While he was at the counter Gwen's eyes followed him. What a nice young man, she thought. A pity Rebecca hadn't gone with him instead of that sadistic guy she'd been with.

Kevin returned with two glasses of coke. He spilled a little as he set them down, then hurried to grab some napkins at the counter and wipe the table.

"It's hard to imagine Rebecca with anyone like, like you described," Gwen said.

"I know. The next time I met her for coffee, she said she couldn't see me anymore. When I asked why, she said 'boyfriend's rules.' So, I asked her about him—what she saw in him, you know? She dropped her eyes. I can remember her lips kind of trembling. At first, she wouldn't answer, she just shook her head. And when she turned, I saw this bruise on her neck. I said, 'Did he give you that?' She rubbed her neck as tears rolled down her face. She said, 'I can't leave him.' I asked why. She said, 'You don't really know me, Kevin.' I asked her what she meant, but she just shook her head and said, 'That's all I can say.' I guess she figured I wouldn't understand."

"Could she have meant 'domination and submission'?"

"It was pretty obvious she had to obey his rules. I don't know, maybe she liked it that way."

"That's not the picture I got from her at all. I heard her sing at a friend's—a beautiful, radiance about her. I can't imagine her being with anyone who wasn't somewhat evolved, as she was—or seemed to be."

"I know. And well, she seemed happy enough, until the last couple of times I saw her. And get this. She never touched so much as a cigarette when I knew her. But that day we met for the last time, I saw tracks on her arm—injection marks."

"Heroin?"

Kevin nodded. "I touched her arm, and she pulled away. I think he made her do it, maybe just for the high he got from making her obey him—whatever the cost."

Gwen felt sick herself to think what had happened to this lovely girl. Had Rebecca defied this guy in some way that made her pay with her life?

Kevin said, "I feel terrible about what happened to her. I cared about her, you know."

"There's going to be a memorial service for her at Tyson's. That's where she used to sing. Would you like to come?"

"Sure. Sure, I would."

"Maybe you could say something about her. Nobody in that group knew much about her, except her marvelous singing."

"I'd be glad to."

"You didn't see her after the time she said she couldn't see you anymore?"

"Only once. I ran into her, and she waved, but she wouldn't stop to talk. So, who killed her? I don't know."

Gwen nodded. They were silent for a few minutes, each puzzling out the different aspects of her personality.

"That time you met this boyfriend, did you catch his name?"

"No. I don't know if she even knew his last name."

"Would you recognize him?"

"I think so."

Finally, Kevin said, "I don't know if I've been much help."

"You've been an enormous help. Do you mind if I write an article about what I learned from you?"

"Not at all. Anything that might help snare this guy."

They exchanged phone numbers and promised to let each other know if they got any leads or new information.

Gwen left glad that she'd had the opportunity to get another glimpse into Rebecca's life and saddened to think that for whatever reason this lovely young woman found it necessary to compromise herself so severely.

~~~

Gwen wrote the article, but first she imparted this news to Tyson. "Come in, sit down."

They sat on the floor, with crossed legs, across from each other.

Tyson got out his paraphernalia to have a joint.

"I just saw this friend of Rebecca's. You're not going to believe what I have to tell you."

He was shocked to discover how she was treated by her boyfriend.

He stopped rolling the joint he had in hand.

"You mean the boyfriend made her take heroin?"

"I don't know if he made her. But apparently she did everything he told her to."

"The poor kid."

"By the way, I invited him to Rebecca's service. I hope that's OK."

"Fine."

"He said he'd be willing to talk about her—the Rebecca he knew."

"That's great. We know so little."

Tyson continued rolling a joint. "Want to share this with me?"

"Yes." She leaned forward, with her elbows on her knees. "But you have to know, I've only done this once before, and that was a long time ago."

"Really? How did that go?"

She shrugged. "Nothing happened."

"Well, this is the good stuff. I think something will happen. But not too much," he smiled.

"OK."

"You have to hold it in for a few seconds."

"That much I know."

They remained seated as they passed the joint back and forth. Finally, Gwen began to feel different. She couldn't exactly describe it, but she tried.

"Lighter, less stressed. And I'm seeing pictures go by where each page looks slightly different from the last."

"Like a movie?"

"More like a flip chart."

"What are the pictures about?"

She laughed. "Bugs Bunny. Enlightening, huh?"

"Just keep paying attention. But relax too, just go with it."

"I feel like dancing."

"Go ahead."

She began to move, first still seated, swaying from side to side. Then encouraged by Tyson, she rose and began moving around the room. Before she knew it, she was spouting poetry and Tyson was cheering her on and clapping. Suddenly, she stopped and looked at him.

"Your hair's out of focus," she said seriously. Tyson burst out laughing.

She flopped back down on the floor beside him and asked what she'd spouted off— "You know, the poetry."

"I'm not sure I understood it all. Something about the goodness of people and how beets are good for you."

"Oh dear, how banal. I was hoping it was profound," she laughed.

Feeling safe, unjudged by Tyson, it didn't embarrass her that she had recited rubbish.

~~~

The memorial service for Rebecca was being held at Tyson's on Friday night. Gwen told Mark that she'd be home late. He grunted but didn't argue.

She went because she cared about this woman—a radiant spirit with an ethereal voice. But as a reporter and knowing people would have an opportunity to say something about Rebecca, she hoped to learn more about her.

She told Tyson she'd bring some food, so at five o'clock she stopped in the deli and bought the makings for sandwiches.

She arrived early to arrange the food in Tyson's kitchen. Soon after Sheila arrived with a cake.

"What's the cake for, and the candles?" Tyson asked.

"It's not a birthday cake," Sheila said. "I thought we could light the candles on it in a moment of silence, if that's OK with you, and then everyone could have a piece of it—sort of a communion."

"That's a lovely idea," he said.

Even before seven o'clock people started piling in. More subdued than usual, they found seats on chairs, or cushions on the floor, talked quietly or sat in silence. Gwen watched those who entered, recognizing most from her previous visits to Tyson's, Rebecca's friends and those who'd been there before. Some she'd never seen. Tyson said they'd attended the Friday evening chants in the past, just not recently. Sophie sat at Marjorie's feet, weeping softly into her lap.

Gwen watched anxiously for her new friend Kevin to appear. But by the time they started he had not come.

Tyson got everyone's attention by striking a little gong.

Then he said, "I'd like to play a song that Rebecca wrote. Maybe you'll help me with the words."

As he sang his eyes filled with tears, and soon he stopped singing; it was only the guitar that he could control. But someone else remembered the words and finished it with him.

When the song ended, he said, "Rebecca touched us all with her voice, her spirit and her love. We come together tonight to celebrate her and say goodbye to her. We all have our memories and thoughts, so now would be a good time to share them."

A box of Kleenex was passed around, as sniffles and tears accompanied the anecdotal remarks of those present.

After about fifteen minutes, Kevin made a tardy entrance, mumbling an apology. Gwen wondered if he was habitually late.

When it appeared that everyone who wanted to say something had, Tyson asked if anyone else would like to speak. As Kevin raised his hand, Gwen rose to introduce him.

Kevin said that he felt honored to participate in this gathering. He went on to talk about his friendship with Rebecca and how they'd met at church.

Then people asked him questions. "Did you ever hear her sing?"

"Oh yes, remarkable voice. She wanted to go professional, you know. Nothing was going to stop her."

"How well did you know her?"

Kevin coughed. "Well, like I said, we were friends—good friends. She talked a lot about how it was back in her hometown in Nebraska. I think I knew her as well as anyone. We used to take long walks in the rain and talk about anything from loneliness to love. And she wrote songs. She was a very sweet person."

"Well, thanks for coming in, Kevin. Will you stay for refreshments? Tyson said.

"I will. Thank you."

Sheila brought out the cake with twenty candles on it—no one knew exactly how old Rebecca was, so she had to guess. She explained that the cake was to celebrate Rebecca's life, and that partaking of it was like a communion of all of her friends.

Kevin approached Gwen and whispered, "I didn't want to interrupt the service, but Rebecca wasn't twenty."

"How old was she?"

"She'd be eighteen in November. November seventeenth."

"You knew her pretty well."

"I did. I'll miss her a lot."

On the other side of the room Tru said to Sophie, "Did you know she went to church?"

"No, I didn't."

The evening ended with Tyson playing *Amazing Grace.* The song without the singer.

~~~

Tired and sad, Gwen went straight to bed when she got home. Mark followed her, and made overtures, which she rejected. He caressed her for a while, which she tried to discourage, but he was not put off. Finally, saying nothing, she pushed him away and turned over.

He spoke quietly. "You're just never available anymore. We used to have great sex. Great talks. Now you're never home. You're slipping away from me."

She lay still, feeling guilty, but certainly not in the mood for sex. "I love you, Gwen."

"I love you, too."

~~~

Gwen wanted to do a feature article on Rebecca. She needed more background and decided to contact the parents. This would be very sensitive, and she would try to handle it in that matter. Perhaps they wouldn't speak to her at all. It would be better if she could talk to them in person, but that wasn't possible.

She didn't have a phone number. What was the name of the town she was from? Somewhere in Nebraska. Had Kevin mentioned it? She'd didn't think so. She'd have to contact him. He said he worked at the Free Store. But which one? Finding Kevin would be her first order of business.

She was about to leave the Chronicle when Sheila called. "Anything new?" Sheila asked.

"I want to do an article on Rebecca. I need to talk to her parents. First, I need to find out what town she's from so I can get a phone number. I'm on a hunt to find Kevin—maybe he knows. He works at one of the Free Stores."

"I'll help you."

"You will? Splendid."

"I'll take the one on Cole," Sheila said.

"Then I'll look for him at the other two.

It was Sheila who located him at the Cole Street store.

She approached him, introduced herself. "I heard you speak at Rebecca's service. It was good of you to come. My friend Gwen—you remember her—would like to do an article on her for the paper. Do you know what town in Nebraska she was from?"

"Oh, let me think. It starts with a 'G.'" He tapped his fingers on the table. "Geneva, that's it. Somewhere near Lincoln."

"Great, thank you. Gwen wants to talk to her parents, get some more background."

His smile was gone.

Something was niggling at her, just out of reach.

She thanked Kevin and said 'goodbye'. She couldn't wait to tell Gwen.

Since Geneva was a small town, it wasn't difficult for Gwen to get the phone number of the Barton's' from information. A woman answered the phone.

"Mrs. Barton?"

"Yes."

"Are you the mother of Rebecca?" She couldn't bring herself to say, *Were* you the mother.

"Yes. Who are you?"

"My name's Gwen Harris. I'm calling from San Francisco. I'm so sorry about what happened to your daughter. I knew her briefly. She had a beautiful voice. She sang in a small group of us every Friday night. Her spirit and voice uplifted us all."

No response.

"Is there anything we can do to help you in this trying time?"

Silence. Then, "I don't see how."

"Perhaps we could meet with her father. I understand he's coming out to claim her body."

"Oh, no. He's already been. He went out to talk her into coming home before she died."

Gwen was startled. "Oh, I didn't realize."

"He brought her body home today."

"I see."

"Who are you, anyway?" This was the part she dreaded.

"I'd like to write an article about her that would—"

"You're a reporter!"

"Yes."

The woman hung up.

Gwen sighed. She hadn't gotten very far, in fact hadn't found out anything at all about Rebecca's background. But what was that about the father coming out before Rebecca died? She'd have to check with Tyson, but she thought he'd told her that the coroner said the father had just arrived to claim the body.

She called Tyson. "Can we meet somewhere?"

"Sure. What's up?"

"I'll tell you when I see you."

"OK. How about the Tea Shop?"

"Fine. Four o'clock?"

"See you there."

When they met, Tyson said, "You sounded kind of urgent."

"Tell me again, what did the coroner tell you about the father?"

"Just that he was coming out to claim the body."

Gwen nodded. "Did he say when?"

"I don't think so. Why?"

"Because the mother said he came out here before she died to talk her into coming home."

"Oops. Maybe I didn't understand the coroner, or maybe he didn't get it straight about when the dad arrived."

Gwen looked at her watch. "It's four fifteen. Maybe we can still catch the coroner at his office and clarify the facts."

They left the Tea Shop and went to the phone booth on the corner.

After procuring the number, Mark got through to the office. "Coroner Turkle speaking."

"Hello, Mr. Turkel. I called the other day about my friend Rebecca Barton, who, as you know was murdered. Could you tell me again when her father arrived in San Francisco?"

"He called from the airport yesterday to say he was here to collect her body."

"From the airport—are you sure?"

"He said he'd just gotten in."

"Thank you."

When he'd hung up Gwen and Tyson stared at each other.

"If he came out here to talk her into coming home, why would he lie to the coroner, about just getting here?" Gwen said.

"Something fishy here."

"Maybe he's our killer."

"Or afraid the police will think he is," Tyson said.

"Yes," Gwen said. "And Kevin suspects the boyfriend, too."

"Oh, God."

~~~

When Marjorie heard Tru coming in she said to her, "Sit down and have a piece of my coffee cake, Tru."

"It smells wonderful. Did you make it?"

"I certainly did. Fresh out of the oven." She cut a slice for Tru and one for herself.

"You and I know that if Sophie was ever going to be happy again, Rebecca's killer has to be found."

Tru nodded in agreement.

Marjorie said, "We know the grocer's killer is one suspect. Can you think of anyone else who might have killed her?"

"Yeah. Her father."

Marjorie dropped her fork. "Her father! Why?"

"'Cuz Rebecca told Sophie he's an asshole. He beat her and raped her."

"Oh, my God! Sophie told you this?" Marjorie twirled her braid rapidly.

"Yes. And there's a third one."

"Who?"

"Her boyfriend." Tru said.

"Her boyfriend—why?"

"Let's just say he wasn't very nice to her."

"The saints preserve us!" Marjorie shook her head back and forth. "That poor child."

They were silent for a while—Marjorie trying to process what she'd just heard, Tru eating a few bites of the coffee cake.

Tru looked up and said, "Do you think a woman would be strong enough to strangle her?"

"Very doubtful. Why? Do you have someone in mind?" Marjorie said.

"No, just want to eliminate fifty percent of the population if we can."

"I think we can."

Marjorie decided to go see Sheila at the vintage clothing shop. Not close friends, but they knew each other from their political involvement.

"Marjorie, haven't seen you in ages," Sheila looked up from her table near the front door of the vintage clothes shop.

"Can you leave your post for a bit?"

"Sure. No clients so far today."

They walked to the Indian tea shop a few doors down. They sat at an outside table.

"She lived in my house," Marjorie said over a cup of tea so hot it burned her tongue.

"I didn't know that. We've been trying to find that out," Sheila said.

"Did you know Rebecca was a witness to the grocer's murder?"

"No! No, I didn't." Sheila slammed her cup down on the saucer. "I only knew her from Tyson's, where she sang for a group of us."

"Both Rebecca and another housemate, Sophie were witnesses. Since Rebecca was murdered Sophie's afraid she'll be next, in case it's the same guy who killed the grocer. So, she won't leave the house," Marjorie said.

"That's awful."

They sipped their tea and watched two girls kissing each other at another table.

"Rebecca sang at my friend Tyson's every Friday night. We miss her a lot," Sheila said.

"We miss her too. She was a lovely girl."

"Listen, I think we ought to put our heads together. I've made a friend who's a reporter for the Chronicle. She's doing some articles on the Haight, but she's sort of a detective, too, and has gotten very interested in getting to the bottom of these murders. I'd like you to meet her."

"Fine." said Marjorie.

CHAPTER 10

When Mark arrived home that evening the smell of something good met his nostrils. He found Gwen in the kitchen, complete with apron and wooden spoon in hand.

"You're home early," he said.

"I was out so many evenings, I thought it was time to spend an evening at home."

"I second that. And what are you cooking? It smells delicious."

"A recipe Denise used to cook when she lived here. Crab cacciatore."

"I can't wait."

"I thought you deserved a decent home-cooked meal after all the take-out and restaurant food," Gwen smiled.

"I already know I'll love it." He put his arms around her from behind, as she attended the food on the stove, and nibbled her neck gently. In between trips to the stove, she nuzzled in his arms.

As Gwen served the meal, Mark opened a bottle of wine. When he took his first bite, an expression of pure joy covered his face along with a murmuring of pleasure.

"Do you like it?" Gwen laughed. "I can't tell."

When the meal was finished, they lingered at the table over a glass of wine.

After a pleasant silence Mark said, "How are things in Hippyville?"

Gwen had decided not to bring up anything about work, especially the Haight.

She resisted reacting to this term. "Oh, Mark, let's not talk about that tonight."

"But you're always bubbling with something to say about it."

"Not tonight. Let's just relax."

"OK," he smiled.

"You can tell me about *your* work. How's everything going at *The Haven* now that things have settled down there? Has it returned to a quiet retirement home?"

"Much calmer. And lots easier for me now that there's no assailant running around the place. By the way, I ran into your aunt, and she says to tell you she misses you, hopes you'll visit her soon."

"Oh, gosh, yes, I have to do that."

They remained over their wine a bit longer, and then Mark said, "Want to catch the early bed?"

"The dishes—"

"Let the dishes wait," he said, pulling her gently into the bedroom.

Since she'd resisted him so strongly the previous time, she decided she'd make up for it tonight. She wanted to make Mark happy.

She'd had enough wine to be physically and emotionally relaxed. It didn't take them long to be divested of their clothes.

Gwen took the initiative, caressing Mark from head to toe, slowly and consciously. He, in turn, found every erotic zone of her body with his tongue, his strong hands. Soon they were transported into the fireworks they both loved. Her body anticipated his entry, and when he was inside her, her back arched as she knew it would. Riding in mutual gratification, it wasn't long before they reached an exultant finish. When it ended, they were left sated and content.

In the ensuing days her warmth, her easy smiles seemed to engender the same in Mark. How easy it would be to make him a happy camper.

She wanted her relationship with him to work, and she admitted to herself that she hadn't been entirely fair with him. She had stayed out late a lot, hadn't always let him know when she'd be home or where she'd been. In short, she'd been cutting him out of her life. No wonder he'd become sharp with her, caustic and cynical. She intended to do her part to bring things back to normal, back to the time when they'd been so very happy together.

~~~

Running into Tru on the stairs as she was going down and Tru was coming up, Marjorie said, "Tru, there's someone I'd like you and Sophie to meet," Marjorie said.

"Who?"

"Someone I know. Her name's Sheila. She and a friend of hers knew Rebecca, too. The friend is on a serious hunt to find Rebecca's killer."

"Cool. When can we see her?"

"How does tomorrow suit you?"

"I'll ask Sophie."

Tru continued her climb upstairs and went in the room they shared.

When she suggested the meeting Sophie was hesitant. "Who are these people?"

"Women who are trying to find the killer, or killers."

"Why do they want to talk to us?"

"Maybe we can help. Maybe some little thing we didn't think anything of could be a clue. Who knows? Come on, Sophie, please."

"I'll think about it. Come on out in the backyard with me, Tru." That was the only outing Sophie had these days.

"You think I want to get a *tan*?" she said gesturing to her dark skin.

"You can sit in the shade by the pear tree."

"Ok, if you'll agree to meet these people."

On the following day, Gwen and Sheila arrived at Marjorie's. As they entered the house on the first floor, Gwen picked up a whiff that wasn't pleasant. Trying to put her finger on it, she thought it must be 'old house smell'. Then she realized it was the odor of the unwashed. Kids who didn't bathe often enough, clothes that weren't washed, and old over-used sleeping bags. As they were shown through the door on the second floor, the odor was replace by the smell of fresh flowers from Marjorie's garden.

Marjorie ushered them into her parlor. After introductions and Tru's lemonade was served Sophie and Tru seated themselves on the floor while the adults found more commodious seating. The walls, Gwen noticed, were decorated with nine by twelve calendar pictures, set in cheap frames. Colorful scenes of various seasons, they were shiny, but somehow cheerful and homey.

As soon as the conversation turned serious Marjorie expressed an opinion that the killer could be the same as the one who killed the grocer.

Gwen said, "It's possible. Both murders were close together, but in the case of the grocer, the killer was after money."

Marjorie explained. "You didn't know, but Rebecca and Sophie were in the store and witness to the murder."

Gwen looked up in amazement.

"Oh, no, I didn't know. That would certainly make him a prime suspect."

Sheila said, "I just found out yesterday. That's why I thought we should all share our information."

"And why Sophie is afraid to leave the house," Marjorie added, putting her arms around the girl who was seated at her feet.

"I see," said Gwen, quickly grasping the vulnerability of Sophie.

Tru spoke up. "Another suspect is her boyfriend. Did you ever see the bruises on her neck?"

"No, I didn't," said Gwen.

Sophie spoke for the first time. "Rebecca told me this guy caused them,"

"Did anyone ever meet this person?" Tru inquired.

"Kevin did, A boy I met in the park who was a friend of hers." Gwen turned to Sheila. "You all met Kevin. He was at the memorial service."

"According to Kevin this boyfriend treated her very badly."

"Why did she stay with him?" Gwen inquired of the group.

There was a pause, then Sophie spoke softly. "He threatened to kill her."

A gasp arose among them.

"Oh, God. How many more suspects are there?" Sheila groaned.

We have one more," said Sophie.

"Who?"

"The father. He was a brute. He beat her and then he raped her."

"I can't believe it!" Sheila wheezed. Struggling to find her inhaler in her voluminous purse, this went on for some time, interrupting the discussion. Finally, locating her inhaler brought her breathing somewhat under control.

"There's some question as to when the father arrived in San Francisco," Gwen said. "The coroner told Tyson that the father called from the airport the day after her death, saying he just got here. But the mother said he left three days *before* Rebecca died to convince her to come home."

"He was here before she died?" Tru asked in amazement.

"That's right. Rebecca told me she saw him at her concert. She looked like she'd seen a ghost," Sophie whispered.

"So, he was here, he could have done it!" Marjorie declared.

"Then he lied about just getting here," Sheila added. "Anybody else?"

Marjorie and the girls looked at each other and shook their heads. "We've learned a great deal today and are very grateful for your sharing it with us," Gwen said.

Sheila added, "We had no idea about the father."

"And we really didn't think the man who killed the grocer was a likely suspect for Rebecca's murder," said Gwen. "But as she was a witness, that changes everything."

"You gave us information, too. I had no idea that the father was in town before Rebecca died," Marjorie shook her head. "And lied to the coroner about when he arrived. Very suspicious."

"I think it was great that we got together. Let's keep in touch and continue to share whatever we find out."

"I agree with that." Marjorie said, as she saw them to the door.

~~~

Gwen went away with her head spinning with all the possibilities of who could have killed Rebecca. She thought about her next move. The father was back in Nebraska, the man who shot the grocer was unknown. She didn't know who the boyfriend was, but maybe Kevin could tell her more, describe him. Then maybe the police could arrest him, at least for rape, if not for murder.

She found Kevin at the Free Store.

"Hey, Kevin. When do you get off work?"

"In about an hour."

"Mind if I wait? I'd like to talk to you some more."

She watched him help customers find what they needed. When he wasn't busy with them he was sorting clothes. People dropped off bags and boxes containing everything from discarded towels to used clothing. It was the workers' job to sort them.

"Need some help?" she offered.

"Sure. Thanks. You can put the dresses over there, the sweaters on this shelf, and let's see, what should we do with these?"

He pulled a grass skirt and coconut bra out of a bag. They laughed. "New category."

Finally, another worker came in and Kevin said, "I can leave now."

When they were out the door, he said, "Let's go to my place, OK? I need to freshen up."

Gwen really didn't want to go there, but he was in the driver's seat, so she said, "If it isn't too far."

"Two blocks."

They walked over to Belvedere, and down another block.

"This is it. Come on in."

Like so many other houses in the Haight he was living in part of an old Victorian.

"I'm a sweaty mess. Just give me a few minutes, OK?"

"OK."

He left the room and in a couple of minutes she could hear the shower running. She didn't intend to take much of his time and didn't see why he couldn't wait to take a shower until after she'd left, but that's the way it was, so she would wait.

While he was gone she looked around the apartment. Clean and tidy she saw no TV, but a fairly large collection of books. One was on management, another on *The Best Islands to Live On* and a third on the effects of heroin. He certainly had eclectic tastes. Then she saw one called *Justine*. She remembered it was written by the Marquis de Sade. Well, anyone might read that, she supposed; it was a classic in literature. Nevertheless, she had a feeling of uneasiness.

Completing her tour of the room she spotted something on the side table that was catching the afternoon sunlight. A ring. A small silver rose, with a little ruby in the center.

Just then he emerged from the bathroom, all fresh and clean.

"Hope I didn't keep you too long. Can I offer you something cool?"

"No thanks. I can't stay long. Kevin, I was thinking if we could identify this boyfriend of Rebecca's, maybe they'd arrest him—for rape, at least."

"I doubt if they would. She's dead, can't testify, nothing to prove the case."

Gwen thought about this. "I suppose you're right." To herself she thought *I need to learn a lot more about the law, if I'm going to play detective.*

"That's unfortunate. The guy doesn't deserve to get off scot-free. But he's a suspect for her murder, too. Can you describe him?"

"I only saw her with him once." He rubbed his chin, thinking. "Tall. Dark hair and long."

"How long?"

"About down to here." He indicated his shoulders.

"Anything else?"

"I didn't like the way he treated her."

"Meaning?"

"He'd make her go to the park with him. She didn't want to go, but he threatened to tell the band that the song she wrote wasn't really hers."

"Was it hers?"

"Oh, yes. But what would the band think? They'd probably drop her."

"What happened in the park?"

"He had his way with her. He didn't rape her though. He'd tell her what to do, and she'd do it even if it took a couple of slaps first. She gave herself to him. Poor guy, all he ever wanted was respect."

Her placid face denied her emotions. "She told you this?"

"Yeah, we were close."

She could feel her blouse sticking to her back. "Thank you. I think I have enough. I can give the police that description." She rose to leave, walking toward the door.

He stood in front of the door, blocking it. "Oh, don't go yet."

"I'm meeting someone. He won't like it if I'm late."

"We have a lot to talk about."

"He knows where I am." She tried to laugh it off. "He's liable to show up here looking for me."

"But you'll come back? Maybe tomorrow?"

"Maybe tomorrow." She forced a smile.

Reluctantly, he stood aside. With legs shaking she left his apartment. Almost in shock, Gwen could hardly believe what she'd just heard.

Everything he'd just told her he couldn't possibly know unless he'd been there. Or unless Rebecca had told him. But he'd said earlier that she wasn't allowed to see him. And then he'd referred to the boyfriend as *the poor guy!*

Were Kevin and the horrible boyfriend the same? Had that ring belonged to Rebecca?

She wasted no time going to Marjorie's. Sophie would know. Inside Marjorie's house she clutched at the railing, out of breath and barely able to climb the stairs. Shaking, she willed herself to do it. By the time she reached the top she was ready to collapse.

"Good Lord, Gwen, what happened to you?" Marjorie exclaimed. "Sit down, I'll get you some water."

"It's Kevin." Gwen breathed heavily. "I think he's the boyfriend."

"What! That nice boy you told us about?" As soon as she'd given Gwen the water, she began twisting her braids.

"Yeah," Gwen said bitterly. She gulped the water down. "Is Sophie here? I need to talk to her."

"As always. Poor girl doesn't dare go anywhere. But you can tell me first. You might want to edit it for Sophie. She's so fragile, Gwen."

Gwen spilled her experience with Kevin to Marjorie. Marjorie's eyes were popping. "He's the bad boyfriend? I don't believe it! I mean I do, but what a shock!"

"A shock is right. He seemed like the perfect choir boy."

"He actually said that—that she gave herself willingly?"

"Yup. And the ring—did she have a ring like that?"

"I don't know, but Sophie might."

Sophie was called, and a softened version of the encounter was given to her.

"Sophie, do you remember if Rebecca had a ring?" Gwen asked.

"Oh, my God. She said that jerk made her give it to him! He said it represented her giving her power over to him."

"Do you know what it looked like?"

"It was a silver rose. Did he have it?"

The color left Gwen's face. "Did it have a stone in the center?" Sophie nodded. "A red one. Did he have it?"

"Yes," Gwen said. There was no longer any doubt in her mind that this boy, whom she'd been taken in by, actually admired, was none other than the loathsome boyfriend.

"Did she describe him, physically?"

"No, but I used to help her after he hurt her, and sometimes there were blonde hairs on her clothes."

"Kevin said the boyfriend's hair was very dark." Marjorie spoke. "What color hair did this Kevin have?"

"Blonde."

"That does it," Marjorie said.

"I have to go to the police," Gwen said, rising to leave. She couldn't believe she'd been so taken in by Kevin. He is truly demonic, she thought.

~~~

"We can't arrest someone for possible rape after the victim is dead," Officer Riley leaned back in his squeaky oak chair.

Damn! she thought. It was just as Kevin had said, letting the rapist, who turned out to be himself, completely off the hook for the heinous crimes he'd inflicted on Rebecca.

"He's also a strong suspect in her murder," Gwen insisted. "After everything he did to her, and given that she was murdered, it stands to reason that he might be the one who killed her."

The officer ran his hand across his almost non-existent hair but said nothing.

"You don't have access to the other suspects, do you?" Gwen asked.

"Who do you have in mind?"

"The man who killed the grocer—Rebecca was a witness to that shooting. I believe you already have a report on that. And then there's the father, who claimed he only arrived after she died, but again you know that he arrived three days prior to her death and has now returned to Nebraska."

"So, what's your point?" He was giving his attention to lighting a cigar. Although Gwen wasn't bothered by cigarette smoke, the stench of cigar smoke always gave her a headache.

"My point is the only one of the three who is known and can easily be apprehended is Kevin."

It took some persuasion to convince the young, impatient police officer that Kevin should be arrested.

"I know there's no proof that he killed her, but he's definitely a suspect."

"We'll decide who the suspects are," the officer said, looking at his watch.

Again, she went through the details of her encounter with Kevin. "Remember, he'd said before that she wouldn't speak to him. Now he knows the whole story, and even feels sorry for the guy. 'It wasn't rape,' he said. 'She gave herself willingly to him.' Well, we know that isn't true. She had bruises, which her friend Sophie saw on several occasions."

"As I said, we can't arrest him for rape."

"But his treatment of Rebecca—"

"Write down the names and addresses of the people involved."

He shoved a pad of paper toward her, checking his watch again. Was there a game tonight he didn't want to miss? She gave him both Sophie and Kevin's addresses, as well as the Free Store where Kevin sometimes worked.

"I hope you talk to Sophie. She can fill you in on the details." As she was leaving, she said, "Are you going to do something? Arrest the guy?"

"Thank you for coming in, Miss."

Gwen left in a state of extreme frustration. But at seven o'clock she got a call from Marjorie.

"There was a detective here. He questioned Sophie on every detail you can imagine. She described the bruises and everything."

"Wonderful. Were you present?"

"Yes. He really wanted to know what this Kevin was holding over Rebecca."

"Do you know if they're going to take Kevin in?"

"I think so. He said Kevin would be questioned." It sounds like he has a split personality, Gwen."

"He may totally deny the story he told me and revert to what he said originally—that she wouldn't talk to him."

~~~

A seasoned detective, Fuller had never met anyone quite like him. At least no one who had allegedly committed such outrageous crimes. They sat across from each other in the interview room at the Park Police Station. A uniformed officer stood at the back of the room. Picked up for questioning the boy, or young man was well dressed and quite polite. He was smiling as though eager to participate in the interview.

Fuller said in a laid-back way, "I'd like to begin by your describing your relationship with Rebecca Barton. Please start at the beginning."

"Yes, sir. She and I went to the same high school. We dated for a while. Even went to our senior prom together."

"How did that go?"

Kevin smiled. "Great. We had a good time."

"And then?" Still laid-back, only gradually did Detective Fuller apply verbal screws.

"After we graduated, I didn't see her for a while, not until we happened to run into each other here in San Francisco."

"Did you come out here to find her?"

"Oh, no sir."

"But you did see her. What happened then?"

"We got together."

"Often?"

"Not at first. But after a while, with a little persuasion we were close. Really close."

"What kind of persuasion?"

"I talked to her."

"Did you hold anything over her?"

"Like what?"

"Did you threaten her in any way?"

"Never."

Detective Fuller watched Kevin for a long time, looking for cracks in his facade.

Seeing none, he went on. "You had a sexual relationship."

"Yes, eventually."

"Describe it."

Kevin smiled, looked baffled.

"Describe your sexual encounters with her."

"It involved some sex games,"

"What kind of sex games?"

"Play rape, she called it. But I don't believe in rape—not even play rape. I told her, you have to do this stuff willingly. I'll call out what you're to do, but I'm not going to force you."

"What sort of things did you tell her to do?"

"You really want the details?" he said, flicking a speck of dust off his trousers.

"Yes, I do."

"Well, I'd tell her to take her under things off. And to spread her legs."

"Did she enjoy this?"

Kevin nodded. "She needed it."

"Did you ever hit her?"

"Yeah, that was part of the game."

"And she liked that?"

"Well, you have to understand, officer, there are two levels of pain in domination and submission. On one level it hurts, of course, same as it would if you hit me. But for people like Rebecca, deep down there's a real pleasure, a need to submit. It makes for an interesting psychological study. People like that require a lot of attention. And a lot of understanding. They know that beneath the discipline, they are being cared for. Really cared for."

"And you cared for Rebecca."

"Absolutely."

Detective Fuller leaned forward. "You believe she enjoyed being hit hard in the face and punched in the neck."

"Oh, that's an exaggeration, sir. I never hit her hard."

"Did she ever ask you to stop?"

"Sure. But she didn't want me to. Part of the game."

"Right."

Fuller leaned across the desk. "Did you kill Rebecca Barton?"

"Kill her? I loved her. No, I didn't kill her!"

"Kevin Jones, I'm holding you on suspicion of the murder of Rebecca Barton."

Kevin shook his head. "You got it wrong, sir. All wrong."

CHAPTER 11

Jennie Lopez went back to see Sheila the following week, still undecided as to what she should do. They sat at Sheila's little table by the window.

Sheila was overjoyed. She said, "I'm so glad you came back, Jennie. Wait here a moment. Let me see if I can find some place private."

"Can we use your back room?" she asked the owner of the store. "It's that girl whose boyfriend killed Pop," she mouthed.

The owner indicated she could go in back.

"Come with me, Honey, we'll have more privacy back here."

When they were in the back room, crowded with vintage clothes, smelling of moth balls and dust Sheila started coughing, but this time she found her inhaler quickly which squelched it.

"I have to tell you, Jennie, a young girl was murdered a few days ago. She was a witness when your boyfriend shot the grocer."

Jennie's eyes widened.

"Oh, no! You don't think, you don't think, oh my God, that Bud had anything to do with it, do you?"

"It's quite possible, Jennie. She was a witness. Killers don't like witnesses."

"Oh, my God."

"There was another witness, Jennie. If your boyfriend is getting rid of witnesses, she's at risk, too."

Jennie put her head in her hands and began to cry. She took a much-used handkerchief out of her purse. Sheila noticed that it was a leather purse, on which was branded *I belong to Bud*. Probably made by the artisan down the street, she mused.

Finally, Jennie said, "I don't know what to do."

"You don't want anyone else to die, do you?"

"No,oo," she wailed.

Sheila waited to see if Jennie would come up with the right solution.

Finally, the girl said, "You think I should go to the police, turn him in."

"Yes. Yes, I do."

"That's not so easy, when you love someone."

"I understand."

Jennie twisted the handkerchief, looked down, then furtively glanced up at Sheila. Tears filled her eyes and trickled down her cheeks.

"He'll kill me. He said he would if I tell."

"He can't if they get him first."

"Maybe. But until they do, or if they don't—Oh, Sheila." And she began to sob.

Sheila took her hand. "I'll go with you."

But she'd no sooner spoken when the wheezing started. Sheila reached for her inhaler, but it was empty. In minutes she was having a full-blown attack.

Jennie spoke up. "Is there something I can do for you?" Sheila shook her head.

Jennie waited a few moments and then she said, "Well, I can see we're not going to the police today." She got up to leave. "I hope you feel better."

"Wait, Jennie. Just let me make a call." Between wheezes she continued. "I know someone who will go with you if she's free. She's very nice, Jennie. I'm sure you'll like her."

"Oh, I don't know. Please don't bother."

"Just sit tight, Honey."

Sheila put in a call to Gwen at the Chronicle.

"I hate to ask you this, but Jennie, the murderer's girlfriend, is finally willing to talk to the police."

Gwen heard a lot of wheezing.

"It's hard to understand you, Sheila. Are you OK?"

"It's my asthma, I'm having an attack." She stopped to breathe. "That's why I'm calling. I told Jennie I'd go with her to the station, but I really can't." More wheezing and breathing. "Do you think you could?"

"When?"

"Before she changes her mind."

"Where are you?"

"Where I work."

"I'll be there in fifteen minutes."

When she arrived, she whispered to Sheila, "They had to let Kevin go. Not enough evidence to arrest him."

"Rats."

Sheila introduced Jennie to Gwen. Wanting the girl to be comfortable with this new person, they sat and went over Jennie's story together.

"What's your boyfriend's name, Jennie?" Gwen asked gently. "Bud. Do you think they'll arrest me?" the girl squeaked.

"No, I don't. You're coming in on your own to turn him in. Did you know he was going to kill the grocer?"

"No! I didn't even know he had a gun. I ran out of there when he shot the man."

"Then I don't think they'll arrest you. I know this is very hard for you, Jennie."

"I love him—at least I did," she wiped into her eyes with her handkerchief.

"Sometimes, life requires us to be very brave, when it's very hard, Jennie." She waited for a response from Jennie, who was just looking down into her lap, with an occasional sob. Finally, with pleading eyes the girl looked up at Gwen. "Will you go with me?"

Officer John Bailey recorded Jennie's statement. He showed neither compassion nor criticism for her not coming in sooner. When he finished, he asked her to write out a statement and left her with pen and paper.

Jennie turned to Gwen. "But I just told him everything," she sighed. "Why do I have to write it out?"

Gwen shook her head. "Probably to make sure your story is consistent. I don't know. Just do it."

Jennie sighed and tackled the task. A different officer entered the room, identifying himself as Detective Pierce. About fifty years old, he possessed a prominent mustache.

After he introduced himself, he said, "What's your boyfriend's name?"

"Bud."

"What is his full name?"

"He doesn't like to say, but he told me it's Bud Smith."

"Smith?" The detective looked dubious. "When did you last see him?"

"A couple of nights ago. He hasn't come back."

The detective plucked his mustache and continued doing so throughout the entire interview. "Where did these assignations take place?"

"These what?"

"Where did you two get together?"

"At my place."

"Always at your place?"

"Yes."

"Why do you think he took off now, and not right after the murder of the store owner?"

"I, I don't know." Jennie squirmed in her chair.

"Where do you think we can find him now?"

"Where he lives, maybe. But I don't know where that is."

"Where else might he be, his hangouts?"

"He goes to a pool hall downtown, and there's a bar." She gave him the locations as best she could.

"Does he have a job? Where does he work?"

"I don't know." She dropped her eyes, twisted her skirt.

"Do you have a photo of him?"

Jennie hesitated. Would this picture get her in trouble? From her purse she brought out a snapshot of the two of them together. Someone had taken it while they were smoking grass. They were each holding a tote, and they looked stoned.

The officer gave her a look but said nothing.

Jennie squirmed in her seat. "What if you can't find him?" she asked, digging in her purse to locate her handkerchief.

"First we'll do a local search. Can you give us the names of anyone he hangs out with?"

Jennie blew her nose loudly. "Usually, when he meets his other friends he goes alone."

"You don't have any mutual friends?"

"Not really. Can I go now?"

"How well do you know him? His politics, religion if any."

"We don't talk about those things. I don't know." Jennie frowned. "I know what he likes to eat, what TV shows he likes. Stuff like that."

"What else do you know about him?"

Her lips quivered. She looked at Gwen. Finally, she said, "He's an Angel."

"Hells Angels?"

She nodded. Having divulged this, her eyes widened in fear. The detective asked, "How does he feel about the hippies?"

"He can't stand them. Thinks they're all queers or perverts. And freeloaders. We're not part of that scene at all," she said with a touch of pride.

She hesitated. "But sometimes the Angels are hired as security for the musicians."

The officer nodded and stood up. "I think that concludes our conversation for now."

Jennie jumped up like a jack-in-the-box. "He'll kill me if he finds out—"

"I understand your concern."

Jennie nodded vigorously. "What if you can't find him?"

"We will do this quietly. Officers in plain clothes will be on the case. It will be very discreet."

"What if—"

"And if we don't find in the next couple of days, then we'll put out an APB—an all-points bulletin."

"Then he'll kill me for sure!" Jennie yelled.

"We can offer you witness protection."

"What's that?"

"First we'll send you to our safe house in Santa Rosa."

"Santa Rosa—where's that?" Jennie worked her handkerchief so vigorously that it tore.

"About fifty miles north of here. You'd be safe there. But for now, we'll be looking for him in the places you mentioned. And we'll be discreet."

He used that word again. Jennie didn't know what it meant, but she nodded dumbly.

"I can't go back to that house! Not now." She looked at Gwen.

"Let's go see how Sheila's doing. Maybe you can stay with her tonight."

"Be sure to leave the address where you'll be," the officer said.

When they left, Jennie was somewhat comforted as to her own safety, but not at all happy about turning in her boyfriend.

"He was going to give me a patch for my birthday."

"What kind of patch?"

"The Angels all wear patches, depending on their rank. And they can give their girlfriends a patch too, if she's his P.O."

"His what?"

"Property of."

Gwen winced.

"I guess that won't happen now." Jennie said. There were tears in her eyes.

Walking back to the Haight, Jennie was getting hot, and removed her sweater. She was wearing a T-shirt which said, "I am the property of Bud."

She showed it proudly to Gwen. "I painted it myself."

Inwardly Gwen groaned. How deeply involved this young girl was with what she saw as her savior. Probably the father-figure she'd never had. And this man was one of Hells Angels.

With growing awareness, she felt somewhat responsible for the girl's safety, since she'd helped to convince her that she should turn her boyfriend in, a boyfriend who would surely seek revenge if he had a chance. It was important that she be kept safe.

They went to the shop where Sheila's shingle hung in the window. Sheila wasn't there. The owner of the store said she'd gone home sick.

"Do you have her address?"

The owner looked suspicious. "And who are you?"

Jennie was hanging out near the door. Motioning to her Gwen said, "Perhaps you've seen Sheila talking with this girl before—Jennie. She really needs to see her now. It's vitally important."

The woman hesitated, then picked up the phone. "Sheila, do you feel like company? That girl Jennie is here with a woman. They want to see you. . .OK, I'll tell her."

"She lives at 44 Page. She said to come on over."

It was a short walk, and Sheila met them on the porch. Her attack was over.

"How are you feeling, Sheila?" Gwen asked.

"Fine now. The attack didn't last long, but while it did—" She rolled her eyes. "Come on in."

Jennie followed Gwen and Sheila timidly into the house.

As they were seated Sheila said, "Tell me what happened. I can't wait."

Gwen filled Sheila in on what had transpired at the police station.

"Jennie, I am so sorry that I couldn't go with you. And Gwen, thank you so much for doing this for me. I owe you."

"No, you don't, but maybe you can help Jennie out for one night. They'll put her in a safe house if they have to put out an APB. She's afraid to go back where she lives after spilling the beans. Do you think she could—"

"Stay here with me? Of course." She turned to Jennie. "It's just the couch, Honey. But at least you won't be alone."

Jennie murmured a thank you.

"I'll leave you two, then. I have some other things to do." Another 'thank you' and Gwen was gone.

CHAPTER 12

G wen decided that Tyson had a right to know that Rebecca and her friend were witnesses at the scene of Pop's murder. And that the killer's girlfriend had gone to the police, given his name and furnished a photo. She went to his apartment.

After asking her in he said, "If they can catch that bastard—"

"But we don't know that he's the guy who killed Rebecca. That's a theory, but not a fact."

"Well, even if he didn't kill Rebecca, at least if they could get the guy who killed the grocer."

"And that's not all. Rebecca had a very abusive boyfriend."

"I didn't know that."

"And he's been arrested as a suspect in her murder."

"Seriously?" Tyson said with growing intensity. "Yes."

"Anybody else?"

"One more."

"Who?"

"Her father."

"Jesus, no."

"Yes."

Tyson sighed. "That's a long list."

"I know. I thought you'd want to be up to date on where that stands."

"Absolutely. Yes, please keep me informed."

"I will."

She stayed, and they chatted for another hour. He told her he was from Colorado and had come to California in the spring.

"Before I came here, the most important things in my life were skiing and playing my guitar."

"You still do the latter."

"I do."

Gwen had been wanting to understand the philosophy behind the Diggers better. She could think of no one better to ask than Tyson.

"What do you know about the Diggers? Besides the fact that they feed a lot of people. Is there some philosophy behind what they do?"

"It goes deeper than feeding the hungry. They want a new social paradigm. They want everything to be free. So, they've set up free stores. But the bigger picture is they want a total liberation from government control. They want people able to make their own choices."

"About everything?"

"That's my understanding. When even so-called liberated folks say, 'You should', they counter with 'There are no 'shoulds'.'"

"Sound idealistic, but doesn't that lead to some serious problems?"

"It could."

"I mean it seems the assumption here is that everyone would act in a responsible way, following a healthy sense of what's right and wrong."

"Of course, they re-evaluate what's right and wrong, too."

"Like what?"

"Maybe multiple spouses. Strong, long-held beliefs about bigamy might be re-evaluated, for example."

Gwen nodded. "Doing what you want could even lead to murder, couldn't it?"

Tyson whistled. "I suppose, but I have a feeling that the murderer or murderers aren't part of the new social order. There are folks hanging out here who have no interest in making a better society, or even participating in the joy of the gatherings, like the concerts. They're just free-loading."

"But they'd still be around. There'd have to be a way to deal with those who committed acts against other people or their property.

They chewed on this a while and then Gwen said, "Are you protesting any particular cause?"

"You sound like a reporter."

"Mia culpa."

"The war. It's so wrong."

She nodded. "Why do you think we got into it? All those young men, they don't even know what they're fighting for."

Tyson was getting really wound up. He'd pace a few steps, turn and make a point to her and pace some more. "Profit and private property— the core belief system of our pervading culture. *That* led to the war. The belief that America can interfere anywhere they please— or not. And that's what the Diggers and others involved in this Great American Dream are trying to change.

He shrugged. "I do what I can, help the Diggers scrounge for food, surpluses. But it isn't just about a free meal here and there. It represents the beginning of a society that's more humane, compassionate. Sheila's a good example, offering free counseling to those who need it." He paused, smiled apologetically. "Oh, you got me started."

"It's a beautiful dream."

"That reminds me of Rebecca's song. Want to hear it?"

"Sure. I'd love to."

He picked up his guitar, tuned it, and began humming. Then he sang:

"Young men go, and young men die. Fallen soldiers, there they lie.
More men go, and more men die, For a cause we know not why.

"That's all I remember."

The melody was mournful, but melodic.

"I like it. I mean, it says what a lot of us feel."

Tyson kept strumming, playing the tune, trying to remember the words. He seemed lost in his thoughts, and Gwen decided it was time to leave.

Walking back to her car she heard a bunch of screaming girls coming down the street in an open convertible. The driver looked no more than fourteen. "Who needs a driver's license?" she yelled waving her arms in the air.

Was this how the philosophy of anti-government would play out?

~~~

The police raided the Angels Clubhouse. Bud wasn't there. They went to the bars and pool halls frequented by Hells Angels. Not there.

"He's bolted," the policeman told the detective.

Jennie spent the night with Sheila on the couch. Sheila could hear her whimpering from the other room. The poor girl, she thought. She betrayed the man she loves, and now she's living in fear of retribution.

When Sheila got up to go to the bathroom, the sudden noise startled Jennie so badly that she leapt off the couch and crouched in the corner. In the morning, Sheila didn't see Jennie anywhere.

Oh, my God! she thought. *Where is she? Did they come and whisk her away while I was asleep? Could I have slept through that, in the bedroom with the door closed?*

She tried to think calmly. Did Jennie run away in fear?

It had to be one or the other. She supposed it was possible that they'd gotten in the door, crept upstairs, and gagged Jennie so she couldn't scream. *While I snored away behind closed doors,* she thought in dismay.

But it was just as possible that Jennie in her state of anxiety and fear had fled.

She called the police.

"Maybe they came and got her," she told the detective.

"Was your door locked?"

"Yes, but they could have used a knife or something to release the lock, couldn't they? I've seen it done in movies."

"Where was she sleeping?"

"On the sofa in the living room."

"And you were where?"

"In my bedroom."

"We'll get on it. And we'll list her with 'Missing Persons'."

Hanging up, Sheila shouted, "Missing Persons! That's an understatement!"

Then she thought, *My God, I have to do something.*

She tried to reach Gwen at the Chronicle, but no, Gwen was not in the office today. She must be in the Haight. She checked out their usual haunts. No Gwen. More pacing, more looking in shops.

She had to get a hold of Gwen. She left a message for her at the Chronicle and tried to find her home phone number. Where was it? Had she ever had it? She paced the streets in anguish. When she saw a park bench, she sat down and tried to pull her thoughts together. What would be the logical course? The day was fading, and still no Jennie.

She called the police. Had they found her yet? Had they checked the place where she lives?

Yes, they'd looked there. No Jennie. No, they hadn't located her yet. Then an asthma attack but squelched by her new inhaler.

The police said they were making it a priority, but meanwhile Jennie could be dead. Where would they have taken her? What, if anything could she do on her own? Nothing. She needed Gwen. Then she remembered she did have her address. She'd go to Gwen's. She'd never been there, but Gwen had issued an open invitation, said come anytime you're on my side of the bridge. Sheila found the slip of paper with Gwen's address on it in her purse.

She didn't have a car. But Gwen had said that the bus stopped very close to her place in Sausalito. She walked three blocks to the bus stop and waited. It was five o'clock, and the next bus wasn't due for fifteen minutes, but it felt like an hour before it arrived. Due to the time of day all the seats were taken, and she had to stand. Between the bus stops and the red lights, it never went a block without coming to a jolting halt, threatening to deck the standing passengers. Finally, they reached the bridge, and it was smooth sailing into Marin down the winding road that brought them into Sausalito.

Getting off at the bus stop she trudged up the hill to Gwen's house, so out of breath from climbing the hill that when she rang the bell Gwen gazed at her in shock.

Bringing her into the house, Gwen said, "Whatever is wrong? Sit down. Tell me. Wait a sec. I'll get you some water."

When she returned, Sheila was using her inhaler. "Just a preventative," she explained.

Then between gasps for breath Sheila relayed Jennie's disappearance. When she was halfway through her account, Mark entered.

Gwen said, "Mark, this is my friend Sheila. She's had a very stressful time and has come to tell me about it. Sheila, this is my partner Mark."

"Would you like a drink? "he said.

Sheila nodded, and Mark returned to the kitchen to prepare the drinks.

"Go on, Sheila."

"We have to do something, Gwen. We can't sit on our hands and let her die! What shall we do? I've been trying to think all day. Gwen, what are we going to do?"

"You said you'd reported her disappearance to the police."

"Yes."

"When was that?"

"This morning, right after it happened."

"Did they go to the house where she'd been living?"

"Yes, but she hadn't turned up there. They said they'd get right on it, but they don't know where to look, what to do."

"We don't know either, Sheila."

Mark returned with the drinks and a plate of cheese and crackers, which Sheila dug into while telling her story.

Sheila turned to Gwen. "I knew I couldn't do anything alone, but with you, Gwen, we could pool our ideas, think of places to look, do our own search."

Mark spoke up. "Well, nothing can be done now. Let's have supper. You can stay here tonight."

"Oh, I couldn't do that."

Gwen said, "Yes, you can. Just as you put Jennie up last night, we're putting you up tonight. It's settled. You'll have to sleep on the couch and I'll drive you back to the city in the morning."

They ate the remains of a left-over chicken and a fresh salad Gwen made.

Later when they'd all turned in for the night Gwen and Mark talked in whispers in the bedroom. It was obvious he'd overheard everything that Sheila had to say.

Gwen said, "If she was kidnapped, how do you think the Hells Angels found out Jennie reported this guy?"

"Broad-band radio, probably, listening to police activity."

"Can anyone listen in to them?"

"You have to have a license, which at least one of them probably has."

"Oh, Mark, this is so terrible."

Mark turned to her. "Why did that woman come here?"

"She's very upset." She could hear the disapproval in his voice. Or was it fear?

"I could see that. I feel for her. And for that girl she was talking about. But what does she expect you to do?"

"I don't know."

"This is a police matter. It would be total folly for you and your pals to get involved."

"The police are working on it," Gwen hedged.

"You're not going to get mixed up in it, are you?"

Gwen didn't answer.

He raised up on an elbow and looked at her. "Well, are you?"

"I'll talk to the police tomorrow and see what they've discovered, if anything."

"And then?"

"I don't know."

"Promise me you'll stay out of it." Again, silence.

"Please, Gwen. I can't stand it—worrying about you all the time. You take such awful risks. Please stay out of this and other cases the police should be handling. You're a reporter, not a detective."

"I have to have something to report on, and right now it's the Haight."

"Promise me you'll stop playing detective."

"I can't, Mark. I can't promise that."

~~~

In the morning after breakfast Gwen and Sheila drove back to the Haight and went to Marjorie's.

They filled Marjorie in on recent events.

"I'm so sorry, Marjorie. I have her in my care one night, and she disappears," Sheila moaned.

"Not your fault, of course," Marjorie said.

"I know, but I feel so responsible."

"Who would know what happened to Jennie?" Marjorie asked.

"The Hells Angels, if they took her, of course," Gwen replied. "But where would they take her?"

"I think they have some headquarters some place, but that might not be an option. One of their homes, maybe," Gwen said.

"It would have to be a bachelor. They wouldn't want to take her home to the wife and kids," Marjorie said.

"Where else might they take her?" Sheila asked. "An empty store?" Marjorie suggested.

"Have you seen any?" Gwen asked.

"Not around here, but maybe somewhere else in the city," Marjorie said.

"Oh, it's like looking for a needle in a haystack," Sheila groaned. "I'm going to call the police, see what they're doing," Gwen said.

"If anything," Marjorie despaired.

Gwen was not able to reach Detective Pierce. "Perhaps he's out there—looking for her, with a team of officers."

"Let's hope so," said Marjorie.

"Well, what are we to do?" asked Sheila.

"It may lead nowhere, but we could go up and down the Haight, ask folks, especially shopkeepers if they've seen any Angel with a girl," Marjorie said.

"It wasn't even light out when she disappeared," Sheila said. "I doubt if anyone saw them."

"She's right," Gwen said. "Nevertheless, it wouldn't hurt to do some inquiries, and to tell people what happened. Then everybody will be on the lookout."

"Let's do it."

Marjorie tried to enlist the help of Sophie and Tru. Sophie would not leave the house, but Tru was eager to assist.

During the day, they divided up the twenty-four square block that comprised the Haight, and each took a section, talking to astounded shopkeepers and hippies alike. Even the most spaced out were shocked and wanted to help.

The three women told everyone to call the police if they saw or heard anything suspicious.

When they met again at the end of the day to share their results, none had encountered anyone who knew anything, but at least they'd put out the word, and hopefully, it would lead to some results.

~~~

Home at five o'clock that evening, exhausted and discouraged, Gwen fixed herself a vodka tonic and sat down on the big easy chair to relax. Just as she took the first sip, she saw a note on the side table addressed to her. She recognized Mark's handwriting.

Picking it up, she read, "I'm moving out, Gwen. I love you, but our relationship is no longer working for me. I will continue to pay my rent until you find another roommate. I'm sorry, Mark."

All color drained from her face. For a moment she sat paralyzed. She could hardly take it in and had to read it twice. Mark was leaving her? Why? It didn't take long for her to figure that out. But she never thought his objections to what she was doing would lead to such dramatic consequences.

Her work was important to her. But so was Mark. She imagined a life without him—coming home to an empty apartment, no one to do the things they'd done together—the picnics, the drives along the coast. She put her hand on the phone.

She thought of the long talks and the great love-making. Tears filled her eyes recalling the time he'd bought the practically new Hudson for her, when her VW had met an untimely death. How good he'd been to her.

She considered calling him and promising to do what he asked. Couldn't she bend a little? But was it just a little?

What was it that made her want to dig into the mysteries of the city, help solve cases? Could she be happy if she went back to reporting the openings of new buildings and working on the society page? She remembered doing just that, and how she'd longed to be doing something more important. If she backed away from investigative reporting, she'd probably at least be able to report on local news, even The Summer of Sex and Drugs, as some called it.

She tried to imagine herself just reporting, no emotional attachment to the awful things that were happening. Nothing to help solve the crime. No interest in the outcome. Just a bystander reporting the facts. Somehow this wasn't her. She knew she couldn't do it. She recognized that she'd developed a passion for investigative reporting. Even if it meant going out on a limb.

She moved her hand away from the phone.

CHAPTER 13

Gwen and Sheila were posting signs on the telephone poles and asking shopkeepers to put posters in their windows. Many windows still held the poster Tru had distributed, asking for information about Rebecca. But the shopkeepers made room for a second poster asking about Jennie's disappearance. "What is the Haight coming to?" they asked.

So many shopkeepers cooperated that Marjorie made three trips to the printer's to renew their supply.

When nothing came of their efforts Sheila moaned, "This is a job fit for the FBI."

Gwen shared her despair.

Without insiders' intelligence, undercover agents, weapons or resources, it seemed more and more likely that their search would become a dead end. What had become of Jennie? Was she even alive? It sickened Gwen to think about it.

"If she just ran off somewhere, it pisses me to think she didn't even tell me first," Sheila fumed.

"If that's the case she was probably afraid you wouldn't let her go."

"Or didn't want to wake you," Gwen said.

"As if waking me were worse than what I'm going through now."

In the days that followed they pursued any lead they got. Most were bogus, or well-meaning, but going nowhere.

~~~

Driving home one evening a driver honked loud and long; in passing he gave Gwen the finger. Usually unperturbed by such rude behavior, she felt the tears run down her cheeks. Reaching her living room, they escalated into a full-fledged crying jag. With only Alfi to comfort her, she said, "Do you miss him too?"

One evening when she came home, she saw Mark on the front lawn playing with Alfi. Her heart jumped. A very familiar sight. But one that didn't fit the present. For a few minutes she stayed in the car and watched Mark throw the frisbee and the very excited Alfi more than happy to retrieve it and bring it back to Mark for another go. This had been a ritual between them when he was living with them. She'd never gotten her kiss or tried to converse with Mark until Alfi'd had his frisbee time.

She tried to stay calm as she got out of the car and approached the house. He smiled as she came forward.

"I came to pick up the rest of my clothes, and to give you a check for rent."

Her heart sank. Of course, that was all it was. What was she thinking?

"Would you like to come in?" she asked as he handed her the check. "No, I already got my stuff."

"Oh."

"I'll be off. By the way, I walked Alfi."

"Thank you."

And he was gone.

In the lonely evenings she missed Mark the most. When the phone rang a part of her hoped it was he. But it never was. Every night Alfi sat by the door, alert and expectant, waiting for his master to return. He was even more diligent and expectant after Mark's visit. It was enough to break Gwen's heart. She'd lure him into the kitchen for food, or play with him, but he always returned to the door. It had been their routine that she walked him in the morning, and Mark did the same in the evening. Now, when she took him out at night, he whined. Something wasn't right. He knew it.

She'd go to bed early, just to put Mark out of her mind, but it was hard to sleep. Although Alfi came into the bedroom when she went to bed, after a while she could hear him pad back to the front door, to resume his vigilance. Waking early in the morning she showered and got ready for work. During the day it was easier to take her mind off him. She had a job to keep her busy.

~~~

The women had set up a little office in Sheila's living room. There they assembled flyers and posters, kept records of where they'd been posted them and met to confer. The police were contacted frequently. The women knew the officers considered them pests.

A typical response was "Look, we're doing everything we can. There's an APB out on her with the picture she gave us."

Gwen wanted to ask them exactly what they were doing, but she suspected that that was going too far.

"She has a mother in Marin," Sheila said to the others, lighting up as she munched on a cookie. She'd put out a plate of them, but as the other two were not imbibing, Sheila finished them off herself. "I wonder if the police got a hold of her."

"We don't even know her last name," Marjorie said.

"It's Lopez. I was with her when she told the police, Gwen said." Writing for both the Chronicle and *The Oracle*, Gwen focused on Jennie's disappearance. She contrasted this dire side of the Summer of Love with the bright, loving side—the Diggers providing free food every day for those who needed it, the Street Theatre, singing in the park. Yes, even the balloons, ribbons and flowers. It was a world of incongruities.

She stopped by the Free Store to see Hank. He was trying to find a place to put a new batch of donated diapers.

She got right to the point. "A young girl has gone missing, Hank. She was the girlfriend of the guy who shot the grocer. She was with him when he did it. After she went to the police she stayed with a woman I know that night but disappeared before morning. You have your ears to the ground, Hank. Have you heard anything?"

He shook his head. "Afraid not."

"It's been a whole week. We don't even know if she's still alive."

"Did the boyfriend kidnap her?"

"She could have gotten scared and run off. Or possibly one of the Hells Angels got her. The boyfriend was one of them."

"Oh, my God. They're a scary group. Most people give them a wide berth. But sometimes you hear of something good they did. I was at a concert in the park one time, and there was this little girl who was lost and crying. One of them picked her up, calmed her down and helped her find her mommy."

"That's a sweet story."

"Listen, I'll keep my eyes and ears open for anything I see or hear about this girl."

"Would you? I'd appreciate it."

She gave him her number and they promised to stay in touch.

CHAPTER 14

In the little office they'd set up at Sheila's, Gwen said to the others, "The Swans are playing tonight. Do you want to go?"

"I don't know. It's hard, after Rebecca," Marjorie said.

"I know. But I have a plan."

"What's that?" Sheila asked.

"You know how Hells Angels guard the concerts. I was thinking I could strike up a conversation with one of them, maybe get to know him, go out with him if he asks me."

"Oh God, that sounds risky!" Marjorie said. "I know. But we can't just sit on our hands."

Sheila nodded. "I can tell, you have some plan up your sleeve."

"OK, I am going to approach an Angel, like an airhead teenager, all gaga about them."

"Oh, Jeez. And then?" Sheila asked.

"I don't know."

"You don't honestly think any of them will give you information on Jennie, do you?" Marjorie said.

"No. But if I stay with it, maybe I'll find out something."

"You mean extended dates?"

"Maybe."

"Oh, Gwen, you're way braver than I am," Sheila said.

"Or foolish."

"That too," her friend agreed. "Anyway, let's go, OK?"

"Just don't dress like a hippie. They hate hippies." Said Sheila.

"Then we're on."

"I'll bring a picnic," said Sheila.

At eight o'clock they met and headed for the park.

"I just had a thought," Gwen said. "I think I'd like to do an interview with the bandleader. About Rebecca's burning desire to play with them, how she finally got to, etcetera. And then do a feature story."

"You mean a sob story."

Gwen made a face.

"I guess, but it might help find Rebecca's killer."

"And it wouldn't hurt the band either," Sheila said.

The band was setting up as they approached the stage. The one called Janet seemed to be in charge. As they stood by the stage, she came over to them.

"Can I help you?"

Gwen introduced herself as a reporter and friend of Rebecca's. Before she said anything, the woman closed her eyes and crossed herself.

"It's terrible what happened to her. She could have really gotten somewhere, you know? By the way, my name's Janet."

"I wonder if I could talk to you sometime about Rebecca, and perhaps do a feature article on your band and weave in Rebecca's wish- come-true."

"Sure, glad to. Maybe it would help find the creep who did it."

"Name a time and place."

"I could meet you in the Haight tomorrow afternoon."

They agreed to meet at four o'clock at the Indian tea shop next to Lyon's Leather.

As the women left the stage looking for a place to sit, they saw a group of Hells Angels hanging out. Easy to identify, they were all wearing their trademark, black leather jackets or vests. The women spread their blanket not too far from a group of them.

The meadow soon filled up, and the band was tuning up. While they enjoyed the picnic Sheila had prepared, a group of young people all in Renaissance costumes paraded among them with tambourines and Irish flutes.

"It feels so good to be back in the joyful side of this summer," Sheila said.

"Amen to that," agreed Marjorie.

"Mind if I leave you for a while?" Gwen asked.

"What are you going to do?" Sheila wanted to know.

"Go over there." She nodded toward one of the Angels. "Maybe I'll get some info."

"Just like that?"

"No, not all at once. I'll have to play it by ear. I'll be back."

"Oh, Gwen, be careful, OK?" Sheila said.

Gwen sauntered over to an Angel who was no longer with his club members, as they'd fanned out and were watching the crowd. Some of them stood in twos and threes, but others, like the one Gwen was headed for, were alone.

He was tall with a muscular build, dark hair and eyes. Gwen noted the similarity of this man to Mark from the back, but he had a formidable face. Nevertheless, she approached him. Adapting what she thought would pass as the demeanor of an awestruck teen-ager she said, "I'm looking for my sweater. If someone found it and turned it in, do you know where that would be?"

He shrugged. "Try the Lost and Found."

"Where's that?"

"Not sure."

Conversation over. He'd barely glanced at her. A new tact was called for.

She sighed. "These concerts are great, aren't they?"

"Yeah."

"What's your favorite band?" Then he turned to look at her. She saw a scar on his face. Was it from a knife?

"The one I'm listening to."

"Well, I like Jefferson Airplane, especially the singer, Janis Joplin, and The Grateful Dead."

"This one's pretty good. All girls. Last time I heard them they had a new singer—great voice."

She wanted to come across as a flirt and a girl just out for some fun, but right away he'd brought up Rebecca. Was this an innocent remark?

"I heard her too. So sad that she died."

"Yeah. What do you know about that?" he asked.

"Not a lot—just what was in the paper."

"Can't think of her name."

"Rebecca, wasn't it?"

"Yeah, that's right."

She knew she was treading on dangerous ground. She didn't want to reveal too much of her knowledge of Rebecca, but on the other hand if he'd seen her carry around that sign, asking if anyone knew anything about her, then he'd smell a rat if she came across as knowing nothing.

She was glad when a group of hippies came by singing "If you're going to San Francisco be sure to wear some flowers in your hair." It gave her a chance to change the subject.

"They're a happy bunch."

"Crazy kids. They ought to go home."

She didn't want to argue with him, so she said, "I bet they're breaking their parents' hearts."

"Totally irresponsible. Just freeloaders."

"I guess so."

He pulled out his cigarettes. "Want one?"

She offered him a bright smile and said, "No thanks."

"These kids have turned the park into a pig sty. You ought to see the garbage they leave after a concert."

She nodded her head in agreement.

"They come from all over the country, just invade the neighborhood and expect somebody else to take care of them. Pigs, that's what I call them. Riff-raff of the city."

"Pretty irresponsible," she agreed.

They chatted some more and then he said, "Look, if you're interested, we could meet after the show, go for a drink somewhere."

Gwen happily accepted. Then she said, "I better get back to my friends now. See you later. Oh, where, exactly?"

He pointed to a tent. "There."

In case he was watching her, she strolled over to a food tent, bought a couple of cokes before returning to her friends. No point in putting them at risk.

"So how did it go?" Marjorie asked. "Got a date after the show."

"Tonight?"

"Tonight."

"You work fast," Sheila said.

"If I can win his trust, maybe I'll find out something about Jennie. But this is not a one-night project."

"I hope it works," Marjorie said.

"Me too."

"Listen, it will be late—too late to take the bus. Why don't you stay with me tonight, Gwen?" Sheila offered.

"Thanks, but what if he wants to walk me *home*? I don't want him to know where you live."

"Oh God, you're right."

"I'll be OK."

They enjoyed the concert, but all of them were thinking how sad it was that Rebecca was not up there with them.

And Gwen was thinking of something else, too—what was she getting herself into, going off with a possible kidnapper?

As the concert ended, even in the cool air, she began to perspire. She said, "Well, here goes."

"Are you nervous?"

"Kind of."

"Call me in the morning. And be careful," Sheila said.

"I will."

Gwen headed for the tent where they were to meet. She saw a lot of the Angels still keeping an eye on the departing crowd and serving as bodyguards for the band. The one she was looking for was nowhere in sight. She waited, watching the couple who manned the tent pack up their wares.

"Pretty earrings," she said, looking at several. "What kind of feathers are they?"

"Turkey. Half price, if you want a pair."

"I'm sorry, I'm meeting someone. Another time."

The couple finished loading their jewelry into two large suitcases and left. The crowd was thinning out, and Gwen began to think that she'd been stood up. Getting nervous about being alone in this vast nearly empty space, she waited another five minutes and decided to leave.

"Hey, wait up," came a voice from behind.

She turned and saw him leisurely strolling toward her. "I thought you weren't coming."

"Got held up," he offered as explanation.

Nervous alone and now nervous with this Angel, she decided the latter was worse.

He took her arm and turned her toward a different exit than she would use to go back to the Haight.

She pulled away. "I'm going to the Haight. That's the other way."

"I've got a car. It's parked over on Downy. My favorite bar's downtown."

Her heart was thumping. "No, I think I'll pass. It's late."

"Well, do you know a place that's still open in the Haight?"

She breathed a sigh of relief. "I think so. On Ashbury."

"Let's go there."

They walked side by side through the dark park while the Angel continued to bad-mouth the 'immigrants', as he was calling them now. When they finally reached the lighted streets of the Haight, Gwen welcomed the light. People were still mingling about, and everything looked OK again.

Still, every fiber in her body wanted to flee, to plead tired and leave his company. But she was investigating a crime, and it would defeat the purpose if she left now.

They found a bar called *Pickles*, which she'd seen from the outside, but had never been in. It was crowded and the noise was spilling out into the streets. As they waited near the entrance for a table or booth, Gwen watched agile waiters weave their way past standing customers, trays held aloft on uplifted arms. A smoky haze filled the room and spilled into the street.

"What's your name?" she asked.

"Rake. And yours?"

"Connie."

They were finally seated. After another long wait, someone took their order, and still longer before two beers were set in front of them. Awkward silences ensued, as Rake had run out of pejoratives about the summer people.

While they waited Gwen tried to think of things to say that wouldn't trigger suspicion. She asked him if he were a football fan and what team he favored. Nil. She asked if he had a motorcycle.

"Have to, to be in the club. Gotta have a Harley, a fast one."

That topic kept them occupied for a while. "I got it used, but it was like new. It can go 2,000 rpm when I'm cruising—2500 if I push it. She's a sweetheart. Starts like a charm, turns on a dime."

"You love it."

"I sure do."

"You have it nearby?"

"Are you kidding? I wouldn't trust to bring it around these pigs. They'd destroy it."

She nodded, though she wanted to strongly disagree. "I bet it's exciting to ride on it."

"You ever been on one?"

"No," she giggled.

"I'll take you for a ride sometime if you want."

Gwen swallowed. *Did she want?*

"Really? I don't know. Maybe." She could feel the perspiration building.

"Gotta a phone number? I'll call you."

Oops. She hadn't thought of that and had to think fast. To buy time she took a gulp of beer. She couldn't give him the Chronicle number, and she didn't want him to have her home number either.

"I don't have a phone, but maybe you can reach me at the Free Store on Cole. I help out there." Starting tomorrow, she would.

"Oh, you help these pigs out, do you?"

Big mistake. Another swallow. "Well, not for long. I got some of my own clothes there, so a little payback, I guess," she finished lamely.

He cooled then, and she kicked herself for mentioning the Free Store. Still, what else could she have said, since she had to be somewhere where he could reach her and didn't want to put her friends at risk by giving him their numbers.

"I'm actually looking for a real job." She was breaking out in a sweat.

"What kind of job?"

"Oh, salesgirl or typing." Had she blown it completely?

"You won't find anything around here. Too many invaders. You gotta go downtown."

"I guess you're right."

She could feel him watching her as she took a few swallows of beer. Then he said, "What made you come over to me tonight? You didn't lose your sweater, did you?"

She blushed and looked down. "No, you found me out. I just always admired the Hells Angels. Wanted to meet one."

"Why?"

"Because you seem so, so . . . ." She decided this was the time to be coy.

"So what?"

"Gee, I don't know." She squirmed in her seat. "Um, masculine. I don't know, the black leather jackets, the bikes—"

"Kind of turn you on?"

Where was this going?

She smiled and drank more beer.

He tried to summon a waitress. "Let's have another round."

"No, really. It's late. I should go."

He didn't argue. In a few minutes he'd paid the bill and they rose to go.

When they were outside, she said, "I go this way."

"OK. I'll be at the park again on Thursday, if you want to come by."

"Maybe," she smiled.

He turned and went the other way. Gwen took a few deep breaths. Thank God he hadn't asked to take her home.

On the drive back to Marin, Gwen couldn't help wondering how far she'd take this investigation. Maybe another evening of drinks after a concert, and then what? The drive across the bridge and down the winding road, dark and lonely this time of night, offered a backdrop to her growing doubts as to the wisdom of the mad adventure she was about to embark on. A deer jumped out in front of her, startling her more than the deer. Slamming on the breaks, she waited for the animal to leave the road. Taking some deep breaths, she drove slowly the rest of way up Main Street to her house on Third.

The house was cold and dark. She heard something fall and jumped. Frightened, she flattened herself against the wall and waited. Then Alfi came padding toward her, wagging his tail. Her heart still pounding she knelt down and hugged him.

"What did you knock over, Alfi? You scared me to death."

When she returned from taking him out, she realized he'd had to wait too long. He'd made a puddle on the bedroom rug.

"I can't leave you alone so long, can I, Alfi?" She said snuggling him. "I'll have to find a dog-walker to take you out in the afternoon. Won't that be fun?"

CHAPTER 15

The next morning, she called Sheila as promised. "I'm glad you're still alive."

"So am I."

"How did it go?"

"Not bad, actually. I had to wait for him at the tent. By the time he showed up, the meadow was practically empty, and I was scared. We went for a beer and thank God he didn't offer to walk me home."

"What was he like? What did you talk about?"

Gwen tried to answer Sheila's questions.

"Are you going to see him again?"

She could hear Sheila munching. "Probably, Thursday night."

"Aren't you scared?"

She lied. "A little."

On Thursday she didn't want to leave Alfi alone for so many hours. She decided that she'd wait until noon to leave the house. Giving him a second outing before she left, Alfi watered the bushes, raising her hopes that he could hold it until she came home from the concert. She told him that soon he'd be a lucky dog to have a new friend, who'd give him an extra walk every day.

She checked in at the Chron to see if there were any notices or letters to the editors for her. There was a message on her desk that her boss wanted to see her.

She knocked on Mr. Vandermeer's door, and he beckoned her in.

Sans his usual smile, she wondered what was up.

"Sit down, Gwen. I hate to spring bad news on you when you're working so hard to cover both the glory and the horror of this special summer, but you have to know about this."

He was holding a letter in his hand. "What is it?"

"It's a letter from the father of the young woman, Rebecca Barton. Apparently, someone sent him a copy of the feature article you wrote up about his daughter."

Every muscle in her body was tensing up. She'd had a feeling it might get her in trouble, but had dismissed it; finally, it had slipped her mind.

"It seems they took umbrage at your mention of the time discrepancy between when he said he told the coroner he arrived for the girl's body, and that the mother told you he'd gone out before she died to get her to come home."

Gwen winced. "Oh."

"Oh, indeed. They're suing the paper, and you as well."

"Oh, God."

"Now understand anyone can sue anyone for anything, but it doesn't mean they'll win. As long as the truth can be verified, I don't think they'll have a leg to stand on." He managed a smile.

"What should I do?"

"We'll try to settle this out of court. I suggest you get the coroner to confirm and put in writing what the father told him."

"I'll do that."

She left his office limp and sickened that her call to Mrs. Barton had led to a lawsuit. To be honest, she didn't think the Barton's out in Nebraska would ever see the article. And she'd included the discrepancy in the father's arrival time in the paper to stir up interest in who the killer could be. She didn't point a finger at the father she hadn't ruled him out, either. She'd mentioned other possible suspects and asked that anyone knowing anything contact the Chronicle.

Contacting the coroner wasn't difficult, and although he was at first fuzzy on the date, he did remember that the father had said he'd just arrived at the airport. Checking some paperwork related to the girl's death established the day he'd heard from the father.

"Can you put that in writing, sir?"

"Why? What's up?"

"It's really important. The man is a suspect in his daughter's murder. Getting his arrival time is crucial."

The coroner agreed.

Gwen breathed a sigh of relief. At least her part of this unpleasant assignment had been done. Now she could wait for the bomb to fall— the official papers announcing the suit.

Composing and typing up a new article, attending a meeting and catching up on the small stuff pretty much consumed the rest of the day.

Changing her clothes and leaving the Chronicle she headed over to the Haight to share a bite to eat with Sheila. Sharing the threat of the Barton's suit with Sheila she apologized.

"I'm sorry. You prepare this nice meal and I unload on you. I'm afraid I'm poor company."

"Hey, you have to have somebody to talk to. I'm a pretty good listener."

"Yes, you are, and a dear friend."

An hour later she walked to the park alone, and over to Rake with a blanket.

"You're back," he said.

"Mind if I set up squatters' rights here?"

"Fine by me."

She spread out her blanket. Patting it she said, "You can join me if you like. Or do you have to stand all night?"

"Stand most of the time—hired security."

Gwen stood too. They talked about the band, how it wasn't as good as the Swans, except maybe the bass player, who was really good.

Rake pulled some money out of his pocket and asked her if she'd go get them something to eat.

"Haven't you had supper?" she asked.

"Nope."

"OK. What would you like?"

"Two hot dogs with mustard and a beer. Get something for yourself."

"Thanks."

She skipped away, happy to be with her Angel, or wanting him to think so. Since she'd had supper with Sheila, all she got for herself was a coke.

"Not a beer drinker, huh?" he said on her return.

"Not right now."

"You're not one of them, are you?" He said pointing to a group with ribbons, long hair and bare feet.

"Heavens no!"

"But you said you worked in the free store—that's a hippie joint."

That was temporary, I told you." She twirled her hair.

"Do you eat that garbage stew they brew up every day?"

"No, I don't. Do I act like a hippie?"

He looked her up and down. "I guess not."

In a few minutes he sat down on the blanket saying, "I guess they won't miss me for a while."

Gwen put on an act of a giddy school girl, all excited to be with an 'Angel'.

"How often do you guys ride on the highway? Vroom, vroom. That is SO exciting to see."

"Depends. Every weekend if we can."

"And during the week?"

"Not the whole club together. Some guys have families."

"Families! You mean they're fathers?" She said in mock surprise.

He laughed. "What did you think? That we only come to life when it's time for a rally?"

"Gee, I don't know. Is that the only time you use your bikes?"

"No, I ride alone, too. We all do."

"But not here."

"Right."

She looked at him, sweating in his leather jacket. "Aren't you awfully hot in that jacket? Do you have to wear it?"

"It's the uniform. Commands respect."

Or fear, Gwen thought.

"Do you mind if I look at the emblem on the back of it?" He turned so she could see it.

"It's so cool. Are they all alike?"

He took it off. "No. This patch with the skull and one gold wing is for all Hells Angels, but this one shows which club we're in."

"Does that depend on where you live?"

"Yeah, different regions, different states."

"What are the other patches for?"

"Some are for achievement." He stopped and looked at her. "You ask a lot of questions."

Oops. "Just admiring you guys."

They were silent for a while, and Gwen concentrated on the band. Rake put his jacket back on, stood up and began his surveillance again. Had she made a mistake, asking too many questions?

Finally, she said, "If you're tired of my company, I can go."

"No need." But he said it without looking at her, as he lit a cigarette.

More silence. Had she blown it all together?

Finally, she felt so uncomfortable, she did get up to leave. "See you," she said, walking away.

He called after her. "Meet me at the tent when it's over?" She turned but didn't answer right away.

"We can go back to Pickles," he said.

She agreed, but her inner voice kept saying, *Is this a good idea?*

Again, she waited by the tent. Again, he was late. This time, he didn't try to lead her in the other direction—they headed straight for *Pickles.*

In the bar he said little. Not much of a talker, she'd felt it necessary to keep the conversation going. But she had to be very careful about asking questions, especially the kind that would arouse suspicion. She decided general interest about the bikers was fairly safe.

"Can anyone join?"

"No."

"How do they choose who you let in?"

He looked at her hard. "Why you want to know?"

"Just asking. I've just always admired the Angels, ever since the first time I saw a whole school of them roaring by."

"School?" He laughed. "I think you mean club."

"OK, club. Anyway, the discipline, the power, the pure numbers—"

He laughed. "You fancy being a biker bitch?"

"What!"

"A biker's ole' lady."

"Oh, my gosh! What's that like?"

"Why don't you come to a party tomorrow night—see for yourself?"

"Really?" She jumped a little in her seat.

"I'll give you the address."

"You mean just show up—alone?"

"Yeah. Lot of girls do. Some just for one or two parties, some stay with us for a few weeks. Some become wives."

"Wow."

He scribbled an address on a napkin. "About eight o'clock. Tomorrow."

"Will you be there? I mean I don't want to crash a party."

"I'll be there. I'll take care of you." He gave her his first real smile.

She took the napkin. "That would be exciting."

"Let's have another beer."

"I can't. I have a dog. He's a real love, but he can't hold it so long. The other night when I got home, he'd made a puddle on the rug. I have to get back earlier tonight. But I am going to hire a dog-walker, so hopefully that won't be a problem for long."

"You ought to put up some signs, on telephone poles, advertising for one."

"That's exactly what I plan to do."

Rake nodded. "Where do you live?"

She'd dreaded the question. If she lied and he found out, she could be in deep trouble. If she told him the truth, he'd wonder what she was doing in the Haight. Despite this, she decided on the truth.

"I live in Marin."

"Way over there?"

"Yeah."

And right on cue: "Watcha doing in this neck of the woods?"

"I just come for the concerts."

"Marin, huh? I like to ride out there on my bike all the way to the ocean."

"Really? Some people think it's the prettiest place in the world."

"It's pretty, alright. Nothin' like the city. All those redwoods, farm country. When I ride alone, that's the place for me."

It was getting late. She said, "I need to get home. I didn't drive today, I'm taking a taxi home."

"I can drive you there. I do have a car."

"Oh, thank you, but it's way out of your way."

"You shouldn't be out alone so late at night."

He was either more of a gentleman than she'd thought any Hells Angels would be, or he was up to no good.

"There've been a couple of murders," he added.

That made her shiver. She wanted to ask how much he knew about them but thought better of it.

He got the waitress's attention and ordered the beers.

"Now you'll get home sooner, so you can take time for another beer," he smiled.

She couldn't very well pursue her investigation if she turned coward.

"I'll have to make a phone call before we leave. Call my roommate, she'll be worried."

He shrugged. The beer came. They talked about the concert as they drank it.

When they left, he said, "I'll get the car. You can walk with me, or you can wait here."

"I'll wait here and call my roommate at the corner phone booth."

Figuring that he wouldn't dare do anything amiss if he was aware that someone knew who she was with and where she was, she made the call to her old friend Eric. Eric, who had bailed her out of trouble more than once, and who lived on a houseboat in Sausalito.

"Is it alright to stay with you tonight? I'm not interrupting anything?"

"No, come right over. I want to hear what kind of trouble you're in now."

Parking on the other side of the park, it took Rake twenty minutes to come back with his car— twenty minutes in which she could have changed her mind. But she was waiting for him when he drew up in an old Ford. Somehow, she was expecting something grander that would announce his status as a Hell's Angel. Of course, she realized all Hells Angels weren't rich—probably none of them. In fact, she suspected they put more money into their bikes than into anything else.

They talked more about motorcycles as they drove toward Marin. When they crossed the bridge, she said, "Take this first exit. It winds its way down to Sausalito."

Gwen lived on the south end, but she told Rake to keep driving through town.

As they drove down Bridgeway, past the waterfront, the restaurants and all the quaint shops, Rake was quiet.

When they reached the north end she said, "We're getting near the turnoff."

"What kind of place do you live in—house, apartment?"

"Houseboat," she lied.

"Houseboat? Never met anyone who lived on a houseboat."

"There's lots of them around Marin. Here's the entrance," she said as they approached Eric's community. "You can drop me off here."

"I'll drive you back in."

"No, the roads are rough—big potholes."

"Then we'll walk."

Stay calm Gwen. "Not this time. Goodbye, and thanks for the ride," she said firmly, got out of the car, and waved goodbye. She didn't want him to know where she'd be staying, or where Eric lived.

With wobbly legs she hurried down the poorly lit road, unsure if he'd followed her. When she stepped on the dock it made a loud clatter, heaving up and down as she traversed it. She was relieved to reach Eric's door.

He was delighted to see her. Bringing her inside he gave her a big bear hug. A large man, strong and deeply tanned from working outside on boats, bikes and nautical equipment, Eric possessed a girth of considerable size. Complete with beard, last year he'd played Santa Clause in the Christmas parade. Once her mother's friend, when Gwen returned to California, she and Eric became buddies. Generally jolly, but when it came to concerns of his god-child, as he liked to think of her, he became quite serious.

He offered her a beer, but the two she'd had was her limit. "I'll just have water."

He popped the cap off a Budweiser for himself and poured her a glass of water.

"What kind of mischief are you up to now?" he asked.

Over the drinks Gwen told him everything. She filled him in on Jennie's story, and Rebecca's too. He'd heard a little about the grocer's murder, but that was all.

"You mean you let this Hell's Angel guy drive you over here? You know what they are, don't you? Lawless—murderers."

"Not all of them, I'm sure."

Eric shook his head. "When are you going to learn, girl? You're going to get yourself killed one of these days."

"I know. And then you'll have to buy a suit to come to my funeral. But wait, you can get one at the Free Store!"

"This isn't funny, Gwen."

"I know." She told him about Jennie and how she'd disappeared after turning in her boyfriend.

"See, if I can convince him that I have a crush on him, and act like a silly schoolgirl, maybe I'll get some information as to what's become of Jennie."

"Your Jennie is probably dead by now, and you will be too, if you keep up this nonsense."

"Let's change the subject, shall we?"

"Have you heard anything I said?"

"Yes, sir. And I know what I'm doing has its risks. I'm trying to be very careful. That's why I didn't let him take me to my place. Now, want to hear some good news? We're being sued by the dead girl's parents."

"Have you considered another occupation?"

"What? Oh." Ignoring this, she continued. "Both the Chron and me personally. But as my boss says, anyone can sue, that doesn't mean they'll win."

Eric shook his head.

"What's new with you?"

Eric sighed. "I finally got a car."

"Really? Great."

"Yeah, an old Chevy, but it runs."

"So now you can come and rescue me without borrowing one."

Eric groaned.

"Oh, I almost forgot Alfi! Can we go get him?"

"Sure."

Squeezing his hand she said, "You're such a dear friend, Eric."

"Hmph."

On the way to her apartment Eric said, "How's Mark?"

She winced. She didn't want to talk about that, but here it was. "He left me, Eric."

"Why?" Nothing subtle here. "He just didn't like my lifestyle."

"Can't blame him."

They were silent for a few moments. Then Eric reached over and touched her hand. "I'm sorry to hear that. Really sorry."

"Me too."

Alfi, of course, was delighted to see his mistress. After giving him a chance to relieve himself, they were back in the car with him, returning to the houseboat.

"Well, time to put our tired bodies to bed." He got out the bedding for the couch as he'd done for her before. The gentle rocking of the houseboat was like a cradle. Barely had her head hit the pillow than she fell asleep.

In the morning she called Sheila. Someone had to know who she'd been with if she disappeared tonight.

"Rake invited me to a club party."

"You're not going, are you?"

"I think I will. I know, it could be dangerous."

"*Could* be. I'd say for *sure* it's dangerous."

"Well, if he wanted to harm me he had every opportunity in that empty park. Anyway, it might be fun."

"Oh Gwen!"

She knew she wasn't nearly as confident as she sounded.

CHAPTER 16

She felt a sore throat coming on at her Chron office that day. Still, Gwen resolved to go to the party. Debating what the appropriate attire would be, she settled on a simple cotton dress and loafers . No beads, no accessories. As the hours passed she tried to calm her nerves.

Although she had studied the map carefully, she realized she'd be driving into a part of the city she wasn't familiar with—called Dogpatch. Still light out when she left home at eight fifteen, by the time she was in the general neighborhood of her destination the sky was black. Finally, she found Tennessee, where streetlights were few and far between. She strained to see numbers on a building. Driving slowly, she was looking for the 900 block.

Her nervousness had given way to focusing on driving, but as she neared her destination, Gwen began to feel anxious. What would she say? What would the other girls be like? Would Rake be there? And what about all the men, how would they treat her? But above all, would her visit be at all fruitful, would she find out anything about Jennie? She warned herself not to expect too much the first time.

She knew she was close to her destination when three motorcycles went roaring by and pulled in about a block away. When she caught up with them, she saw about thirty bikes parked in front of the club. Yes, this had to be the right place.

A one-story simple cement block structure, it held nothing of architectural interest. A sign, with the skull logo pronounced it Hells Angels. She found a parking spot about a block away and walked back. Gwen took a big breath, pulled the door open and walked inside.

Smoke and the tangy scent of sweat permeated the interior. She was in a dimly lit bar, noisy with a cacophony of loud talking, the sound of pool balls striking each other and a baseball game on TV. Amongst the dissonance someone was playing country music on an electric guitar.

It took a few moments for her eyes to adjust to the darkness. Scanning the room she searched for Rake. Not in sight, she felt her heart start thumping.

A girl dressed in patched jeans came up to her. "Can I help you?"

"I was looking for Rake. He said he'd be here."

"Just a minute." The girl left. Was she coming back?

Gwen stood by the door, as others, both men and women took note of her. Did she look out of place or was it just that she was new? The air was thick with smoke and testosterone. At least that was what Gwen was thinking, as tough-looking dudes, most in leather filled the room.

Finally, the girl came back. "He'll be here in a minute." Gwen didn't appreciate the delay but at least he was here.

The girl smiled. "I'm Sandy. Can I get you something to drink?" Sandy appeared to be about Gwen's age. "No, thank you. I'll wait."

"Why don't you have a seat?" She was directed over to a table.

Not wanting to appear rude, Gwen followed her to a table where three other girls were sitting. Two were clad in bell-bottom trousers, the other in jeans. Gwen felt uncomfortable in her dress. The chair available left her with her back to the rest of the room.

"What's your name?" one of them asked.

"Connie."

"Girls, this is Rake's friend. Have a seat, Connie." Sandy said.

After introductions the girls returned to their conversation about nail polish.

"I like Sally Hanson; it's the cheapest."

"But Revlon doesn't chip as fast."

Gwen barely listened. Where was Rake?

"You need to use a top-coat to set it."

One of them turned to Gwen. "What's your favorite brand?"

"I don't know. I have some Revlon and some Maybelline. I never thought about which lasted the longest."

She wondered what was keeping Rake. Another girl asked her if she would like a beer.

"No, thanks. I'll wait for Rake."

"He might be awhile."

She wanted to ask why, what was he doing? But she kept still.

Her bladder often over-reacted to tense situations. "Could you tell me where the Ladies' room is, please?"

"Sure. Just go way to the back, and it's on your right." Sandy pointed in the general direction.

Threading her way between tables and men standing around talking, she saw a door to the alley that was open. Gwen could see three men unloading something from a truck. When they saw her, they closed the door.

If they hadn't closed the door, Gwen wouldn't have thought anything about it. But because they did, she couldn't help wondering if the goods they were unloading were contraband. Drugs, maybe. Was this what Rake was so busy doing?

After using the facility, she returned to the table, where she found the girls deep in conversation about the next rally.

"Has Rake invited you?"

Gwen shook her head. "No."

"He will, if you hang out long enough," Sandy said. "Have you ever ridden on the back of a bike?"

"No, but I'd like to."

"I just loved my first ride on a bike—better than a roller coaster," Sandy said.

She felt hands on her shoulders, knew it was Rake. Hiding her annoyance at his tardiness, she turned to him and smiled.

Smiling back, he said, "You made it," with no apologies.

"Yup."

"I see you've met some of the sisters." He pulled her to her feet. "Let me show you around."

He took her hand and led her to the bar where he got a couple of beers for them. Her throat was getting so sore, the beer made it worse. "Want some chips?"

"Not now."

He walked her over to the pool table. "Do you play?"

"No, I don't." She was beginning to feel terribly inadequate in this environment. "Do you?"

"Yeah, great game."

She sensed that he was glad to be with her, eager to show her the game.

With his arm around her shoulder, they stood watching men chalk their sticks, bend over the table, and take their time in calculating just how to attack the ball. Observers as well as players were deep in concentration. Everyone watched while the man calculated his move and finally made his shot. As the ball found its mark observers shouted their congratulations. It was clear they took the game very seriously.

Gwen said, "It must take a lot of skill to hit the ball just right."

"You got to use the right amount of muscle—too little, it won't go far enough, too much, it overshoots the goal. And of course, the trajectory—gotta get that right."

Gwen tried to pay attention, though the game didn't interest her, and she was beginning to think her trip to Dogpatch was a waste of time.

Finally, they left the pool table. As they walked around, Rake introduced her to a few of the *Angels.* She could feel them sizing her up, looking her up and down. Not exactly surprised, nevertheless she found it distasteful.

She pretended to be enthusiastic about everything Rake and his friends said. Although she didn't really expect to see him here, she couldn't help looking for Bud. The picture of Jennie and Bud together was burned in her mind.

After watching a poker game for a while, he took her to the bar, where they sat on the stools watching a baseball game on TV. The volume was so loud that it made conversation difficult. Rake acknowledged her presence from time to time by squeezing her hand or putting his arm around her shoulder, but for the most part his eyes were on the game.

While Rake consumed four beers, Gwen hadn't finished her second. "You're not much of a drinker," he commented.

"I have to drive home, remember."

"Yeah, right. Don't want you to get a ticket."

She was also trying to stay alert to any nuances in what Rake or the others said, and to keep an ear peeled to information that might possibly lead to Jennie's location. She knew they wouldn't talk about it in her presence, but nevertheless it didn't hurt to stay alert.

While Rake was focused on the game, Gwen heard a couple of men talking a few feet away.

"Yeah, well that's why he was kicked out."

"Right."

Who was kicked out, Gwen wondered. Out of the club?

During the commercial Rake turned to her and said, "Have you decided if you want to go for a bike ride?"

"You mean the rally this weekend?"

He looked surprised. "You know about that."

"Yes, the gals mentioned it."

"No, I didn't mean a rally. I meant just you and me—for starters." She smiled. "I'll think about it."

The truth was she thought she'd be safer in a group of mixed company than with this man alone, although she had to admit he seemed harmless enough.

About eleven o'clock Gwen decided it was time to leave. Rake walked her to her car. When they reached it, he put his arms around her.

"Did you have a good time?"

"It was really interesting. And I liked meeting the girls."

"Glad to hear it. Was it what you expected?"

"I didn't know what to expect. It must be great to have a club and clubhouse with friends to hang out with."

"Yup. These folks are family."

"That's wonderful."

"Come again, OK?"

"When?"

"Tomorrow night, if you can."

"Another party?"

He shrugged. "When it's not a rally weekend, we meet up at the club. That's all."

"I'll think about it."

He leaned forward expecting a kiss.

She pulled back. "I don't want to give you my cold." He backed off.

She unlocked her car and opened the door. "Drive safely."

He held the door for her, and when she was inside, closed it. "See you tomorrow."

She hadn't said 'yes' but he seemed to think she had. Not a bad guy, she thought. Not her type, but no one she need be afraid of. That is, unless he discovered her real mission.

Driving home she was thinking she wasn't any closer to discovering what happened to Jennie than she'd been before. Was getting involved with the Angels worth the trouble, and the risk?

~~~

The next day Gwen decided to go to the house where Jennie had been staying. She'd made a note of the address when Jennie had given it to the detective. When she'd first disappeared, the police had gone there and established that she wasn't there, but Gwen wanted to see if she could find out anything about her from the other residents.

The house was several blocks from the hub of the Haight, on Fell. It was a quiet neighborhood, lacking the shops and pedestrian traffic she was familiar with in the Haight.

She found the address—another old house needing a facelift. The same style of architecture was used in every house on the block. Peeling paint on the siding, steps and the porch gave it a forlorn appearance.

Gwen rang the bell. After several tries a young man wearing only a towel opened the door.

"Yeah?" he said.

Not knowing how else to begin she said, "I'm looking for Jennie Lopez."

"She don't live here no more."

"Do you know where she went?"

The young man turned his head to the side, then back again. Finally, he said, "She disappeared."

"That's what I heard. I'm a friend of hers and I want to find her. Can I come in and talk to you, and anyone else who might be here?"

He hesitated. She felt he was appraising her, thinking it unlikely she was a friend of the forlorn Jennie.

"Yeah, I guess." He opened the door and let her in.

"Is this a rooming house?"

He shrugged. "About eight of us live here."

"Is anyone else home?"

"I'll call up."

He walked halfway up the stairs and yelled, "Anybody home? If y'are, come on down. Somebody here wants to talk to you."

Gwen heard some chatter and then the sound of footsteps on the stairs. It must have been curiosity that made them respond to the call.

Two girls about Jennie's age. In fact, one of them resembled Jennie, small and thin. The young man left the room.

Gwen said, "Hello, I'm looking for people who knew Jennie. Did you know her?" she asked with a smile.

"Yeah, we did. She used to live here," the larger girl said.

"Do you have any idea where she might have gone when she left here? It's important that I find her."

They looked at each other and said simultaneously, "No."

"Do you know why she left?" Gwen was careful to pose her questions gently, with a friendly smile.

"She just disappeared one day."

"Do you think she was afraid to stay here?"

The girl stopped talking and looked suspicious. "Why do you want to know?"

Taking on the role of Sheila she said, "She came to me for counseling. I care about her—a lot."

That seemed to satisfy the girl. She nodded.

One girl said nothing, but the other one, large and vocal spoke. "Maybe. She was afraid of her killer-boyfriend."

"Do you think she left here to find a place to hide?"

"Either that or he got her."

"You mean—"

"Killed her. Or maybe his buddies took her somewhere."

"Hells Angels?

"Yeah."

The girl who'd been silent turned and walked back upstairs, leaving her friend to handle this intruder.

"Where would they take her?"

"Who knows?"

"Has this guy or any others come here since she left?"

The girl hesitated, then she said, "Yeah, the first night she didn't show up here, a couple of guys burst in here, ran through the whole house looking for her. We were all pretty scared."

"Did they talk to you?"

"Only to Jared. One of them shook him up a little. He kept telling them she wasn't here. Finally, they left."

"If she did get away safely, do you know where she might have gone?"

"Well, she wouldn't have gone home. That's for sure. Once she said something about an aunt in Orinda. But I don't know her name and I don't know if that's where she went. She just disappeared, didn't tell anybody anything."

Gwen scribbled her phone number on a piece of paper and handed it to the girl, "If you find out anything else, please call me."

She left feeling she'd accomplished nothing. Just one little thread that might lead somewhere—if the aunt's name happened to be the same as Jennie's she might be able to contact her.

She went back to Marjorie's and asked to use her phone.

"I might be able to reach a relative of Jennie's. Long shot."

Marjorie stood by while Gwen got numbers from 'Information' for any Lopez's in Orinda.

There were three— Jose, an 'S'. and an Emilia. She tried Emilia first. Although she let the phone ring many times, there was no answer.

Next, she tried Jose. A woman answered.

"I'm trying to locate the aunt of Jennie Lopez. Would you know how I can find her?"

"Who?"

"The aunt of Jennie Lopez."

"Never heard of her."

Dial tone.

Gwen sighed and made her third attempt—S. Lopez. A man answered. Gwen repeated her inquiry.

"What's the girl's name?" he said.

"Jennie Lopez."

"My sister has a niece, her husband's niece. Don't recall the girl's name."

"But her last name wouldn't be Lopez, would it."

The man thought about this. "No, reckon it wouldn't be."

Two more attempts that evening resulted in no answer at Emilia's.

CHAPTER 17

Although she was still on the hunt for Jennie, Gwen realized there was another reason she wanted to go back to the Angel's clubhouse. She wanted to know more about the women, try to understand why they chose this life. She decided to accept Rake's invitation to come back the next night. The women had been friendly last time, and she'd remained rather distant. This time she'd talk to them, pretend she was interested in joining their ranks. As soon as she entered, she headed over to the table where the girls she'd met were sitting.

She was greeted in a friendly way. A pitcher of beer was on the table along with a couple of unused glasses.

"Hey, welcome back. Have a beer."

A glass was poured for her. After some general chit-chat about the club and what the patches meant, Gwen dared to ask, "Did you ever know a girl named Jennie?"

Eyes dropped. Tongues stopped. Silence.

"Just asking. She was a friend of a friend of mine, and she wondered what happened to her."

"What do you know about her?"

Gwen acted innocent. "Me? Nothing. Except this friend wants to know why she doesn't answer phone calls. Stuff like that."

"What makes you think we'd know?"

"She was going with an Angel. Thought you might have heard something."

More silence. Then Sandy spoke up. "Look, you gotta understand, if you're some guy's property, you stand by your man no matter what."

So they did know about her, and maybe what had happened to her.. Gwen remembered the T-shirt— property of.

"Yeah, Jennie forgot that," the girl called Pat said.

"Have you seen her recently?" Gwen asked.

A few shook their heads.

"Do you know what happened to her?"

Shrugs. But *did* they know?

"We're not included in all the men stuff."

"We don't even speak unless spoken to."

"It's not that bad. I do."

"Well, at home, yeah. But not with the Angels. You just don't go butting into their conversation."

The talk had veered away from the subject she was interested in.

"Look, if you're getting involved with Rake, it's our job, as your sisters, to let you know what the rules are."

"OK. Like what?"

"Always treat your man with respect. Do what he tells you to do. Try to anticipate his needs."

"Yeah, like Rake smokes. When he pulls out a cigarette, light it for him. He may or may not allow you to smoke."

She laughed. "I don't have a lighter."

"Get one."

"And watch your tongue. No backtalk, no arguing and no swearing. You may hear him swear up a storm, but he wants you to be a lady."

"Smile a lot. Be cheerful. Learn how to cheer him up when he's down."

"Yeah, be a good listener."

"And offer sex."

"Often."

"Don't ever refuse him that."

No wonder Jennie had said, "We don't like Hippies." Hippies were free, free to express themselves in whatever way they wanted.

They must have noticed her look of disbelief. One of them said, "Don't knock it, girl, until you try it."

Another added, "You're probably wondering why we'd give up our own voice to obey our old man. But you don't know how wonderful it is to be cared for, protected, maybe even loved."

"The surrender brings you kind of a . . . peace. Not to have to worry about stuff, no more hustling, no more trying to make it all work by yourself in a world that's gone crazy."

"And the rallies are a real high. Hanging onto the back of your old man while he revs up that muscle machine, and then roaring down the road three across with a trail of twenty more behind. Nothing beats that—not even sex."

"Oh, come on, Shirl. Don't go that far!"

"Hey, speak for yourself."

"OK. Well, almost."

The girls laughed so hard, others in the room turned to look.

Gwen nodded. She was beginning to understand. The scope of it was vast, more than she could wrap her mind around. Obviously, this life offered something satisfying to these women. Maybe they were looking for the father-figure they never had. It was complicated, to her anyway, and would require more thought.

Just then one of the Angels came toward them and plucked his woman away from the others, drawing her toward the bar.

"That's how we know when we're wanted—when they come and get us."

"Yeah, and when to stay away."

Gwen said, "I heard once that the Angels have gang-raped women." She tried to sound nonchalant.

"No, that's a myth. Where'd you hear that?"

Gwen shrugged. "Can't remember."

At first, no one said anything. Then the tall one with long black hair said, "That's very severe punishment for very bad conduct. And it would only happen if her ole' man makes the call."

Gwen swallowed hard. "It's just within the club, that that might happen?"

"Yeah, but not in this club."

"How would you know, if the men don't tell you this stuff?"

"We see our sisters. She might not tell us in so many words, but pictures are worth a thousand words—like black eyes."

"But gang rape?" Gwen asked.

"Maybe she couldn't walk for a while."

"But she stays in the club?"

"Depends on "her ole' man."

"So many questions."

"Hey, Connie, you worried that might happen to you?"

Gwen realized she'd gone too far, was now embarrassed and ill at ease. She smiled and shook her head.

For a minute no one said anything, then Sandy broke the ice. "And by the way, most girls belong to one man only, but there are a few girls who belong to the club, and any man can have her."

"That way, she gets some variety."

"If that's what's important to her. Not for me, thank you," Pat said.

"And then we have passers-through. You know, a girl might hang out with a guy for a few days or a few weeks and then decide the program's not for her, so she's dropped off at a gas station. Everybody isn't here for life. We're free to leave."

"But most of us stay."

"It's a good life, if you mind your own business and live by the rules."

"Think you can handle it, Connie?"

"Whew! I don't know. It's a lot to take in."

"You don't have to decide right away. I think Rake's the patient type."

"Tell me about him. I don't know him very well. I just met him at the concerts in the park."

"He's the strong, quiet type."

"Yeah, not like Rogue—all lathered up about everything." More laughter.

"He's not violent, is he?"

"Rake? No way. I'd say gentle, but then I don't know him very well, either."

"Does he have other women, or did he recently break up with someone?"

The girls looked at each other and shook their heads in agreement.

"He may have had an occasional fling, but I don't think he ever had a property."

Gwen looked up and saw Rake coming toward them.

He looked at the women. "Did you give Connie the lowdown?"

"We think so, Rake."

"Did you have a nice visit with the sisters?" he smiled as he led her away from the women to a booth where they could be alone.

"Yes, I did."

"I wanted them to fill you in on what it's like to be a member's ole lady. Did they do that?"

"They certainly did."

"And what do you think?"

"I'll be honest. It's a totally different life than I'm used to."

He nodded. "I thought so. It takes some getting used to. No hurry."

Perspiration broke out on her forehead. Was he indirectly asking her to be his 'ole lady? He went on to tell her how old the San Francisco chapter was and how they'd often meet up with other chapters.

Then he guided her over to a table where they were playing poker. He was invited to join, which he did, leaving Gwen to watch as he played a couple of games, and then she said she'd like to leave. He walked her to her car.

She kept the act up. "You were good, Rake. Do you always win?"

"No, just lucky tonight. When we play for money I usually lose," he laughed at himself.

"Aw, that's a shame."

"You ready for a bike ride, Connie?"

She swallowed. Then feeling bold, brave or foolish, she smiled, "Yes, I think so."

He nodded. "I'll pick you up at twelve o'clock tomorrow, at the entrance to your houseboat."

"OK," she said softly.

He drew her toward him. "Still have that cold?"

"Afraid so."

He released her. "Bring a picnic," he smiled.

On the drive home she wondered again what she'd gotten herself into. The motorcycle ride would be scary enough if she were riding it with someone she knew. Triple scary with an Angel.

I could stand him up, she thought. Or meet him and politely decline. But then I'd be chickening out on my mission to discover what had become of Jennie.

There was another reason to continue hanging around the Angels. She was drawn to their strange and bewildering life-style, especially that of the women. She wanted to get to know them, write about them. Fascinating material for feature articles. Maybe a whole series.

~~~

The next morning she wrote an article, stating how the Hells Angels were a big part of the summer scene—present at so many concerts of Jefferson Airplane and the Holding Company, and The Grateful Dead. Strange bedfellows, indeed. She included the names of some their friends like the poet Alan Ginsberg and Ken Kesey, who'd written *One Flew Over the Cuckoo's Nest*. She'd seen them near the stage sharing LSD sugar cubes together.

In another piece she contrasted the free-thinking hippy women to the 'ole ladies' of the Angels, revealing some of their core beliefs about obedience. She explained how they became 'voluntary chattels', proud to be a 'P.O.' —*property of* an Angel.

She came across a statement in the Chronicle archives called *Life as Biker Bitch* and wrote an article which including the statement,

"There will always be a male responsible for the actions of any woman that is a part of this outlaw set. There are also sisters who will harvest any woman to make sure she understands this set. Harvesting a sister means that a more experienced P.O. will spend time with our sister and help her to understand her place in this environment. We help her to remove her old way of thinking and grasp the lifestyle of our outlaw brothers. Teach her to adhere to authority, learn to submit, show respect, speak when spoken to, maintain being a lady, and understand the brand.

I think some women are brainwashed into believing they are superior to men, and that's just not the truth.... Adam from the Bible represents strength, and Eve was created as his helpmate to support her man. That is the same thing we are doing. Supporting our own! A true P.O. will serve the brotherhood in whatever way she is needed. Wipe noses, lace boots, pop collars or any domestic-related things our brothers need."

—*Property Of*

~~~

In the morning she put signs on telephone poles around her neighborhood. "Dog-walker needed afternoons, call 415-332-5863."

Then, remembering to pocket some 'mad money' and the lighter she'd found in her former roommate's room, she drove to Issaquah,

Eric's houseboat community. Concealing her car further up the road she walked back to the entrance and put up a couple more signs while she waited for Rake. Late as usual, she practiced her karate. When he arrived, Rake was proud to show her his bike, and explaining all its visible parts. She studied the iron horse she was about to mount. Painted dark purple and shiny as silver, she couldn't help admiring it.

"It's beautiful."

"That it is."

A little timid in mounting the bike, he told her how to do it—jump and leap over the seat. She felt clumsy and had to make a second try.

"You'll get used to it," he encouraged.

As he gunned the engine and prepared to take off, she knew enough to put her arms around his waist.

"Tighter," he called, as he made a jack-rabbit start.

"Where are we going?" she asked over the din as a cloud of exhaust engulfed her.

"Out to the coast,"

"What?"

"The coast."

They took the freeway to Sir Francis Drake, drove west passed the town of Forest Hills, then through a forest of redwoods called Samuel Taylor Park and out to Olema. There they turned left, passed through Inverness, as Rake skillfully rounded the many winding curves cut out of the forest. Finally, they found their way to the ocean. The ride made her both excited and fearful. Her hands were shaking by the time they reached the beach.

"What a ride!" she exclaimed as she dismounted and removed her kerchief.

"You liked it?"

"Scarier than a roller coaster. But you're a good driver," she hastened to say.

He locked the bike up carefully, then taking the picnic and a blanket out of the boot, they walked down to the beach. Not as busy as a weekend there were still several mothers with children and a few couples.

Being here, in the exact same place as she'd been with Mark at Pt. Reyes made her miss him. With miles and miles of coastline, why had they ended up at the same beach where she'd been with Mark? She couldn't help recalling their first walk along this beach, how he'd stop to write with a stick in the wet sand, "I love you, Gwen."

She tried to brush those bittersweet memories away, as Rake found a spot away from others to plant the blanket, and they sat down.

They opened the picnic she'd brought of ham and cheese sandwiches, a couple of pears and brownies.

"What brought you to the Haight?"

Taken aback, with a sandwich mid-way to her mouth, she shrugged. "Doesn't everyone get there eventually?"

He wasn't buying. "Why did *you* go?"

"It's a phenomenon—something I wanted to experience. And I was in between jobs."

The last thing she wanted him to know was that she was using her experiences to write articles for *The Chronicle* and *The Oracle*.

"What do you do there?"

"Act like a tourist, I guess. And, as you know, I love the concerts. Now, maybe you'll tell me why you like being a Hell's Angel."

He looked at her a long time, and she was wondering if he disapproved of her question.

He loosened a cigarette from its pack. Just in time, Gwen remembered the lighter, pulled it out and lit it for him. He gave her an appreciative smile.

Finally, he said, "It's a brotherhood. Family, loyalty, friendship."

"You didn't have that growing up?"

He looked hard at her again, then said, "No, I didn't. I was an orphan. Lots of us were, or from broken homes, foster homes."

They stopped talking then, and consumed the food, listening to the surf break on the beach, and a couple of kids squealing in the waves.

When they'd finished lunch, Rake said, "OK, so you want to know more about Hells Angels—who gets in, who doesn't."

"If you want to tell me."

"No one who's ever applied to be a prison guard or policemen can get in. Child molesters are never considered. If a guy's invited to visit, he might become a Hang-around. He can attend some events, bring girls. Then if the club likes him, he might become an associate, eventually a prospect, and finally a full patch member—if he passes muster."

"Does that take a long time?"

"Altogether? A couple of years. Sometimes longer."

He changed the subject abruptly. "You know we're not all bad-ass boys."

She looked up, surprised. "I'm sure you're not. I've heard the Angels help kids out."

"Yeah, we do. Give 'em toys at Christmas time—the ones who wouldn't get any otherwise."

"That's great, really great."

Gwen wondered if it were because many of them had endured rotten childhoods.

"Do you work, have a job?"

She noted a stiffening of his jaw muscles; he didn't answer. Was it true that they survived as drug dealers, as she'd heard? Was it drugs she'd seen being carried into the building on her first visit when the door had been shut to conceal their actions?

A long silence ensued. Then he turned from a seagull he was watching to her. "Some of the gals said you were asking about a girl named Jennie."

There was no point in denying it. Her heart must have missed a few beats, but she tried to sound casual. "She's a friend of a friend of mine."

"Why would you think we would know anything about her?" She felt a cold wind pass over them.

She leaned back on her hands to stop them from shaking. "She was going with an Angel."

"What's his name?"

"I don't know."

"Listen, Connie. You don't want to ask so many questions. It could get you in trouble."

She saw a flicker of his eyelids. Frightened, she said, "OK."

They watched sea-gulls dart and fly about, pick at bits of food picnickers had left.

Finally, he said, "Have you put up any signs for a dog-watcher yet?"

"Yes. I'll show you when we go back—right at the entrance."

He nodded. Before long he said, "Time to leave."

His mood had changed. Gwen knew it had something to do with the conversation about Jennie and it made her very uncomfortable. Still, she had to mount his bike, hold on to him and trust him all the way back to Marin. What choice did she have?

The ride back was uneventful. She was wondering if he'd want to see her again.

When they'd dismounted, he said, "Good ride, huh?"

"Yes, very exciting." She gave him a big smile.

"Show me the ad you put up."

They walked over to one of the poles. He looked at it. "You do have a phone number."

How could she have been so stupid as to show him the sign? Embarrassed, and caught in a lie, she tried to recover. "Sorry, I just didn't know you then and I'm reluctant to give it out to strangers."

"Smart girl. But now that I know, mind if I take this?"

He ripped the sign off the pole. "You've got another one of these around, right?"

"Yes." Well, at least he'd accepted her explanation. "Be in touch," he said, as he walked back to his bike.

She waved 'goodbye' and watched him wheel away. What was niggling at her mind? Somehow, he seemed a bit cooler than before. Maybe it was just his personality. She hadn't been able to figure him out at all. Had she put her foot in it, asking too many questions. It was like walking on eggshells, she decided, leading the life of an undercover detective.

Gwen wished she could share her dilemma with her friend Eric, but knowing his aversion to her risky undertakings, she walked to her car and drove back to her apartment. Maybe I'll tell Tyson about it. He'd be a good person to talk with.

CHAPTER 18

After returning from walking Alfi the next morning, the phone rang. The voice of a teenager asked if she was the person looking for a dog-walker. He said his name was Carlos. Yes, he was available every day. He agreed to come over and meet her in about an hour. She gave him the address.

Right on time, the doorbell rang, and Gwen opened the door to a boy of about fifteen. Nice-looking and cheerful, she liked him right away. Inviting him in she introduced him to Alfi. It was clear the boy liked the dog and visa-versa. He lived in the canal district of Marin, where many Mexican families made their homes. She asked him if he had any references.

"On Saturdays I help out at a laundromat." He gave her the name and number of the owner.

"Anything else?"

"I had a job last summer mowing this guy's lawn, but he moved away."

The boy looked eager to please, seemed responsible and mature. "Would you like to take Alfi for a little run?"

"Now? Sure."

He seemed happy to do so.

While they were gone, Gwen called the laundromat. Yes, she was told, he was responsible, and the customers liked him.

"I can even trust him with the cash register. Customers who want their clothes folded pay extra."

He sounded perfect. When he returned, Gwen told him she'd like to hire him. He agreed and would start tomorrow, Monday.

Gwen breathed a sigh of relief. She would still walk Alfi in the morning and in the evening when she got home, but he would get a little attention and a chance to relieve himself in the afternoon.

Two more offers to dog-walk came in, but Gwen was happy with her choice.

Carlos Gonzalez arrived at Gwen's apartment at 4:00 on Monday afternoon. He placed the key the owner had given him in the door and was met by a happy dog. It was a kick taking this friendly lab for a walk. They went down along Bridgeway, on the path along the water, while Carlos gazed out at the many sailboats, focusing on a group that were clearly in a race. Someday he'd own one—a racing boat, maybe a Sun Odyssey or a Jeanneau. He was sure of that. When they returned to the apartment, he gave Alfi a treat.

Now to the real business at hand. With the dog at his feet, he sat at the worn desk in the living room and opened the center drawer. A couple of handwritten letters, and a folder of bills, mostly utility. Beside it was an unsealed envelope. Opening it he saw several five and ten-dollar bills. He put it back and opened another drawer and pulled out a thick folder marked 'Chronicle'. In it were some newspaper clippings written by a Gwen Harris. He scanned the contents. Then he looked at the utility bills again. All addressed to this Harris woman. No Connie here. Going back to the articles he saw that she was writing about the Haight, the death of a couple of folks there, and a missing girl named Jennie. He wondered if this was the kind of stuff Dad wanted to know. Searching further he found one specifically about the Angels.

He picked up another folder labeled "Oracle". Flipping through the clippings his eyes landed on an article headlined "Where is the Killer's Girlfriend?" He read it. It told the name of the killer, identified him as a member of the Hells Angels. The article proceeded to reveal that after reporting the identity of the killer, the girlfriend had disappeared. She left the reader to imagine what had become of her.

On another sheet in handwriting he read, "Possible suspects for Rebecca's Killer." Underneath that he read, "Bud Smith, Rebecca's father, Rebecca's boyfriend."

Carlos didn't know who the last two were, but he knew that Bud was one of the Angels.

He put everything carefully back in the drawers. Except two of the articles. He didn't think she'd miss them. It was easy to memorize the list of suspects.

Before leaving he walked through the rest of the house. Maybe Connie was a roommate of this reporter. He checked the bedrooms. One bed in one bedroom. Very little in the other—some books and boxes. He gave Alfi a goodbye pat, locked up and left. He wasn't sure what to think. Either Connie didn't live here, or maybe Connie and Gwen Harris were the same person.

~~~

Gwen was in the Haight in the afternoon, delivering an article to *The Oracle*. That done, she decided to visit Tyson. Climbing his steps, she could hear him strumming his guitar. She knocked on his screen door and motioned for her to come in.

"Don't stop. It's lovely."

He kept playing for a while, and when he stopped Gwen clapped. "You are really good, Tyson."

He smiled. "To what do I owe the pleasure?"

"It's been a while. Quite a while, I think."

"That it has. I'm glad to see you."

He rose and gave her a warm and lingering hug. How she appreciated it. How much she missed being touched.

Then he put on an LP record of Joni Mitchell. Moving on to the kitchen he called out, "Still have some coffee, but it was brewed this morning. Or tea?"

She followed him. "Tea would be good." She saw what she'd been smelling. "Cinnamon rolls. Yum,"

"Help yourself. One of my roommates made them."

"That's OK. I hinted shamelessly."

He put one on a plate and handed it to her. Taking another for himself, he said, "Anything special on your mind?"

"Yes, actually. I thought you might be the best person with whom to share what I've been up to."

"I'm honored."

The tea was ready, and they adjourned to the living room, sitting cross-legged on the floor, next to each other.

"I've gotten involved with an Angel."

The tea he was sipping spurted out of his mouth. "You? With an Angel?"

"Oh, not romantically. Although he probably thinks that's my interest. No, I'm trying desperately to find out what happened to Jennie."

"Who's Jennie?"

"You don't know? I guess you wouldn't." She filled Tyson in on the whole story of who Jennie was, her turning Bud in and her disappearance.

"I'm on a mission to discover what happened to her. Bud, who killed Pop and may have killed Rebecca was her boyfriend, and he was an Angel. No sooner had she reported him to the police than she disappeared. We figure some of Bud's friends got her."

"You're sure this guy killed Pop?"

"His girlfriend was with him, turned him in."

"So, you've been getting cozy with an Angel in the hopes that he'll tell you?"

"I don't expect it to be that simple. I've been to their club a couple of times, and on a bike ride out to the ocean."

"Find anything out?"

With her mouth full of cinnamon roll, she said, "Oh, and I've met their women. That's another story, but so interesting. They implied that she had been dealt with, whether punishment or death I don't know."

"Where do you think all this will lead you?"

"This is SO good, Tyson. I'm not sure, but I'm doing everything I can to find out." She paused, drank some tea to wash down the roll.

She elaborated more on her adventures. "He's always treated me like a lady. I'm not afraid of him unless . . ."

"Unless what?"

"He finds out my real reason for seeing him."

"And then the shit hits the fan."

"Do you think I'm nuts?"

"I'm not sure you're being wise."

"Same thing."

"Aren't the police trying to find her?"

"They're the ones that let it happen. When she turned him in, they promised their search for him would be discreet, but the very first night she was kidnapped."

She put down her empty cup and leaned against his shoulder. "I haven't heard you say 'Stop!' or 'You're a damn fool'. What do you think?"

"What you're doing is dangerous. I know you know that. Apparently, you think it's worth the risk. I would only ask you to be very careful and put your life first."

She nodded. "Sage advice. Oh, we're being sued by Rebecca's parents, the father anyway." She filled him in. "The official papers came today."

"Good luck with that. How's your boyfriend—Mark, is it?"

"That's the other good news. He left me."

"I'm sorry to hear that." He put his arm around her.

She nodded. "He didn't like what I'm doing. He let it worry him too much."

"Anyone who cared for you might feel the same way."

"I guess. I miss him terribly. Even his bad habits." She tried to laugh.

"Like what?"

"Like taking a half hour to brush his teeth. He'd tie up the bathroom forever when I'm trying to get ready for work. It's not too bad during the day with my work, but the nights are so lonely. Alfi, that's our dog, misses him too."

With her head on his chest he held her while they listened to the music. "Both Sides Now" was playing, and Gwen was hearing *but clouds get in the way*. Didn't they, though.

Moments later he was turning her head gently, inviting a kiss. Whether it was her hunger for intimacy or a genuine interest in Tyson, she responded. His warm, full lips found her eager ones They were lying on the floor now, she didn't remember how they got there, but as he leaned over her, she could feel his long hair cascade around her head like a veil of privacy descending around them. How hungry she felt, realizing how much she missed making love. Fondling followed, and it would have been so easy to continue to the finish. But a small voice in Gwen's head grew louder and she stopped abruptly.

"I can't, I'm sorry."

Tyson pulled away slowly.

"It's just, just that—I'm not sure why."

"You don't need to give a reason."

"Thank you."

They lay side by side on the floor for several moments, their hands entwined. After a while he said, "Want some more tea?"

"No thanks. I better be getting home."

"Don't become a stranger. You're always welcome, you know." They stood, and he gave her a warm hug.

What a good friend he was.

On the way home, she realized that although she hadn't thought of herself as still committed to Mark, apparently, she was. At least she wasn't ready for a new relationship. Maybe her body was—*the body has no morality,* she remembered hearing—but her heart wasn't.

~~~

Martin Vandermeer didn't know where Gwen was, but he wasn't going to just sit on the conflicting information regarding Rebecca Barton's father arrival time in San Francisco.

He went to the police. After some hassle, he was finally led into the small office of a detective, to whom he told the story. Only they had the authority to demand the airlines release the names of the passengers on their flights.

"Why do you want to know? The airlines don't give out that information," Detective Pierce said.

"I know I can't get it. But you can, under the circumstances."

"And what circumstance is that?"

Had they already forgotten the unsolved case of the death of this young singer?

"The father may be the culprit in this case and establishing his date of arrival in San Francisco is crucial."

"Go on."

"The father told the coroner he was at the airport, had just gotten in the day after her death. But the mother told my reporter that he'd gone out three days before her death to bring her home. Now this couple deny that she ever said that."

The detective pursed his lips, took out a file, and checked it.

"The only information we have is that he arrived after the girl's death. That came from the coroner."

Martin took a deep breath and tried to control his frustration. "Yes, but as I say, his wife told my reporter a different story." The officer nodded. "So that makes him a suspect."

"I'm afraid the man is back in Nebraska now," Martin offered.

Detective Pierce rose. "I'll see what I can do."

"I'd appreciate it." He knew it was a long shot, but he asked anyway. "And would you be so kind as to share that information with me?"

"Afraid I can't do that."

It was worth a try. No story here, not until and if the authorities cared to divulge their web of suspects to the news media. Well, if it helped to catch the culprit, he could feel good about that.

~~~

Busy finishing an article at home, Gwen was startled when the phone rang. Although she hadn't heard his voice on the phone before, when he called, she recognized Rake's voice. Yes, she remembered he had her phone number now.

"Hey Connie, I've got something to show you." He sounded excited. "What's that?"

"Kind of a surprise. If you're coming to the city, I can pick you up and show you."

"Well, I have errands to run this morning, and then I plan to visit my aunt this afternoon."

"That's OK. I have to work the concert tonight. After that meet me at Pickles."

"You'll bring it there—the surprise?"

He laughed. "No, I can't bring it. We have to go there. I'll tell you all about it when I see you."

"OK."

As long as she was going to be in the city, Gwen decided to go to the concert. Not making any attempt to locate Rake, she sat and absorbed the sweet fragrance of pot, the joyous voices raised in song and the visual display of people gently swaying to the music. After being consumed by the grim side for so many days it was therapeutic, she decided.

Sleepy and in a state of peaceful joy, she really wanted to just go home to bed after the concert, but she headed for Pickles. This time he was waiting for her.

She would have liked to relax with a drink, but he was eager to show her his surprise. They walked to his old VW two blocks away and headed toward South San Francisco.

"Where are we going and what's the surprise?"

"Two of the brothers and me are going in together to buy this toy store. We're all pretty fired up about it. The old man who owned it was a brother too, so his wife is selling it to us for a song. It's really cool."

"I bet."

"Wait 'til you see it."

Gwen had not been to this part of San Francisco before, and after turning several corners had totally lost her orientation. They seemed to be entering a run-down neighborhood.

Finally, Rake pulled up and parked in a block with an 'L' shaped strip mall. Almost ten o'clock, most of the shops were closed.

"Here we are."

They got out and crossed the expanse of long grass between the street and the shops. They were indeed approaching a toy store; a colorful sign proclaimed, *The Toyhouse*. The neighborhood bar, kitty corner from the Toyhouse was the only establishment still open. Its welcoming lights blinked on and off.

Rake procured a key from his pocket and ushered Gwen inside. He flicked the light switch on and off a couple of times, but no lights came on.

"Damn! The electrician was supposed to come today and fix this. Something about the circuit breaker. But since we're here, let me show you around the best I can. There's a little light from the streetlamp."

Reluctantly, Gwen nodded. Rake took her hand and led her through the aisles, pointing out a shelf of dolls, another of teddy bears.

Showing her a miniature stage, he said, "This is for the puppets— isn't it cool?" He picked up a puppet and pulled some of the strings.

"It appears to be a great little shop."

"Yeah, and we're going to donate ten percent of our profits to the Children's Hospital."

"That's wonderful."

They had traversed the length of the store and were at the back now.

He led her through a curtain into a back room.

"Back here there's even more stuff. The store is well-stocked."

"I can see that."

"It even has guns."

Gwen turned to see Rake had a gun pointed at her. A toy gun, of course. But then she looked at his face. Hardened, as cold as steel, she started shaking. Was it a real gun? She couldn't be sure. Why was he doing this?

She tried to smile. "Rake, put that down. It's not funny."

"No, it's not."

He pushed her toward the stairway that led to the basement. "Go down. Move!"

"Rake, why are you doing this? What's wrong?"

"I think you know what's wrong, Miss Gwen Harris. Move!"

He'd found out! How had he discovered her true identity?

He shoved her again through the doorway, and down the first step. Almost falling, she caught the railing just in time. He continued to bare down on her as he loomed over her, forcing her further and further into the dark abyss below.

Did he plan to kill her down here, where no one would hear the sound, and no one would find her? Terrified, but knowing she had to use every brain cell and muscle she had she tried to think what escape she could manage.

They reached the bottom of the stairs and as he pushed her forward, she stumbled on the uneven dirt floor. Shoving her against a wall the fieldstones cut sharply into her back. Totally pitch black, Gwen could see nothing, not even her assailant. She knew if he planned to shoot her he wouldn't waste any time doing it.

What was he doing? Untangling some rope? Loading the gun?

He shoved her against the wall again. This time, crumbling stucco which covered the stone wall trickled inside her dress and down her spine. The damp cold crawled up her legs, with tremors following. Her fragmented thoughts were firing at a hundred rpms per minute. The darkness! Her thoughts funneled into one purpose—use the blackness as an ally! It was her only chance.

She moved slowly and stealthily to his side, tiptoed away from him and walked in the direction of where she thought the stairs were.

Realizing she'd left him, Rake shouted out to her. "You won't get away. Come back here!"

She heard him start for her, but in the wrong direction. He tripped over something and fell. As he did, Gwen found the stairs, and began ascending them, two at a time. Hoping to escape his clutches, she could hear his steps right behind her.

She was barely inside the main body of the store when she could almost feel him breathing down her neck and knew she was within his grasp. Light and shadows from the adjacent bar played among the puppets, dollhouses and stuffed toys.

She flattened herself against the back wall as he stumbled forward, toward the front door. Of necessity she had to choreograph her moves according to the blinking lights from the bar. She counted three seconds on and three off. When he doubled back, she moved forward and crouched below a large display of games. Concealed for the moment her eyes searched for the next hiding place. Each move must take her closer to the door, but she could only move when she was in the shadows.

Spying an outdoor playhouse, as Rake's steps headed in her direction, Gwen waited for the bar's lights to go off before skittering three feet and ducking inside it. Almost big enough to stand up in, for the moment she felt safe. But how long could she stay here?

Now she realized she didn't know where he was. A feeling of panic came over her. Was he in the front of the store? The back? Right next to her?

How did she dare make her next move without knowing?

For what seemed like hours she stood still, listening, straining hard, watching the play of shadow and light. Was he standing still somewhere waiting for her to make a move?

Then hearing a slight movement which seemed to come near the front of the store, she left the relative safety of the playhouse, moved forward, darted into an aisle of sports equipment before the lights went on. Yes! Somewhere around here there must be a baseball bat. A bat was no match for a gun, but it was better than nothing.

Ping-pong balls, footballs. Where were the bats? Spotting a baseball, she grabbed it. Just as her eyes fell on the bats, she saw her assailant round the corner approaching her aisle.

Feeling him coming closer, knowing if she moved he'd see her, she could only think of one thing. She threw the ball toward the back of the store hoping it would cause some commotion. It did, knocking something over with a crash, Rake took off running in that direction, allowing Gwen to make tracks to the front of the store. While he scoped out the back to find her she was able to make her escape.

But now what? She knew he must have heard the door and would be just steps behind her. Racing toward the light in the bar, she managed to open the door just as Rake came out of the toy store.

Dashing toward the bartender and nearly collapsing on a stool, Gwen managed to get his attention.

Just then the door opened and Rake looked inside. But he could do nothing now, not here. In an instant he was gone.

She cried out, "Call the police!"

"What happened, lady? Are you OK?" the bartender inquired with real concern.

"Call the police— that man was trying to kill me!" She pointed toward the door.

The bartender placed the call. "You better tell them, miss." He tried to hand the phone to Gwen, but too shaken to do anything but try to catch her breath she shook her head.

In what seemed like very far away she heard the bartender talking to the police.

When he got off the phone, the bartender led her over to one of the booths. "You can rest over here."

He called to a waitress. "Donna, get her some water!"

The voice of Nancy Sinatra was blaring through the sound system belting out "These Boots Are Meant for Walking."

When he got her situated, he asked again, "What happened to you?" All she could do was shake her head.

The waitress brought a glass of water and a wet towel. Sliding in beside her she said, "Here, Honey, let me put this on your forehead."

Between shaky breaths 'Thankyou' was all she could say.

"Carla, get my coat, will you? This girl's freezing," Donna asked the other waitress.

The coat came. Gwen allowed the towel, the coat and the arm around her shoulder to give her comfort. She began to breathe more evenly. She laid her head on the table, collapsing into weakness after her catastrophic ordeal. The song pounded in her ears— "And one of these days these boots are gonna walk all over you."

"I wonder why the police haven't got here yet," Donna said.

Rousing herself after a few minutes, Gwen sat up. "I must go. You must be closing up."

"Hey, I don't know what you've been through, but we're here for you. Can we take you somewhere?" Donna said.

Gwen looked at this woman for the first time, seeing in her a gentle, caring soul.

"Could I use your phone?"

"Of course."

Donna led her to the pay phone on the wall next to the restrooms, dug in her pocket and handed her a dime. "Here, Honey, you'll need this."

Gwen accepted, and grateful to find a stool by the phone, she inserted the coin, then hesitated. She wished she could call Mark but discarded that idea. She hated to ask Eric to rescue her, to have to listen to his admonitions, but call him she did.

"Eric," she asked in a small voice, "can you come and get me?"

"Where are you?"

"I don't know, somewhere in South San Francisco."

She turned to Donna. "Can you tell him how to get here?"

"Sure." Donna took the phone.

"Hey, fella, where you starting out from?"

"Marin."

"Marin?" She whistled. "We're a long ways from there."

What followed was a lengthy discussion on the best way to reach Benny's Bar.

Still, no police. Well, Rake was long gone now, anyway. And Gwen was too exhausted to go through a police interview now, anyway.

She watched while the bartender pulled the curtain down over the glass door, turn off the outdoor lights, and put the chairs up on the tables. They were closed. Someone would have to wait the better part of an hour for Eric to arrive. She saw the one called Carla leave.

"I am so sorry to keep you waiting," she said, deeply apologetic.

Donna adjusted her coat around Gwen's shoulders. "We just want to help you. Are you ready for something stronger than that water?"

Gwen was. She wasn't going to be driving, so she looked at Donna gratefully. "Yes."

"What'll it be, Honey?"

"I don't care. Anything."

"How about a martini? You like martinis?"

"Thanks, Donna, but that's too much trouble."

"Not at all."

Donna returned with two martinis. Smiling, she said, "I'll have one with you, it's after hours," She sat down beside Gwen.

Gwen squeezed her hand. "I really appreciate all you're doing for me."

"Don't mention it, Honey. Hey, I've had a few rough spots myself Men!" this last spoken like an expletive.

Gwen wondered if there were any vermouth in the martini. It was strong, but oh, so good.

She wanted to give them both some money, but she'd lost her purse somewhere in the toy store. "I'm sorry, I have no money."

"That's OK."

Where were the police? Why hadn't they come?

Sooner than they expected, there was a knock on the door. Gwen could barely face him.

With one arm protectively around Gwen's shoulder, Donna said, "She's been through a lot, we don't know what, she didn't say exactly, but you take good care of her, you hear?"

Gwen could hardly believe this waitress was telling Eric how to behave. She looked up sheepishly and saw Eric nodding.

"You bet." It was his turn to put an arm around her shoulder. "Thanks for taking care of her. I really appreciate it."

"Me too. You know I do," Gwen added. "Oh, here's your coat." She handed it to Donna and gave her a hug. "You've been just wonderful."

On the way back to Marin, Eric was quiet. From time to time he squeezed her hand or looked at her to make sure she was alright. But for now, he asked no questions, offered no reproach.

As they crossed the bridge back into Marin, Gwen felt she had to humble herself further. "May I stay with you tonight? I can't go home. He knows where I live now."

"Who knows?"

"Well, may I— stay with you?"

"Of course."

Hating to ask for another favor she said, "And can Alfi come too?"

They stopped by the apartment long enough to pick up Alfi, then proceeded to Eric's.

Except to determine what had happened to her he didn't press the question as to why she'd done what she had. She figured he was waiting until they were safely back in his houseboat to admonish her. When she was wrapped in a blanket she told him the whole story, how she hoped her association with Rake would lead her to Jennie, she explained.

How stupid it sounded to her now. How insane.

Eric knew better than to interrupt her. He let her finish, and still he was quiet.

"Well, aren't you going to say something? Aren't you going to ball me out?"

For a moment he said nothing. Then, "Sometimes I think your life is more important to your friends than it is to you."

That simple statement stung more than any scolding would have.

He fetched the bedding for the couch, and suggested she get some shut-eye.

Crawling under the covers in her clothes, and trying to fall asleep, she kept going over the horrible time in the toy store. And only now did she have the time to put together what had caused the change in Rake. It was the dog-walker, of course, who must have been a plant. He had the run of the house, every opportunity to go through her papers, discover her real name and the articles she'd written.

How stupid she'd been, letting Rake know she wanted a dog-walker. She'd walked right into that one. The sum total of her experience sleuthing before this search for Jennie was at Mark's retirement home. In those cases when she herself was in danger she hadn't invited trouble as she was doing now. Well, she'd have to smarten up if she wanted to be a sleuth. Her naivete and inexperience could be costly.

Wrestling with that, she fell into a troubled slumber, only to wake soaking wet as she was reliving the real nightmare in her dreams. And another dream about Jennie. She'd chased her through the streets, with the girl always eluding her.

Poor Jennie had been gone for two weeks.

CHAPTER 19

In the morning over a cup of coffee, Eric said, "The police are looking for him."

"What! You called them?"

"Of course. What did you expect me to do?"

"When did you do that?"

"Last night, after you fell asleep. They got on it last night, searching for him, talking to his buddies. I told them to wait to talk to you until morning, you couldn't go through anymore, but they'll be here soon."

"Alright. I can do it now."

When the police arrived, the first question was *Have they caught him?* And the answer was *No.*

"Their clubhouse was searched, he wasn't there. We got an address out of one of the Angels, but he wasn't there either. Guess he figured we'd be after him and flew."

Gwen told them the story, of how she'd gotten involved with this man and why. She relayed the events of the previous evening, and what she left out Eric filled in.

"How did he find out what you were up to?"

"I was looking for a dog-walker. He knew, and I think he sent a boy, probably the son of another Angel, to fill the job."

"How did he know where to send this person?"

Gwen could feel herself coloring. "I showed him my sign on the telephone pole."

"With a phone number?"

"Yes."

"You'd been using a false name?"

Gwen was surprised to hear Eric say, "Is this line of questioning really necessary?"

The officer pursed his lips and looked skyward. "You're saying the whole reason for getting involved with Hells Angels was to find this Jennie."

"Yes. Well mostly. But also, I'm a reporter. This summer I'm covering the phenomenon of the Haight and the Park. The Angels sometimes serve as guards there, and some are pretty tight with some of the musicians. I'm interested in that too, and their women—why they choose this lifestyle."

"Enough to risk your life?"

Gwen turned away. "No."

"It's doubtful he planned to kill you."

"How can you know?"

"We found the gun on the cellar floor. It's a toy."

"Well, he made a good show of using it."

"And we found one other thing—your purse."

"Wonderful. Thank you!"

"You can retrieve it at the park station in the city."

"Oh. Are the police doing anything to locate that poor girl?"

The officer looked blank. "I'm not the person to ask, Miss."

"Can you tell me who is?"

"You could call the superintendent—he'd know."

The policeman moved to leave. Gwen had one more question. "Officer, do you know anything about that toy store, who owns it, for instance?"

"That toy store has been closed for two months, awaiting a decision in Probate Court. And the utilities were turned off even before that."

He knew there weren't any lights.

"No member of Hells Angels has any stake in it."

Everything, all of it was a lie.

"How did he get a key?"

"Probably got in with some kind of master key. Or maybe he used to work there. Anything else?"

Gwen shook her head. "Just get him."

The policeman left. She now had to face the difficult question of where she should go. She didn't dare stay in her apartment with Rake on the loose, and she couldn't overstay her welcome here. Maybe Sheila would have room for her for a while.

"May I use your phone, Eric? I need to call a friend about staying with her for a few days."

"You're not going anywhere. You're staying here until they catch that scoundrel."

"But Eric—"

"No buts. I wouldn't think of letting you go anywhere else. Unless you told the guy exactly where I live." He looked at her, hard. "Did you?"

"No, no I didn't. Just in this area."

"Well, don't be wandering around the grounds. And take a couple of days off. Your boss will understand."

"You sure you don't mind?"

He grunted. "No."

She had to give him a hug. Tears were running down her face. She wasn't sure why. Maybe she, too needed a father-figure, and Eric had filled that role.

"What was the name of that bar where you picked me up?"

"Benny's. Why?"

"I want to send them some flowers."

"That would be a nice thing to do."

After she'd arranged that, she called Sheila.

Before she could speak Sheila said, "I've been trying to reach you. Where are you?"

"I'm at my friend's Eric's."

"All night? Not a new romance?"

"No, not at all. Listen, I promised I'd keep you up to date. I had quite an experience yesterday."

"Tell me."

Gwen told her the whole story of the toy-store, and why she'd ended up staying with Eric.

"My God, Gwen, when are you going to stop taking such risks?"

"You sound like Eric."

~~~

Two days later she asked Eric to drive her to her apartment to pick up her mail and get a few clothes.

On the way over, she said, "I'd like to get my car, too."

"Don't be foolish. You might as well put up a sign— "Here I am!"

"I didn't plan to park it by the houseboats. I was thinking over by Mollie Stones. The grocery store has a big lot."

"Same thing, too close."

She didn't think Rake knew what her car looked like, but she accepted his advice. As they drew up to the curb by her apartment, Eric said, "I'm coming with you."

Gwen had no objection. A cursory look inside indicated no break-in or any disturbance. Still uneasy, she wasn't sorry not to be staying here so soon after her ordeal.

She gathered some clothes and a jacket. Remembering the money in the drawer, she was relieved to find it was intact and took that, too.

As they left, she turned to the mailbox. Retrieving an advertising flyer and a letter from her aunt in Michigan, she saw a small note fall to the porch floor.

Picking it up, she read, "Meet me at the Molinari Delicatessen on the corner of Columbus and Vallejo in North Beach at 9:00 a.m. on Thursday. Come alone."

It didn't say in reference to what, but Gwen could only imagine that it had to do with Jennie. And if it didn't, well, a deli was a public place so that she wouldn't be in any danger.

"Anything you want to share with me?" Eric asked.

"Uh, no." She shoved the note in her pocket.

All the way back to the houseboat her head buzzed with possibilities. Who was the messenger? And why would he divulge information about Jennie? He said 'Thursday'—that's tomorrow! If she hadn't come by to pick up her things, she'd have missed the note, missed the chance of finding Jennie.

Gwen was not ready to give up. Why would Rake have gone to such lengths to shut her up if they didn't have something to hide? They must have kidnapped Jennie, and then what happened to her? Gwen hated to think. Well, if she was still alive, Gwen meant to find her.

When they got back to Eric's place, he said, I've got to work on this boat. You'll be OK inside?"

"Of course. Thanks, Eric. Thanks for everything."

She was bursting with information and questions. She called Sheila from Eric's phone.

"I have news."

"Tell me."

"She's alive, Sheila! Jennie's alive!" Gwen read her the note.

"That doesn't prove she's alive, and there's no mention of Jennie."

"But don't you see, what else could it be about? And assuming it is about Jennie, what would be the point of meeting me if she wasn't alive? He has something to tell me, I'm sure of it."

"Gwen, it could be a trap. Is he an Angel?"

"What else? How would anyone else know?"

"How would he dare reveal anything? He'd get in big trouble."

"Maybe he was just a friend of an Angel. Or maybe his sense of right and wrong is stronger than his loyalty to the club." Gwen could hear Sheila munching.

"Wow. You're not going, are you?"

"Yes. Yes, I am."

"Wow."

There was a long pause. Gwen could hear the exhalation of smoke.

"Then I should go with you."

"He said to come alone."

"But it's so dangerous. What if you run into some Angels there?"

"In a deli? It's a public place."

"Yeah. But then what? What if he wants you to go with him some place where he promises you'll see her."

"I won't do that."

"Promise?"

"Promise."

"Do you think you can find this place?"

"A deli? Of course." Gwen could hear the door as Eric entered. "I have to go now. I'll call you after I meet him."

Gwen lay awake that night wondering who this person was. He must be a brother, who knew as Rake did now where she lived, because of Carlos. Was this a trap or was this a brother who didn't think what was happening to Jennie was right, and had taken a chance by arranging to meet with Gwen. Would she finally find Jennie? Eric would think she was crazy to get involved. So would Mark. But she was so close.

CHAPTER 20

When the first rays of sunlight peeked through her window, Gwen was awake. She'd lain awake most of the night and felt she hadn't slept more than three hours, but she couldn't sleep any longer. She rose quickly, did her morning routine, gulped down a bowl of cornflakes and pulled on the only pair of jeans she had. Nervous, and not knowing how to kill the hours ahead of her she went outside.

"Can I help you?" she asked Eric.

"No, and I'd prefer you stay inside."

Reluctantly, she returned to the houseboat. She tried to read, gave up and wrote an article for the Chron.

Finally, the hour she must leave drew near. Eric, who'd only come in for lunch was still working in the yard. She dashed off a quick note to him, explaining that she was needed in the city and was taking the bus. She hoped he'd think she meant the Chronicle.

Donning a sweatshirt, as the day was cool, she left the houseboat, taking a circuitous route to avoid passing Eric in the boat yard. She walked to the bus stop, waited fifteen minutes, and was on her way to San Francisco. Once in the city she transferred to another bus that took her to North Beach. She'd only been in this part of the city once before, to attend a poetry reading of Alan Ginsberg at the City Lights bookstore. The closer she got to her destination the more nervous she became.

Stepping off the bus at the corner of Broadway and Columbus she was struck by the many store fronts advertising strip clubs. Billboards proclaimed the same. There on the corner was the well-known Condor nightclub with a bigger-than-life lit-up sign of the famous Carol Doda, red lights blinking from her nipples. Further down the street a barker was calling out to the tourists to come inside. "Topless dancing." Another proclaimed "Candy for your senses."

Gwen had thought that this sort of thing only came awake at night. But sex was big business here—morning, noon and night.

Known as Little Italy, the area was alive with Italian restaurants, confirmed by the aroma of exotic spices all along the street. Tables on the sidewalks overflowed with people of every ethnicity.

She'd looked at a map the night before and located the cross-streets mentioned in the note. Walking further down Columbus she came to the intersection with Vallejo.

And there it was, the Molinari Delicatessen.

The place was buzzing with customers. How was she to recognize the man she was to meet? She bought a cup of coffee, then noticing a few small occupied tables in the back, she waited for a couple to finish their coffee and leave. Then she sat, waiting.

Assuming that the man would recognize her, she sat where she could still see the front door. After a while she wondered if he'd show up at all.

Several customers came and went. Was she wasting her time? Some kind of sick joke? Then a man entered, short and stocky, looked around and spotted her. He checked to make sure he hadn't been followed, approached her table and sat down, shoulders hunched, as if to hide his head like a turtle.

"You want to know about Jennie," speaking so quietly Gwen could barely hear him.

"Yes. Is she alive?"

The man nodded, his jaw muscles contracting and releasing. Gwen breathed a sigh of relief.

"They took her to a cellar here in North Beach. You have to go through an underground tunnel to reach it. The closest way to the tunnel is by going down the stairs in the bagel store—that's a block down the street. The tunnel, adjoining the cellars of the stores, goes several blocks, then crosses under the street and continues."

He paused, looked around again to make sure he'd not been followed.

"Some of the stores have access to the tunnel through their cellars, and some have their name on the door down there. Others don't. The one you want only has '913' written on the door in chalk. At least it did. That's where they took her. Don't know if she's still there. And if she is, I don't know how you'll get in."

"The police—I'll call them to go there."

He shook his head. "They've already been. But the brothers were tipped off, and Jennie was taken somewhere else that day. Doubt if the cops will go there again."

Uneasy, he rose to go. "That's all I can tell you."

"Thank you. Thank you so much."

He shook his head. "Good luck," and he was gone.

He was clearly agitated about divulging this information. He must be an Angel. Who else would know? And didn't he refer to them as *the brothers*? If he was one of them he was taking an awful chance to tell anyone what he knew about Jennie.

A dozen unasked questions swirled through her head. How was she supposed to get in the door? How would she know which door it was if the chalk had been rubbed off? Was it next to a door with a name on it? If she got in would there be someone inside guarding Jennie? But he was gone before she could ask any of them.

Her head buzzed with the information she had and the information she lacked.

She left the deli, walked down a block and saw a bagel shop. It seemed to be the only one around. Her head whirring, should she go in? Despite what she'd been told she decided to call the police. Calling from a phone booth on the corner, she told the responding officer what she knew, receiving a laconic response. "We've been there before."

"Yes, I know, but as I said—may I speak to the detective?"

"He's in a meeting."

"Will you please pass on the information I gave you, and relay how important it is that she be rescued now?"

"Sure thing."

Gwen wasn't convinced that the detective would even get the message. Should she try to rescue Jennie? Well, if not, what had all her other efforts been about? Why had she taken such risks with Rake?

This tunnel was public, wasn't it? Maybe everyone didn't know about it, but shopkeepers did, and perhaps others who knew of it used it to avoid the street traffic.

Like a moth to flame she was drawn inside the shop. A clean and busy place, several people were waiting in line. The wholesome smell of fresh baked goods permeated her senses. Scanning the small interior, she saw two doors. One apparently led to the kitchen or back room. The other could be a closet or the stairway to the tunnel.

Pushing reservations aside, she strode to the door and opened it. Yes, before her lay a stairway leading to a lower level. Without hesitation, before an employee might prevent her, she took the first step down, and closed the door behind her. Then she began the long descent into Jennie's hell, and what might become hers as well. Dimly lit, when she reached the bottom, the narrow passage was even darker. It felt shadowy and eerie.

Having only gone a short distance, she could see a figure coming toward her. A black cutout against a dim background, she wasn't sure if it were a man or woman. She stood still as the figure came toward her, its ominous presence looming larger and larger as it came closer. The stranger was beside her now, and then passed by.

Gwen didn't realize she'd been holding her breath until she let it out in one big swoosh.

Then feeling rather ridiculous she forged ahead. This was, after all, a public thoroughfare, wasn't it? She'd heard stories about this tunnel. Built as a bomb shelter during World War II it had fallen to neglect and now, though not publicly recognized, it still existed and was used by those who knew of it. She had no idea how many blocks or miles it covered.

The tunnel was damp and musty; rusty metal doors lined the left side of the wall. Occasional puddles appeared on the uneven ground where rain had seeped down through cracks in the buildings above. As she'd been told, some doors had the name of a store stenciled on them, others did not. Occasionally, there were numbers on a door—369, further on 741. How far should she go? Another two blocks? Feeling stupid that she'd undertaken this mission with so little information, Gwen was at a loss as to what to do. But she kept walking, hoping to find the chalked numbers 913 on one of the doors.

The tunnel took a turn. Above she could hear a lot of road traffic, and the muffled sound of honking cars. She wondered if the tunnel was going under the street above. Walking on what must have been another couple of blocks she saw a door with the faint trace of numbers on it. Craning to see it in the dim light, she could just make out '91'. Could the '3' have been rubbed off? Based on previous numbers, she thought this must be it, but her uncertainty made her even more apprehensive.

She tried the door. Locked, of course. Dare she call out? "Jennie, are you in there?" she spoke in a loud whisper.

No answer. She pounded on the door, "Jennie, are you in there?" The sound of movement and a knock on the door from the inside.

"Yes! It's locked."

"I'll be back. Be ready to run."

At last she'd found Jennie! She had a plan, but to carry it out she had to leave the tunnel. She would enter 913 from the street level, sneak down the basement stairs and rescue Jennie that way if possible. Surveying her surroundings, she realized that she could hear noise from the street, and there was more light coming into the tunnel. She decided to leave via that end rather than re-trace her steps the other way.

She saw the stairs ahead of her and began the long climb to the top. Reaching the street, she looked around to get her bearings, then headed back to find 913. When she found it, she could see that it was a fish shop with an abundance of fresh fish laid out on ice, outside the shop as well as inside.

Stepping inside, she immediately saw a familiar face—one of the Angels she'd met at the clubhouse. *Oh, my God*! Hoping he hadn't noticed her she returned to the street.

So this is why Jennie was kept where she was. An Angel owned this store and had access to the cellar below.

She looked at the establishment next door. It was a sleepy strip club—no barker here. But the front door was ajar. She stepped inside to an almost black interior. Standing still until her eyes adjusted to the darkness, she could just make out small tables topped with inverted chairs. Stepping cautiously along the side of the room she thought she was completely alone. Suddenly a figure loomed in front of her. Gwen's heart almost stopped. She audibly gasped.

"Hey, lady, didn't mean to scare you. You here for the audition?" She nodded dumbly.

"Just go across there, behind those curtains and down the little corridor. On your left will be the office. Joe's in there."

"Thank you."

Whew!

She followed his directions. Once behind the curtains, she meant to keep going to find the stairs to the cellar. But a door opened, and a man appeared.

She put on her best fake smile. "Are you Joe?"

"That's me."

"The man out front said I should see you about a job."

"Come on in."

He motioned her into the office.

What had she gotten herself into?

He looked her up and down, appraising her figure. "You bring any costumes with you?"

"No, sorry."

He picked up the phone. "Zelda, honey, bring up that costume Lulu left when she jumped ship."

Gwen blanched. *How was she going to get out of this one?*

"While we're waiting, you can sit down and fill out an application."

She sat, while he looked in his drawer for a form. She tried to keep her mind on anything but the mess she was in. She studied Joe. He looked to be about fifty, with greying hair and a paunch. She surveyed her surroundings, noticing the tiny room had no window. She saw cobwebs hanging from the ceiling and a pile of disorganized papers on the man's desk.

He handed her the form, then cleared enough of the desk so she had room to write.

"You need a pen? Here's one." Then lighting a cigar, he sat down in his chair, rocking back and forth as the springs creaked in tune with his humming.

"What's your name, Honey?"

"Annabelle."

"Well, Annabelle, you fill that out and then we'll talk." He smiled pleasantly.

She nodded.

Barely believing that this was happening, she picked up the pen and looked at the paper. The usual things were there—name, address, phone number. Then a lot of space for previous experience. Experience as a stripper, of course.

With a jerky hand, she began to fill it out, with lies. Except for experience.

The costume arrived.

"You think that'll fit, Honey?"

She picked it up, full of sequins, it was skimpy and itchy. "No, it's too large for me."

"You sure?"

"Quite sure."

"Why don't you go ahead and try it on, anyway? It'll give me an idea of how you look, you know? Maybe do a little number."

With pounding heart she said, "To be honest, I've never been a stripper. But I've studied modern dance, and I've, well, seen some strip shows in Vegas with my boyfriend. I liked how the dancers moved and went home and practiced."

"Well," he tapped a pencil on his desk, and flicked his ashes in an overflowing ashtray. Finally, he said, "I gotta have somebody with experience, you know? Maybe you get some and come back. OK?"

Gwen smiled. "OK."

She rose to go. He opened the door for her, and she proceeded to return the way she'd come. *Whew!* When she was sure he'd closed the door, she retraced her steps, passed his door and kept on going further into the dark abyss.

A bare hanging lightbulb of minimum wattage appeared hanging near the back wall. Moving toward it she could just make out a door below. Was it locked? No, she could open it. Gazing into the chasm below, she could just make out the descending stairs. Stepping cautiously down each step and wondering if the door at the bottom was locked, she reached the floor below. Turning the knob, she found she could open the door, at least from the inside.

Thank heavens for that. She closed it silently and surveyed the space. Large, with a few low wattage bare bulbs, she could just make out racks of costumes, props and cleaning supplies. Across the room she spotted crates of whiskey, gin and vodka. Assorted boxes were everywhere. A ladder led to high shelves where more boxes were stored.

With a plan in mind, she moved the ladder from lightbulb to lightbulb, unscrewing it just enough to kill its illumination.

She opened the door to the tunnel slightly and put some sponges inside the doorframe to keep it from closing. When everything looked as ready as it could be, and she could think of nothing else to be done, she sat by the door and waited. This might take a very long time. Maybe they only fed Jennie once a day and had already done that. Or maybe she wouldn't be fed until evening. However long it took, Gwen was determined to be there.

She must have waited about twenty minutes when she felt the blare of lights. Looking behind her, she could see the stairwell light had come on and someone was coming down. Hastily, she hid behind the costumes. The dust and musty smell made her want to cough. From this position she could hear a light switch turning on and off.

"Damn! What the hell?" a man's voice shouted.

Peeking between two skimpy outfits Gwen could see someone rustling through the cleaning supplies. The stairwell bulb cast just enough light for him to locate what he'd come for.

She could only pray he didn't notice the door that was ajar.

After what seemed like a lifetime the man gathered what he needed, ascended the stairs and turned out the stairwell light.

More waiting, while her breathing returned to normal. Going over her plan once more, she tried to assess the risks and think of anything she might have overlooked. Where would she take Jennie if she did manage to get her out of there? She couldn't take her to Eric's. It wouldn't be safe to bring her to her apartment. She should call the police and let them handle it. But she wanted to get Jennie's story, and offer what comfort she could, if only for an hour or two.

It would still be light out for a couple of hours. What if she took her home for a short time, cleaned her up, fed her and then called the police?

While still in this reverie she heard the sound of keys turning in the lock next door. Gwen was on her feet. As the door opened and someone went in, she was right behind him, pushing the door open before it closed.

Astonished, the man was not prepared for what happened next. Gwen executed a karate kick that sent him sprawling. Almost overwhelmed by the stench of urine, she grabbed the frightened Jennie, pulling her out the door and into the adjoining cellar. Quickly she took the sponges away and closed the door quietly. Knowing the man could outrun them after he recovered, she had devised this plan to put him off the scent. Hoping the door was locked from the outside she led the girl back behind the costumes, where they sat on the floor.

The girl was filthy. She began coughing, hard and long. Gwen pulled her as far away from the door as she could to conceal the sound. She thought Jennie either had bronchitis or worse. They sat down on a couple of crates behind a rack of costumes, where Gwen cradled her in her arms listening carefully for sounds from next door. Shortly she heard a door slam; Gwen held her breath, indicating to Jennie that she should be quiet too. They froze as they heard the door handle rattle on the room they were in, but the door remained secured. Thank God!

Finally, Gwen said, "I think we're safe."

Gwen felt they should get out of there as quickly as possible, less the Angel figured out her plan and come down through the strip joint and discover them. She held her, while Jennie shook and whimpered.

The girl started blubbering, trying to speak. "Don't try to talk now, Jennie."

"How did you find me?"

"I'll tell you later. Right now, I want you to just think about staying calm and following directions for getting out of here."

The girl squeezed her hand tightly. "You're coming with me, aren't you?"

"Yes. Now listen. We're going to walk up those stairs. They lead to a strip joint."

"A strip joint?" Jennie squealed.

"Yes. Now we're going to walk through it and out the front door like nothing happened. I want you to just act normal and try not to look afraid. Do you understand?"

"I guess so."

A noise from the door above made them both freeze. As the stairwell light came on Jennie buried her head in Gwen's arms. Two men came down, one with a flashlight, shining it against the bare bulbs.

"See. They're all out."

"Must be something wrong with the circuit."

"Do you know where the box is?"

"No. If you have what you need for now, we'll call an electrician tomorrow."

They went back upstairs, killing the stairwell light. "All clear, Jennie. They're gone."

Jennie shook so hard and long Gwen had to hold her tight to help control it. The poor girl had been through so much, and the bombs were still exploding around her.

Upstairs they could hear a few people moving about and sounds of laughter. Yes, the place was surely coming to life.

"We're going to go now." She heard a quiver in her own voice.

They stood up and felt their way across the room toward the stairs.

Taking Jennie's hand Gwen led her up the steps. At the top she said, "Ready?"

"Uh huh."

"We're going to be cool, right? If anyone asks us anything, let me do the talking."

As Gwen opened the door, they could hear girls in the dressing rooms laughing and getting ready for their act. Gwen thought she remembered how to get back to the corridor where Joe's office was. From there they could exit the same way she'd come in.

But it all looked so different now. Curtains had been pulled back, revealing a stage. Chairs had been placed around the tables. Customers were beginning to file in. The tinkle of glass was coming from the bar she hadn't seen before. With lights on, however dim, it was an entirely different scene than it had been in the morning. Feeling disoriented, she paused, considered her options. Where was that corridor, Joe's office? She didn't know, and they couldn't just stand here. They must look like they knew what they were doing.

Thinking as fast as she could, it appeared the only thing to do was to boldly cross through the open space of tables.

They started across the floor. An unfamiliar man approached them. "Can I help you, ma'am?" He said, appraising Jennie in her filthy clothes.

Gwen put on her brightest smile. "Just came to wish my friend 'good luck.' We can't stay. Just trying to find our way out," she laughed.

"That way," he said, pointing to an exit. "Thanks."

They proceeded to traverse the floor, zig-zagging between the tables. She could feel the man's eyes following them. There were the doors, and there was the outside light. Just a few more steps and they'd be out of here.

But home free? She didn't want to think what might happen if one of the Angels was going in or out of the fish shop next door.

Outside, they walked to the corner. Gwen directed Jennie to turn left, although that didn't lead to the bus stop.

"We just want to play it safe," she said. "A few blocks out of our way won't hurt."

She hailed the first taxi she saw and pushed Jennie inside. "Can you take us to Marin?"

"Sure thing."

As the cab pulled away from the curb Gwen breathed a deep sigh of relief. They'd gotten away. They were safe. For how long, she didn't know.

"Are you sure you don't want to go back to your mother's, Jennie?"

Jennie shook her head. "She doesn't want me. I doubt if she noticed I'm not living there anymore."

"Oh, Jennie. That can't be true."

"I have an aunt in Orinda. Maybe she'd let me stay with her."

"We'll call her from my place," she said.

When Jennie started to spill her story, Gwen hushed her. "Not here, Sweetie. Wait 'til we're alone."

She'd become so suspicious, she was afraid even the cab driver could be an Angel. They rode the rest of the way in silence, with Jennie leaning on Gwen's shoulder and Gwen holding her hand. Now in the light of day, Gwen noticed that Jennie had a twitch in her cheek. She didn't remember seeing it the time she'd taken her to the police station. When they were safely inside Gwen's apartment drinking hot cocoa and eating cookies at the kitchen table, Gwen said, "Now you can tell me, everything that happened."

"They took turns bringing me food."

"Start at the beginning, Sweetie—the night you were staying with Sheila."

"Oh, God, I was so scared. Finally, I fell asleep, and all of a sudden, I felt a hand over my mouth. This guy whispered, 'Come quietly or you're dead.' I was so scared. So I did."

"Then what happened?"

"He took me downstairs, still with his hand over my mouth. And he had my arm twisted around to my back. It really hurt."

"Didn't any of the kids downstairs wake up when you went down?"

"No. You have to open a glass door between the bottom of the stairs and the living room. And I couldn't scream."

Gwen nodded.

"Then he shoved me in the back seat of this car and got in beside me. There was another man in the front seat, and we drove away. This man beside me," she started sniffling, "he called me terrible names, like traitor, canary, even filthy slut. I was so scared, Gwen." She started shaking.

"I know."

Jennie was reliving the experience and crying. Gwen suggested they go sit on the couch. There she put her arm around the girl. When Jennie had gotten quiet Gwen said, "Then where did they take you?"

"I don't know. Almost right away they blindfolded me and tied my hands behind my back. When we got to this place—I think it was a house, they made me go down the basement."

"How long were you there?"

"I don't know, maybe a couple of days. Then they blindfolded me again and took me where you found me."

"Were you properly fed, Jennie?"

"Well, they brought me something every day, nothing you'd choose if you had a choice. Usually, stale bread and peanut butter, or oatmeal— stuff like that."

"Just once a day?"

"Yeah."

"Two of them took turns bringing me food and sometimes they'd empty my pot. I knew them from before." She started coughing, from deep down. When she finished, she said, "One of them spit on me."

"Do you know their names?"

"One was called Jimmy and the other one was Rogue."

"I'm so sorry. Were you always free to move around the room?"

"Not at first. I was tied to a chair. But then they realized I had to use the can, you know? And nobody wanted to stand guard around the clock, so they untied me."

"I didn't have time to get a close look. Did you have a mattress, anything to sleep on?"

Jennie shook her head. "Just the floor. They brought me one blanket."

"It was always cold in there."

She started coughing again, and Gwen wondered how serious it was. "The room always smelled, because they only emptied my pot about once a week."

Gwen squeezed Jennie's hand. "Did they ever hurt you?"

The twitching began again. "I got raped."

"Once?"

Jennie shook her head. "I lost count." The twitch in her face continued

"Oh, good heavens!" Gwen's hand went to her mouth. "Who did this to you?"

"Both of them, when they felt like it. I stopped fighting them."

Gwen pulled Jennie to her. "I am so very, very sorry."

"But that wasn't the worst. The worst was they said if the police found Bud, I'd be dead! They held that over me the whole time." She was shaking.

"Oh, God."

"I turned him in so he *would* be caught, and now I was praying that he *wouldn't* be."

"And if he wasn't found? Would they let you go?"

"I don't know."

Gwen wondered why they kept her alive. Maybe they thought this form of torture was worse than death and would eventually kill her. Or maybe they planned to take her to Bud when it was safe and let him finish her off. Either way, the outcome couldn't be good for Jennie. She thanked her lucky stars she'd been able to rescue her.

"Is there anything else you can tell me?"

Jennie shook her head. "No. Well, once in a while a third guy came. He was nicer than the others. He's the one who brought me the blanket, and a couple of times he gave me a candy bar. He never said anything, but just the way he looked at me, I knew he felt sorry for me."

Gwen thought immediately of the man she'd met at Molieri's.

"Did they ever enter the cellar by way of the stairs that come down from the street level?"

"At first. Then they boarded it up. I could hear them pounding stuff on the other side, I think to make it sound-proof. Maybe in case I screamed. After that, they had to come the other way."

Gwen remembered the door to the tunnel. Heavy and thick, maybe soundproof.

"I am so very sorry for all you went through, Jennie."

"Yeah, well, it wasn't your fault."

The phone rang.

"It's Martin, Gwen. I have good news. It's about that lawsuit that the dead girl's parents started."

"Yes?"

"The airline's log states that Mr. Barton arrived at SFO on flight 363 on August 9th. That's three days prior to his daughter's death. The lawsuit's been dropped. And the local authorities have taken Mr. Barton in for questioning."

"That's wonderful! Oh, thank you, Martin. And I have good news, too. Jennie is safe. I'll tell you all about it in the morning."

Returning to Jennie Gwen said, "We may have found Rebecca Barton's killer. It could be the father."

"She was one of the witnesses in the store, right?"

"Yes, she was."

Jennie pulled her thin legs up under her chin and hugged them. "Gwen, I have something awful to tell you."

The girl's eyes were wide in fear, and her face was twitching again. Suddenly she pulled away from Gwen and threw herself down on the couch.

"Tell me." Gwen waited patiently for the girl to recover and sit up. Wiping her nose on her sleeve and sucking her breath in Jennie said,

"He killed her. He killed that witness."

"Who did? Who killed Rebecca?"

"Bud did." Jennie sobbed.

"Are you sure?"

Jennie nodded.

Gwen felt the color drain from her face.

"We went to the ice-cream shop, 'cuz I wanted a banana split. We were waiting in this long line and I recognized this girl, and nudged Bud. He pulled me out of there and said, 'Is that the girl? Was she one of the ones in the store?' I was so scared I just nodded. And then we got out of there."

A fountain of anger was building up in Gwen. For moments she could say nothing. All the effort put into discovering who Rebecca's killer was, barking up the wrong trees, Rebecca's father, Kevin. And all the time Jennie knew. She took some deep breaths and focused on how young and vulnerable this girl was, the terrible fear she'd faced in reporting Bud.

"The next afternoon he came over. I could tell right off that something was wrong. He headed for the bedroom. He got in bed, but he couldn't—you know. He just tossed and turned. When I asked him what was wrong, he said, 'Shut up.' Then he got up and took a shower. When he came back he pulled down the shades and just sat in the dark smoking one cigarette after another. After a while I had to go to the bathroom, and when I got back he was gone. I never saw him again. Then the next day it was all over town that this girl had been killed. I knew he did it."

Jennie began to cry. Through her sobs she managed to say, "I should have told Sheila when she told me a witness had been killed, and then when you took me to the police, it was too late— I'd already lied to Sheila. I'm really sorry. But I was so scared."

"It's all over now, Jennie. You're safe. And you're going to stay safe." It was still too much for Gwen to wrap her mind around. She had to put it on hold and changed the subject.

"You must be starved. Do you like spaghetti?"

Jennie stopped crying. "Yes."

"Well, that's what we'll have."

Jennie watched Gwen as the meal was prepared. "It smells so good."

"You can help me. Why don't you set the table?" Gwen handed her the plates and utensils.

She was thinking about the revelation Jennie had divulged. So, it wasn't the father. Probably he'd lied to avoid being a suspect, not realizing that his wife had told Gwen a different story. Then she thought about the Rebecca's abusive boyfriend who'd even threatened her life and turned out to be Kevin! He wasn't the killer, either. They couldn't even convict the asshole on rape and assault.

When dinner was ready Jennie gobbled it down.

"I've never had anything so good. And I never had garlic toast before."

"Did you like it?"

"Yes."

After finishing the meal Gwen suggested Jennie take a bath. "Really? Here?"

"Yes." Gwen took her to the bathroom and turned the water on. "Do you like bubbles?"

Jennie nodded. Gwen had a reason for the bubbles. They were made from dish soap. Her hope was that Jennie's attempts to clean herself would be assisted by the soap.

When the bath was ready, Gwen left Jennie alone. There were things that must be taken care of.

First, she called the police, to report the events of the day, including the location of Jennie's incarceration, and the fish shop above, run by an Angel.

"I need to find a safe place for her to go. The girl thinks her aunt will take her, but lacking that, a safe-house was mentioned before. Do you have the address?"

"I'll find out," said the officer on duty. "And get back to you."

"Thank you."

Then she called Sheila.

"I thought you were dead! You never called back!"

"I'm so sorry. One thing led to another. But I'm safe and so is Jennie."

"You rescued her? She's alright?"

"She's safe."

"Where is she?"

"Here, in my bathtub."

"You're kidding."

"No, I'm not. She was filthy. Hadn't bathed in all that time. And she's oh, so thin. She wasn't fed properly."

"I don't know how you did it, but bless you, Gwen. You're an absolute saint!"

"No, just foolish and stubborn."

"Anyway, you accomplished a miracle."

"I'm afraid she's sick. She has a terrible deep cough. She had to sleep on the floor with only one blanket—for over two weeks, Sheila."

"Oh, Jeez. Where was she? How did you find her?"

"It's a long story. I hate to cut you off, but I'm expecting a call from the police, about the whereabouts of the safe house they said they'd provide. I'll fill you in later."

"Don't forget."

"Promise."

Gwen had barely hung up when the phone rang. It was Detective Pierce.

"I understand you rescued the Lopez girl."

"Yes."

"Where is she now?"

"Here at my home."

"I can have her picked up and taken to our safe house within an hour."

"She thinks her aunt in Orinda might take her, but if that's not an option—"

"Too risky. If they found her at your friend's house, they're likely to find her at her aunt's."

The detective was probably right. "I see. Look, she's been through a lot. They threatened to kill her if Bud was caught. And she's sick— bronchitis or worse."

"She'll be well taken care of in the safe house. They have a very caring staff."

"And clothes—she'll need clothes."

"They have that too."

Gwen had to be satisfied.

"A social worker will call out there to interview her. She'd like to talk to you, too, to get a full report on what she's been through."

"I'll be happy to talk to her."

"There's another reason she should be in the safe house. Miss Lopez is a material witness. We need to know where she is, so that when the killer is caught, she'll be available to testify against him. If she desires, we can offer her a witness protection plan.

"I see. So will that be all?"

"One more thing: No doubt she will be called to a hearing herself, as an accessory to the crime."

"What! Oh, no! Surely, she isn't. There are witnesses who saw her scream and run out of the store. She had nothing to do with what happened to that poor grocer."

"Nevertheless, a hearing is a possibility."

"This poor girl has been through hell—imprisoned, poorly fed, repeatedly raped. Surely the law won't put her through more torment! Besides, she's a minor."

"All these things will work in her favor. Don't worry too much, Miss. But we do need her to sign a paper indicating her commitment to testify in court."

"When?"

"I'd like to present her with the papers tonight."

"Tonight! Officer, she's been through so much, and now she's going to another strange place. Can't that wait?"

Detective Pierce hesitated. "I suppose it can. But we can't lose track of her."

"I understand."

When the conversation was over Gwen's mind reeled with what poor Jennie was still expected to go through. To attend a hearing in which she'd be accused of being an accessory, as well as to testify in court against the killer. Witness protection or not, she could slip through the tracks as she had the night she was kidnapped. Well, she wasn't going to worry Jennie with any of this tonight.

She went to her closet and found a dress for Jennie—a little big, but at least it was clean. Then some underwear, socks and a sweater.

She tapped on the bathroom door. "Are you about through in there?"

"Yeah, I'm getting out."

"I have some clean clothes for you."

"Oh, great. You can come in."

Gwen stepped inside and lay the clothes on the little table. "I hope they fit."

"You're super, Gwen. You really saved my life, and now this." Wrapped in a towel, but still wet, she gave Gwen a bear hug.

"You've been through hell. You deserve every kindness you can get."

Gwen caught sight of herself in the bathroom mirror. *My God, I look awful.* It was no wonder. She'd been through a lot lately herself, and very little sleep last night. She'd make up for that tonight. Taking a fresh washcloth, she cleaned her face and ran a comb through her hair.

When Jennie finished dressing and the two were in the living room, Gwen said, "Jennie, I talked to the police in San Francisco, and they think you should be in their safe house."

"Let me call my aunt first. I think she'll let me stay with her."

"I mentioned that to the detective, but he thought you'd be better off in the safe house."

Jennie started to shake her head. "I want to go to my aunt's."

Gwen put her arm around the girl's shoulder. "I know how you feel. But the police are afraid that if the bad guys could find you at Sheila's they might be able to find you at your aunt's."

Gwen could see the twitch coming back in Jennie's face, and the inner struggle.

"The detective said the safe house has a wonderful staff. They'll give you clothes, medicine and everything you need."

Jennie had a coughing fit, and for a few minutes it looked as though she'd pass out from the sheer exhaustion of it. Recovering, she nodded in submission. Gradually, her breathing slowed. She reached for Gwen's hand, and the two sat quietly until a plainclothes policeman came to the door and Gwen let him in.

Jennie looked terrified, almost as though she were being captured again. But the grey-haired policeman smiled kindly at her. Jennie glanced at Gwen, who nodded encouragingly, and back at the policeman. Her face lost its look of terror, replaced with a tentative resolve to trust.

Gwen moved to give Jennie a goodbye hug. As she did so, the girl clung tightly to her, but there were no more tears.

The policeman opened the door. As the two walked out Jennie called back over her shoulder, "Will I ever see you again?"

"Yes. I'll call you soon. Take care, Jennie."

Tears ran down Gwen's face as she shut the door. The poor girl. Would she be traumatized for life; would she ever be able to get over the horrors she'd experienced? And what of her future? How long would the police provide protection for her? Would they give her a new identity, send her to a new town?

But for now, at least she was safe. She has a lot of growing up to do, but I believe she will come around and testify against Bud.

And now I have to get out of here, Gwen thought. It had been risky bringing Jennie here when it was almost certain that Rake, and by association, Bud knew where she lived. But she couldn't imagine bringing her to Eric's. Now, it was time for her to return to Eric's, but she was oh, so tired after so little sleep last night. She'd lie down for a few minutes.

~~~

A huge gush of cold air washed over her. Was she having a nightmare?

"Thought you'd get away, did you? Not this time, bitch!"

No, it was real. Rake! Not again! He dragged her to her feet. Adrenalin kicked in and she was wide awake. About to scream, he slapped some tape across her mouth before she could. Fighting to get away, she kicked him, attempted to knee him in the crotch.

"Little hell-cat, aren't you?" He shoved her hands behind her back and tied them together.

Pushing her forward and out the door, they were hit in the face with incoming leaves. It was totally dark, she must have slept for hours. He forced her to his car and shoved her in the front seat, tying her to it before going around to the driver's seat. Gwen looked desperately for someone to come to her rescue, but there was no one in sight.

Driving up the nearly deserted winding road to the freeway he sped north, on past Corte Madera and San Rafael.

Her mind was racing now on how she could escape. When she made struggling noises in her binds he turned the music up. It was useless to attempt anything further in the car.

Rake took the Sir Francis Drake exit, headed west through the small towns of Ross, San Anselmo and Fairfax. Where was he taking her?

Still he drove on. Out in the country now on winding roads past bare hillsides, Gwen no longer recognized her surroundings.

There was no doubt why he was so angry, what had fueled his wrath this time. Jennie's rescue, of course!

They passed a sign to the town of Woodacre. He was slowing down. It seemed obvious he was looking for something, and then yes, there was a crossroad. He made a right-hand turn, and within a short distance another right onto a narrow dirt road. Bare hillsides were replaced by a forest of redwoods. Gwen began crying out behind the gag.

He continued driving over bumps and potholes until they were swallowed by the forest. Then pulling off the road, he got out of the car and over to Gwen's side. He undid the rope that bound her and pulled her out of the car.

This was her chance to run. She attempted a karate kick, but it went afoul—she was too close to him. Twisting her arm behind her he held her tightly while he retrieved a coil of rope from the back seat.

Giant redwoods loomed above them, obliterating even the light of the moon. Throwing the rope over his shoulder, Rake pulled her along, off the road, through the woods. She tried her best to pull away, but in his iron grip it was useless.

He pushed her up against a tree, held her there with his body as he deftly un-looped the coil of rope.

With all her strength she managed to pull away and run. As he rushed to catch up to her, she turned and kicked him square in the crotch. Moaning he fell.

Knowing she couldn't outrun him, she hid behind a large tree. He lay for only moments, stumbled on to find her. For a minute he seemed lost, stood still, but then he seemed to sense which tree she was behind, and discovered her quickly.

Again, she employed karate, but this time he blocked her kick, and grabbed her painfully by the arm.

"You like this tree? Then this tree it is."

Again, he pinned her to it, jabbing both an elbow and knee into her as he readied the rope, adroitly secured her to the tree.

When he'd finished securing the knots, he looked at her. She could see fury in his face. "The game's up. Know what I mean, bitch?"

She shook her head.

"Then you have lots of time to work it out. You can think about it while you starve to death!"

With that he turned and left.

She could hear the crunch of leaves and sticks as he walked back to his car, and then the sound of the engine as it gradually faded in the distance.

Now she stood trapped in total silence, save for the sound of sporadic dripping from the trees, as fog condensation fell on the leaves, the rope and her.

Surveying her predicament, she could feel the tightness of the knot that tied her hands together. She knew the rope ran around the tree, where he'd spent some time back there tying it. How many other knots were there?

She was determined not to give up, though every cell in her body told her there was no way out of this nightmare.

The September night was now dropping drastically in temperature.

A chill ran through her right down to her bones.

She fought against the confines of her bonds for what seemed like hours. Exhausted, she allowed herself to rest for a time. Then somewhat revived, she tried bumping her rear end against the tree to the extent that she was able. Maybe this way she could gain some slack. Something hard in her pocket made her stop. What was it?

Oh, yes, the cigarette lighter still in her pocket from the time she'd brought it to light his damn cigarettes! She was wearing the same jeans she'd had on the last time she'd seen him. She continued bumping anyway.

Then it hit her. If only she could get the lighter out!

Her hands had been tied behind her back. With renewed energy, she fought to loosen the tie around her wrists until she thought they must be raw. Finally, she was able to reach into her back pocket, but not far enough to grip the lighter. Leaning backward a little and to the side, yes, she could touch it!

With further gymnastics she was almost able to grasp it. But first she'd have to get the knot that was tying her hands undone.

Now there was hope—at least a little. When she'd gathered some strength, ignoring the pain she twisted her hands until the fingers of one hand could reach the knot. For the next hour she wrestled with that knot. Crippled by her restrictions, she could not get quite the right angle to untie it.

Suddenly she heard something crashing through the woods. Had Rake brought reinforcement? What would they do to her now?

Ready to scream, she saw it. A deer, a buck. He stood stock still when he saw her, then turned and walked away. Her heart was thumping wildly, and her breath was coming in spurts and gulps.

Sapped of all strength, she crumbled into the arms of her restraints.

~~~

Eric tried to calm himself. A mixture of fear for Gwen and anger at her for leaving the grounds despite the danger pervaded his mind. Where the hell had she gone? Why couldn't she follow a few common-sense rules of behavior, at least until this villain was apprehended?

He felt responsible for her. As a friend of her mother, ever since that special woman had mysteriously disappeared, he'd felt protective of her daughter. Granted, when the child was whisked away to Michigan to be brought up by a relative, that feeling had abated, but since she'd been back in Sausalito it had been rekindled.

He tried to think; where would she have gone? Home, to get some of her belongings. Stupid. She knew he'd take her there if she asked. Nevertheless, without anything else to go on he called her home number.

No answer. He drove to her place. She wasn't there, but her car was. He went to the police and got the same kind of response Mark had gotten. There was nothing to do but wait.

~~~

Rousing herself, Gwen thought *I have to stay focused*. Taking deep breaths, she managed to get a measure of control over her thoughts.

She attacked the knot again. Almost crying in pain from forcing her shoulders to once again bend backward as her arms went behind her and clenching her teeth with the pain in her raw and swollen fingers, she forged ahead. This time she managed to loosen the knot and free her hands!

By no means released, at least her hands were free, and she had a little freedom to use them. The first thing she did was remove the tape from her mouth. Stinging pain as she ripped it off, but oh, the relief. She moistened her lips, tried to forget how thirsty she was.

Now what was the next step? She checked her pockets. Anything of use? Some 'mad money'. What good was that here? Again, vestiges of another time with Rake.

And that lighter. It was her only hope for escape.

She wanted to burn the rope away, but could she do that without burning herself?

She procured the lighter from her pocket, held it tightly in her hand and debated where to start the fire. Several inches away from her body, on the side would be the best. She flicked the lighter and followed the flame as she lowered it to the rope and watched the fire try to engage it. Repeatedly, the flame went out and she had to re-light it. But the rope wouldn't catch. The dripping trees had made it too damp.

She stopped to think. If she kept doing that, she was afraid she'd run out of lighter fluid.

The only place where the rope might be dry was right across her stomach. Her loose sweatshirt had somewhat overlapped the tightrope. Would it be dry enough to light? And how could she do it without burning herself? The rope that looped around her was still secure and tied behind the tree. Gwen kicked, moved her body as much as she could but nothing she did provided any slack to her confinement.

In a few moments she hit on a solution. Her shoe! If only she could reach it and wedge it between herself and the rope. She put the lighter back in the front pocket of her jeans. With one foot she kicked the shoe of the other foot off. But with the restraints of the rope across her chest she couldn't bend down to reach it. Maybe she could raise it with a bare foot. Employing the same method, she removed one sock with the other foot.

Using her bare foot she attempted to grasp the shoe between her big toe and the one next to it. Succeeding in this, she began to raise the shoe toward her hand. But half-way up, it fell back to the ground. Once more she managed to clutch it with her toes. She brought it up slowly, higher and higher. But again, when it was almost within her reach, it fell and bounced. And this time it was further away from her feet. She couldn't reach it with either foot.

After closing her eyes and breathing deeply, she scanned the nearby ground spotting a stick. About a half inch round in diameter and two feet long, she clasped it with her toes, raised it and clutched it with her hand. Now she could just barely touch the shoe with the stick. After several attempts she couldn't reach quite far enough to get the stick inside the shoe to drag it toward her feet.

Stumped for the moment, she soon remembered she had another shoe. Pushing it off with her bare foot she carefully hooked it with the stick, and holding her breath raised it to her hand. Success!

Holding her stomach in as much as she could she managed to wedge the shoe between her body and the lash that bound her.

Now for the lighter. Not a job for the weak at heart, Gwen couldn't afford to give thought to the consequences if the plan went awry. Retrieving the lighter, she held her breath as she flicked it on and lowered it to the rope. The flame was small—she realized the lighter was almost out of fluid. Watching it touch the rope she waited for it to engage with the bonds. It caused no great flame but burned slowly through the fiber. Still, she kept the tiny flame alight as it sawed through her restraint.

Finally, the flame went out. But it had burned through the hemp enough that she was able to pull the tether apart and quench the ember. At last! The rest was fairly simple. She was able to loosen and step out of her shackles.

Relieved, she wanted to shout for joy, but knowing she was not out of the woods yet, she focused on what she needed to do now. Re-installing the shoes on her feet, with legs shaky and stiff Gwen set off to find her way out of the prison of these woods. As much as she wanted to run, it was still dark; her footing was tenuous and slow.

Frightened as she'd been when Rake was dragging her along, Gwen had not paid attention to her bearings or the direction in which they had come. Now, she was uncertain. If only she could find the dirt road on which they'd traveled. With no sound of cars to guide her, after walking some distance she feared she was going in the wrong direction. Surely, she'd have come to the dirt road by now.

Still dark, with no light to guide her, she tripped over a root and fell. Shooting pains shot from her ankle upwards. She tried to rise, but the pain kept her down.

After all that work when she thought she was finally free, she lay trapped again, this time by her own body. She lay shaking, shivering and sobbing on the damp ground in the cold autumn air.

CHAPTER 21

In the early morning Mark drove up to Gwen's apartment. As he went up the walkway, he saw that the door was open. He walked in and called for Gwen. No answer. He peeked in the bedroom to see if Gwen was still asleep. Not there. Her bed was made. She was probably out giving Alfi his morning run, and the door hadn't properly latched. He was amazed at all the leaves that had blown in in the short time she'd been gone. He decided to sweep them up. Finding the broom, he swept them out of the house, then from the porch as well.

She'll probably be back soon. He decided to wait on the porch. He wanted to talk to her, see how she was doing, and if anything had changed.

It was getting cool, but wanting to be here if she showed up, he went inside and settled down with a copy of *Life* magazine. Turning to an article on civil rights, he was barely able to concentrate, he found he'd finish a page, realize he didn't know what he'd read and have to read it again. Where was she?

One hour, two hours went by. Still no Gwen. Had she taken to staying out all night? Gwen had not slept in her bed last night. If she didn't sleep here, where did she sleep? And with whom, he couldn't help wondering. And where was Alfi?

Just on a chance he called the Chronicle. No, she hadn't come in to work.

He decided it was pointless to wait any longer. What had made him think a possible reconciliation was in order? He wouldn't be any happier with the hours she kept now than he was before. He rose to leave.

Just as he opened the door, the phone rang. Whether it was purely out of curiosity or a distant hope that some explanation would be forthcoming, he picked up the receiver.

"Hello."

"Who's this?" A female voice. "Gwen's friend, Mark."

"This is Sheila. Is Gwen there?"

"No, she isn't." He remembered a woman named Sheila who'd come over one night in distress. Perhaps this woman could shed some light on Gwen's whereabouts.

"Well, she called yesterday," the woman said. "She was OK then. No more trouble with the Angels."

"The *who*?"

"Hells Angels."

"Jesus! What's she doing with them?"

"Oh. She hasn't told you? Well, I guess I shouldn't be talking about it then. But since I've opened my big mouth, let's just say she was determined to save Jennie, and that meant getting involved with the Angels."

"She's with them now?"

"I don't know."

Mark could feel perspiration run down his arms, his back and his face. The memory of that night Sheila had been at the house and Gwen refused to promise she'd stay out of the hunt for the missing Jennie — it all came back and reminded him why he'd left.

But he couldn't leave things the way they were now. Gwen was in danger. The woman he still loved was in trouble. He knew it.

After getting Sheila to fill him in on more of the details, Mark left the apartment and headed for the police station. Giving his report to a sleepy officer, he was losing patience.

"Look, don't you get how serious this is?"

The officer stuck out his protruding chin and rubbed his prominent nose. "I get that this woman voluntarily spent time with someone associated with Hells Angels. I also get that she's been with this person before." He shrugged. "So, she's not home."

"But it's more complicated than that." He tried to remember exactly what Sheila had told him. "She's been trying to find out what happened to a girl that's gone missing. The girl's boyfriend killed someone in the city, and after the girl reported him to the police she disappeared. Gwen Harris has been looking for her. If the Angels know this, they wouldn't like it. God knows what they've done to her."

Mark almost broke down at this point.

"What murder was this?"

"Somebody in a mom and pop store last month in the city. The girlfriend was with him when he pulled the trigger, told the police, and then she disappeared."

"Haven't heard about that one."

Mark was ready to scream. "Look, are you going to do something?"

"Like what?"

"Look for Gwen Harris?"

"Where?"

"I don't know!"

"I suggest you get some rest and come back tomorrow is she's still missing. Too early to file a missing person today."

Half-crazed, he left the police station.

Maybe she'd gone to her old friend Eric's. He remembered collecting her there after some previous mess she'd gotten into. If only he could remember which houseboat Eric lived in.

He headed south to the end of Sausalito, then took a right. Issaquah, yes, that was the name of the place. He parked, walked through the lot and scanned the docks looking for a familiar houseboat. Approaching what he thought might be the right one, the loud barking of a dog inside confirmed that he was in the right place. There was no mistaking Alfi's bark, and Alfi must have caught his scent. She must be staying with Eric.

But no one answered the door. Alfi kept barking, but Mark could not get in.

He walked back to the car, wishing he'd gotten Sheila's phone number. Maybe she knew more than she'd said. Maybe she could help. What had Gwen said about her that night— that she was a counselor over in the Haight?

He drove to the Haight, walked the streets, went in some shops, asked if anyone knew of a counselor named Sheila. It was like the proverbial needle in the haystack, but it was the only thing he could think to do.

Finally, someone in the pipe shop told him there was someone down the street who had a sign in the window—free counseling.

He looked for the store, for the sign. And there it was, he'd walked right by it, the vintage clothing store. Sheila was not at her table. In fact, he saw no one at all. Racks of old clothing filled the room. A shrunken old woman emerged from between the racks.

"Can I help you?"

"I'm looking for Sheila."

"She hasn't come in today. If you're in need of immediate counseling, you can always go to—"

"No, no, that isn't it." He realized he must look desperate.

Mark sized up the owner of the clothing shop and decided he had to trust her.

"Look, someone we both care about a lot is missing. She's in danger. I have to reach Sheila. Could you please call her for me?"

The owner hesitated briefly, then picked up the phone.

Mark tried to hear the muffled conversation between the shopkeeper and Sheila. Then the woman turned to Mark. "She wants to talk to you."

Grasping the phone quickly, he said, "Sheila? It's Mark. Have you heard anything?"

"No. Nothing."

"We need to put our heads together. Can you come to the shop?"

"Yes. Sure. Give me ten minutes."

It seemed like an hour, but Sheila came hurrying in, out of breath. "Thank God you're here."

The owner let the two of them go to her back room. This time Sheila employed her inhaler before the dust and mothballs affected her.

Standing among stacks of large boxes and racks of clothing Mark said, "Tell me, tell me everything. Start at the beginning, or at least a couple of days ago."

Mark bumped a stack of boxes and the top one fell to the floor. He jumped, realized his nerves were shattering.

Sheila took a big breath and proceeded to censor what she told Mark, omitting her foray into the toy shop.

"Jesus! But she said she was safe?"

"Yes, she called from her home, I think."

"We have to do something," Mark said. "Maybe she's in hiding."

"Where?"

"I don't know. One of her friends?"

Mark breathed a sigh of deep frustration. "I just left her friend Eric's. Her dog is there, but she isn't."

"Have you reported it to the police?"

"Yes, and they won't do anything. Too soon." He turned to Sheila with another thought. "Before yesterday—was she seeing anyone in particular among the so-called Angels?"

Sheila hesitated. "Yeah, there is someone—Rake. She'd been with him a few times, at their clubhouse, and on a motorcycle ride out to the ocean."

Ready to explode, he managed to contain his rage. "I have to go back to the police."

"Why not try the sheriff?"

He thanked her and left. Of course, what was he thinking? That was the arm of the law most likely to help. The whole county needed to be searched. In fact, both Marin and San Francisco counties were involved.

He got her phone number, saying he'd call her if he got any news.

~~~

As a dim morning light began to permeate the redwoods, Gwen woke with a start. Had she really fallen asleep in that cold, wet place with a captor likely to appear at any time? How long had she slept? She didn't know.

Her thirst was enormous, and her ankle and hands were throbbing. Gritting her teeth, she used a nearby stick to help her up. It hurt to put weight on that foot, but she had to get out of here.

In the distance from the main road she could hear the sound of cars that were absent in the middle of the night. Judging by the direction of their sounds, she knew which way to go to reach the main road.

Painfully, she took her first steps. Looking for a better stick to help her walk, she found one that was thick and about three feet high. This would do. It was taking so long to reach the dirt road that she thought she'd either set off in the wrong direction during the night, or her painful ankle made it feel further than it was.

Finally, with the dirt road in sight, she allowed herself to rest on a redwood tree stump.

Glancing down at her ankle, Gwen could see that it was badly swollen. She could feel it throbbing and wished she could elevate it with ice. But that was not to be—not now.

Allowing herself only a brief respite, she began limping along the dirt road. Now, hopeful at last that she might reach safety, but still no cars, no sign of life save the occasional squirrel or a crow.

Her body cried to her to stop walking, she could barely stand the pain, but if she did, she feared her ankle would grow so stiff and swollen that she couldn't walk at all; she pushed on. In the distance the sound of cars was growing louder from the main road. Finally, she could see it. And there, when she reached it, she allowed herself to collapse at the side of the road in sight of anyone who might come by.

The first vehicle to pass was an old pick-up truck headed west. The driver stopped and ran across the street.

"What's wrong, lady? You OK?"

"I've hurt my ankle."

He knelt down beside her and looked at it.

"That's a badly swollen ankle, that is. Can I give you a lift?"

"I need to go the other way—back to Sausalito."

"I can go that way. Ain't in no hurry."

"Yes, I'd be grateful."

He made a U-turn in the road and brought his truck close to Gwen, helping her to the truck and lifting her onto the seat.

She was panting from that mere bit of exertion. "You can relax now, Lady. You're in good hands."

She managed to gasp, "Thank you."

"You been lyin' there long?"

"No, just a few minutes."

"How'd you happen to twist your ankle? Take a fall, did you?"

"Yes."

"You don't look so good. What are you doin' out here alone? Do you have a car somewhere—run out of gas?"

"No."

He was curious, but realizing she wasn't in any state to talk about what happened, he talked about himself instead.

"Me, I'm on the way out to Pt. Reyes, I mean I was. My day off. Like to go to the ocean, watch the waves come in. Kinda soothing, you know? I work at the Cheese Factory, in packaging. You been there?"

Gwen shook her head.

"You're shivering. I'll turn on the heater. It'll make some noise, but you'll soon be toasty."

Country roads turned into more urban ones. Soon Gwen was recognizing the towns she'd passed in her agony in what seemed like days ago but was just last night. How different everything looked now that she was safe, now that the sky was blue.

"Hey, I got some cheese, right here, right in back. Want to try it? It's real good."

"Water," she managed to say. "Do you have any water?"

"No, ma'am. I'm sorry. Will an apple help?"

"Yes." Weak with exhaustion as well as her other travails, Gwen gladly accepted.

With his eyes on the road, he reached one hand behind the seats and pulled up a bag.

"Here, take anything you want in there. There's some good bread, too. I was gonna have it for lunch out at the beach, but I can get more."

Biting eagerly into the apple, it's juiciness spurted into her mouth.She'd never appreciated a piece of fruit so much. "Go ahead. Eat the other stuff, too."

"No thanks. Not hungry, just thirsty."

"There's a thermos of coffee in the back, should have thought of that before."

He reached back and brought it up for her. She poured some in the cup and drank it. "Thanks so much for everything. I'm really most grateful." She remembered a line from a play, something about the kindness of strangers.

"You're welcome. Glad to help a lady in distress. My ma used to tell me to do something nice for somebody every day. Well, I haven't lived up to that, but I do what I can."

She smiled at him and touched his arm. "You're an angel." Then she realized what she'd said. Well, he was a real one.

"Hey, nobody ever called me that."

His face turned red, but he was grinning ear to ear.

They were on Sir Francis Drake, now, going through Ross. "Where can I take you? Wanna go to the hospital?"

"No, thank you. Just home, if you don't mind. In Sausalito, if that's not too far."

"Nope. That's where we're going, if you're sure you don't want that ankle looked at."

"I'll put ice on it when I get home."

As they entered the freeway driving south Gwen thought about how she had to face Eric. He must be tearing his hair out with worry. She had just disappeared yesterday while he was only a few feet away outside.

Well, she'd just have to face the music. She directed the driver to go into the Issaquah parking lot as close as he could to Eric's houseboat.

"I'm staying with a friend who lives here."

He helped her out of the car and down the dock to the door of the houseboat. The winds were up, causing the houseboats to rock and sway on the turbulent waters. Halyards lashed the masts of nearby sailboats creating a clamor familiar to all sailors.

Gwen knocked. No answer, she knocked again, waited. Inside she could hear Alfi barking desperately. But she had no key to open the door.

"He might be out in the yard. Would you mind looking?" she said. "It's over there."

She sat on the porch steps and waited, her ankle throbbing. Coming back to her he said, "No one there."

Vastly disappointed she said, "Then I'll have to go to my place." They left the houseboat to Alfi's woeful wailing.

"You shouldn't be alone, Lady."

She didn't answer, gave him directions to her home on the other end of town.

"This is it. Right here on the corner."

The man pulled up to the curb, ran around to her side, and helped her out of the truck.

Leaning on his arm, as they were struggling up the walk-way Mark came out of the house and raced down the steps.

"Gwen, thank God you're safe!" He supported her from her other side.

She attempted to introduce the men.

"Mark, this is, this is—oh, I'm sorry—I don't even know your name."

"Pete."

"Pete found me, a long way from here."

"Then I'm very grateful." He extended his hand to Pete's.

"Just helping out the lady."

Gwen slumped on Mark's shoulder. He bolstered her up and asked, "Where was she?"

"Lying on the side of the road, by Roy's Redwoods out on Nicasio Valley Road. Something awful must have happened to her, but she didn't tell me what. Lucky, I found her when I did."

"Let's get you inside," Mark looked at Gwen more closely.

Gwen pulled the mad money out of her pocket. It was useful after all.

"I can't thank you enough," she said to Pete. "Take this, just a token, of my appreciation."

"Oh, I couldn't, Lady. Just doing my good deed for the day."

"Please—the gas, you went way out of your way."

Pete shook his head. "I'll leave you in your husband's care. I'll be on my way now."

They heard him drive away. A rattley old pick-up truck disappearing around the corner. And he was gone.

Mark helped Gwen up the stairs, inside the house and on to the couch.

She wondered what he was doing here in her apartment but that would come later.

He was dying to get her story, where had she been and why? What had happened to her to make her hands and wrists so raw? But first things first.

"Let me see your ankle." He held her swollen leg up. "Ow!"

"I'll get some ice."

Fashioning an ice pack for her with a towel, he applied it to her ankle. He saw her wrists, swollen and nearly raw, and held them in his hands. *My God, what has she been through?* His eyes questioned her.

"I fell." That was all the explanation she offered.

"I think we should go to the hospital."

"I'll be OK, Mark," she murmured.

He looked at her haggard face, her shaking body. "I'd feel a lot better if you were checked over and your ankle X-rayed."

She closed her eyes and slumped over against his shoulder. "Just let me rest, Mark."

He held her then, gently rocking her back and forth.

Interrupting the peaceful quiet, the phone jangled in their ears. "Shall I get it?" Mark asked.

"Yes."

Gwen strained to listen. Then she heard, "She's safe, Eric. Yes, I'm here with her at the apartment." A long pause, then, "She's been through a lot, a long story, but she's safe. I'll ask her call you when she feels a little better."

Gwen buried her head in her hands. "Poor Eric, he must have been so worried."

"He certainly was. He came to your apartment, went to the police station. He must have been there just before I was."

After a few minutes Mark raised her legs on the couch and placed the ice pack on her ankle. He brought a blanket from the bedroom and made her as comfortable as he could. Then quietly, he went to the phone.

~~~

After about an hour of shut-eye, Gwen was awakened by the soft tongue of Alfi licking her hand. So glad to see him, but so sleepy, she fell back to sleep after a brief pat on his head. Faithful Alfi remained by her side.

Later, Mark spoke to her gently. "A deputy from the sheriff's office is here, Gwen. He needs to talk to you."

In a deeper sleep now, waking from the nightmare of the previous evening, Gwen sat up with a start and let out a cry.

"It's Ok, Gwen. You're safe now."

Her eyes scanned the room in fear. "Where am I?"

"You're home. It's all over."

She faced a different officer than the one who'd interviewed her so recently at Eric's.

"I'm Officer Ryan, ma'am. I'm sorry to bother you now, but the sooner we get the facts from you, the sooner we can go after the perpetrator."

Oh, why couldn't they leave her alone? All she wanted to do was sleep. But of course, he was right. She nodded, brought herself into the present.

This young officer with his boyish face and blonde hair looked no more than eighteen. Wasting no time with pleasantries he said, "You were alone when he grabbed and gagged you?"

"Yes, sir."

Mark brought up a chair for the officer, stood a few feet away from the two of them. He listened as Gwen spilled her story to the deputy. In stops and starts, back-tracking and out-of-sequence she managed to get most of the story out.

"You knew he was a member of the Hells Angel?"

"Yes."

"And you'd been with him before."

"Yes, a couple of times."

She saw Mark's jaw tighten.

"How had he treated you on previous occasions?"

"He was polite."

"He never hurt you before the previously reported incident in the toy store."

"What!" Mark called out in alarm.

The officer raised his hand toward Mark indicating he had to be quiet.

She shook her head.

"After the first incident did you do anything to protect yourself so that it wouldn't happen again?"

"I stayed with a friend."

"But last evening you were alone when this man grabbed you."

"Yes, I was in this apartment."

"Did you tell your friend you were leaving his or her place?"

"No."

"What made this man turn on you again?"

"I—I'd rescued Jennie."

This opened a whole new can of worms. She tried to explain her determination to save this girl, and why her success had angered this man.

"That's why he tied me up in the wood 'to starve'."

The officer cocked his head, scratched his chin and studied Gwen.

"You're a private eye?"

"No, an investigative journalist."

She'd never used that term before, but it was true. It was what she'd been doing all summer.

She saw Mark wince and turn away, wished this interview was in private.

"Do you know this Rake's last name?"

"No, I'm afraid not."

"Why is that?"

"You don't ask too many questions of the Angels. It didn't seem relevant."

Mark interrupted. "Can't you put out a warrant for this man's arrest?"

"There already is one, since the toy store incident."

Mark was dying to ask what had happened at the toy store but held his tongue, for now.

"Any idea where your assailant might be?"

Gwen shook her head. "I'm afraid not. Maybe someone in the club would know."

As a parting note the officer said, "Let us know if you think of anything else that will help us find him."

When they were alone Mark could hardly restrain himself from asking her why in hell she'd gone after this wild goose chase putting her own safety and life at risk. But he didn't. She was in no condition to enter an argument or brook criticism from him. He'd have to bite his tongue.

Instead he said, "I still think you should see a doctor."

"Let me get a good night's rest, and in the morning, if it feels like my ankle's broken, then I'll go."

"Hmph."

Alfi, still sitting on the floor beside her whimpered gently. It was his turn for attention.

"Mark, when did Alfi get here?"

"Eric brought him over. We talked on in the yard, not wanting to wake you. I told him you'd call when you felt better."

Mark fixed her some hot soup, brought a basin of warm water and bathed her face and arms.

Picking small sticks and weeds out of her hair he said, "I'm so glad you're safe. You've no idea how worried I was. And so was your friend Sheila."

"Why Sheila?"

"We've been in touch."

She wondered how that came to be, but she was too tired to ask Gwen squeezed his hand.

They heard a key in the door, and Carlos entered, accompanied by a gust of dry leaves.

Alfi ran to him, and the boy reached down to pat him. "Hi, ma'am. You're back," he smiled.

"Yes." She controlled her anger. If only she hadn't hired him. "Carlos," she said, "Do you know any members of Hell's Angel?"

The boy appeared baffled by the question. Then he said, "Yeah, my dad."

"Did you go through my files when you were here?"

Carlos colored, swallowed. Then he said, "My dad told me to. I didn't know why. He said he was helping out a friend, who wanted information about you."

"And you gave it to him."

She watched him shift uncomfortably from foot to foot.

"I think you know that what you did was wrong, Carlos. I won't be needing you anymore."

Carlos opened his mouth a couple of times, licked his lips before he got the courage to ask, "Are you going to tell the cops?"

"No, but don't expect a reference."

Carlos nodded. "I sure like your dog, though." He turned to leave.

"The key please," Gwen said.

"Oh, sure." Carlos laid it on the table, turned and left.

Mark questioned, "You sure you don't want to call the police?"

Gwen shook her head. "He's only a kid, doing what his father told him to do."

"How long had he worked for you?"

"Only a couple of days. That's all it took for the information to get back to Rake."

"How did you find this kid? Did you let this Rake come to the apartment?"

"No. The two times he came to Marin, I had him pick me up at the entrance to Eric's place."

"How did you advertise for a dog-watcher?"

"I'd told Rake I needed to hire someone, and even showed him the sign I'd put up on the telephone pole by Eric's, with my phone number. It all fits. He got his buddy to send his son over to apply. The kid was nice, clean-cut. I thought I had a winner."

Mark kissed her hand.

"That's how Rake got my real name, and why— I was stupid!"

Mark offered no argument to this.

"That explains the toyshop, too. And when I outwitted him there— oh, you don't know about the toyshop. Never mind."

Mark couldn't resist. He said as calmly as he could, "Can you tell me about the toyshop?"

Gwen looked at him closely. "Can you withhold explosive expletives?"

His smile was grim, she thought.

"I'll try."

She told him how she'd gone to the toyshop and what had happened there. "This is when I knew he'd found out my real identity."

He listened quietly. But it was as though he'd been reminded in indelible ink why he'd left her in the first place. This plus the strong feelings he still held for her collided in his mind and body creating a tsunami of conflict. When she finished, and before he burst into begging her to stop her insane ventures, he changed the subject.

"Let's have something to eat."

He looked in the fridge and found some left-over meatloaf. "How old is this? Is it OK?"

"Oh, gosh, that must be moldy by now—that was days ago. Will you throw it out?"

"Sure. There's some canned ravioli in the cupboard."

"OK, let's have that. And I think there's some beer in the fridge." Gwen said.

After consuming the ravioli, they moved to the couch. Mark propped her leg up again and replaced the ice. The jangling intrusion of the phone broke the silence.

She could hear Mark's end of the conversation. "Already? That's great." Then after a long pause, "He said that?"

He came back to her. "They've got him—found him at his clubhouse playing pool, of all things. He was flabbergasted that you'd gotten out. Said he was about to go back there and get you—just wanted to scare you a bit."

"Oh, my God! Do they believe him?"

"Doubt it. He's been taken into custody."

"He left me there to starve! Probably thought he was safe at the clubhouse—who'd know? I can't believe it!" With barely a moment she added, "And what about the bastards that repeatedly raped Jennie— Jimmy and Rogue?"

"They got them all in one sweep."

Gwen was seething. "I can't get over it. The bastard went back there and enjoyed a game of pool after leaving me to die."

"Well, you'll be glad to hear this. The San Francisco chapter has been told that if there is a single breach of the law their clubhouse will be shut down indefinitely. So, the officer said, he thought you could relax. He said he didn't expect any Angels would be after you."

"That is good news, very good news."

Mark put his arm on her shoulder, and when she was quiet, he asked, "May I stay with you tonight? And take care of you for a few days? I just think you shouldn't be alone, you're in no condition . . ."

She smiled into his searching eyes. "I'd like that," she said squeezing his hand.

~~~

In the days that followed Gwen's body began to heal. Mark stayed with her, doing what he could to help her out.

Three days after she returned from her traumatic experience in the woods Detective Pierce called Gwen. Mark handed her the phone.

"We have Bud Smith in custody."

"You got the killer! You caught Bud! Wonderful!"

"Our boys have been following some of the members of that club. We figured if the brotherhood was so tight, at least one of them would visit the outlaw, take him food, and so on."

"And it paid off?"

"Last night, over in Oakland, they caught the guy hiding out in a friend's basement."

"That will make a lot of people happy."

"I knew you'd want to know. The Lopez girl, she's recovering, I understand."

"Yes, she is."

Well, finding Rebecca's killer was worth celebrating. She received a call from the safehouse and talked to Jennie, who burst into happy tears. The housemother there told Gwen they'd been informed that there would be a hearing for Bud in early October, and Jennie had agreed to testify.

"In the meantime, we're keeping her here; she has so much healing to do. We called a doctor right away, because of her cough. He gave her some antibiotics, and she's improving. She's getting along with the other women. But she's having bad dreams."

"I'm not surprised. Thank you so much for taking care of her."

Again, Gwen wondered if this girl could ever really heal from such traumatic experiences. But she was glad the safehouse people were willing to help.

She called Sheila, Marjorie and Tyson to let them know of Bud's arrest. Everyone was ecstatic. Tyson wanted to throw a party.

"Are you sure?"

"Of course, I'm sure."

Gwen said, "Marjorie, Tyson wants to throw a party. Bring Sophie and Tru, and anyone else who knew Rebecca."

~~~

Mark remained at Gwen's for a few days to help her out, and Gwen hadn't asked him to leave. But it was time to discuss the arrangement openly.

"Do you want me to stay?" he asked Gwen, sitting at the breakfast table.

Taken aback at this sudden question and not sure exactly what he meant, she just looked at him.

"Stay, for good," he clarified.

She paused before replying. "I don't know." She'd thought about it herself. It felt so good having him back. "It hurts when you leave, Mark."

"I know." He rose, put his arms around her. "We could try again. I've missed you terribly."

"But nothing's changed."

"I still love you." He nuzzled her neck.

She raised her voice, but not in anger. "Is that enough? It wasn't before. You can't stand the hours I keep, the risks I take!"

"Why don't we play it day by day? That is, unless you want me to leave now."

As if adding his vote to Mark's Alfi licked Gwen's hand. She broke away from Mark and said to Alfi, "I know, you want him to stay, of course you do. I don't know, Mark! I just don't!"

"How about we try it for a while?"

"And then I come home someday to find another note?" Tears ran down her face.

"No. I promise I won't do that again. If it begins to look. . ." He searched for the word. "problematic, we'll discuss it openly, before any decision is made."

"I can't have you objecting to everything I do, Mark."

"I'll try not to."

It was all she could ask for. "A trial period then, for two weeks."

"Two weeks."

He led her to bed. Falling all over each other, their celibacy ended. Passion culminated quickly, as they sealed their verbal agreement with a physical one.

CHAPTER 22

On the evening of the party Mark wanted to drive Gwen to Tyson's.

"Your ankle isn't entirely healed yet."

Gwen didn't argue. They parked a block away in the now quiet Haight. The summer of love had ended. The Diggers, carrying a coffin through the streets had performed a mock funeral of the summer of love. The kids were told to go back home. Thousands returned to school. The few who remained could tell the fun was over. Happy people and concerts were replaced with empty streets and an empty park. The lonely, cold evenings sent the rest of them away.

"I'll help you up the stairs," Mark said.

"Won't you come in?"

He shook his head. "I don't know those people."

"I know you'd be welcome."

He hesitated. "Is it important to you?"

"It would be a very nice indication that you're trying to make it work."

"OK, then."

They found a place to sit, and Gwen introduced Mark to the people she knew. He was welcomed with big smiles and handshakes. Watching him, Gwen noticed that he didn't seem to mind the marijuana smoke. At least he didn't show it if he did. He was even friendly with her friends. Yes, he was trying, and she would too. When both people want it to work so badly, she thought, surely there has to be a way.

Marjorie held Sophie's hand as they walked to Tyson's. Although somewhat jittery Sophie was delighted to leave the confines of the house. She twirled in the dry leaves, and Marjorie saw a smile on her face for the first time since the night of the murder.

True and two other girls from Marjorie's house joined them. As they walked up the stairs, Sheila was waiting for them in the doorway.

Smiles and tears intermingled in an atmosphere that was both celebratory and somber. Pizza and beer were consumed as Rebecca's friends recalled happy memories, and Tyson played the songs Rebecca had sung. Even Mark joined in singing, "This Little Light of Mine, I'm Gonna Make it Shine."

Near the end of the evening a newcomer was ushered in. Out of context, at first no one seemed to recognize her. Then Gwen introduced her. "This is Janet from the Swans Band."

A cheer went up the group made the connection.

"I have something you might like to hear," she went on. "The night she sang, we made a simple recording, intending to present her debut song to her at some future date. It was done live, not in a studio, so it includes all the ambient noise, the applause." She stopped. "Would you like to hear it?"

A tremendous shout of assent went up, and a place was cleared for Janet to set up her equipment. She placed a reel-to-reel recorder on the table. In hushed expectancy they waited as Tyson plugged it in and Janet turned it on. The reel started whirring, and then yes, there it was, the clear, pure voice of Rebecca.

Closing her eyes, Gwen felt as though she were reliving the first night she'd been here, the first time she'd heard this radiant voice. How glad she was that she'd invited this woman to their gathering. By the end of the song, snivels could be heard, and Sophie was crying softly in Marjorie's lap.

Finally, Tyson said, "I think that's a good note on which to close this evening."

"Can we get a copy?" someone asked. Others joined in.

Janet agreed to have a few copies made, which she would leave with Tyson.

As the evening concluded, Sheila said, "Did you know she was coming? Did you invite her, Gwen?"

"Yes, I did. As the evening wore on, I was beginning to be afraid that she wasn't coming. I'm so glad she did."

"Did you know about the recording?"

"No, I didn't know. That was a complete surprise."

"A wonderful one."

Gwen said goodbye to her friends and promised to stay in touch. "Well, that wasn't so bad was it?" she took Mark's hand as they walked to the car.

"No, not bad at all. Rebecca was a much beloved member of this group, wasn't she?"

"Yes, she was."

"And what a voice. How very sad that it was cut off so soon."

As they drove across the Golden Gate Bridge back to Marin, Gwen, lost in reverie, mused over the events of the past weeks. The glorious explosion of love, peace and music had met its demise with the end of summer.

Like fireworks it had lit up the sky for a brief time, and then was gone, as short-lived as Camelot. But shoots and vines had sprung up everywhere, as the effects of the summer washed over the country like a tidal wave. San Francisco, and maybe the world, would never be quite the same.

She sighed and took Mark's hand. "It's over."

"What is?"

"The summer."

"Are you glad?"

She thought about that. "Fall is a time for going within, reflecting."

He pulled her hand up, kissed it. "And for slowing down."

She smiled. "A time of endings and new beginnings. Yes, I'm happy. Who knows what this new season will bring?"

The End